Love in the Temperate Zone

L. R. WRIGHT

Love in the Temperate Zone

VIKING

VIKING
Viking Penguin Inc., 40 West 23rd Street,
New York, New York 10010, U.S.A.
Penguin Books Ltd., 27 Wrights Lane,
London W8 5TZ (Publishing & Editorial), and
Harmondsworth, Middlesex, England (Distribution & Warehouse)
Penguin Books Australia Ltd., Ringwood,
Victoria, Australia
Penguin Books Canada Limited, 2801 John Street,
Markham, Ontario, Canada L3R 1B4
Penguin Books (N.Z.) Ltd., 182–190 Wairau Road,
Auckland 10, New Zealand

First published in 1988 by Viking Penguin Inc.
Published simultaneously in Canada

LIBRARY OF CONGRESS CATALOGING IN PUBLICATION DATA
Wright, Laurali, 1939–
Love in the temperate zone.
I. Title.
PR9199.3.W68L68 1988 813'.54 87-40276
ISBN 0-670-81173-4

Printed in the United States of America by
Haddon Craftsmen, Scranton, Pennsylvania
Set in Garamond No. 3

This book is for my daughter,
Johnna Margaret

Part One

1

Only the March rain, cold and relentlessly pervasive, was there to watch on the day that Michelle Paparo inadvertently detonated her marriage.

The rain fell straight down, pulled to earth by its own weight. Dense cloud had sat heavily upon the earth for a week, immobile, as though after spending eons in search of a permanent home it had finally found one, directly above Vancouver. As Michelle made her way through the house with feather duster or vacuum cleaner she turned the lights on, even though it was only mid-afternoon, to keep the grey day outside where it belonged.

It certainly didn't feel much like spring.

It was Saturday. She was alone in the house. Max was at work and their daughter, Lizzie, had gone downtown shopping with her friend Corinne. Michelle was determined to get the house in shape before she had to go on the road again. She'd cleaned the downstairs rooms and done the laundry and was now tackling the master bedroom. She felt disheveled and irritable and had decided that if she couldn't persuade Lizzie to make dinner, she would dispatch Max for take-out Chinese food.

It happened when she flipped the edges of the fringed spread up onto the bed to get it out of the way of the vacuum cleaner. On Max's side she saw something on the floor, protruding a couple of inches from under the bed. Of course she pulled it out; what else was she supposed to do? It was a large manila envelope. Of course she was faintly curious about it; who wouldn't be? But she assumed it was something he'd brought home from work.

And really, all she had on her mind that dull, wet, March day was getting the damned cleaning done.

As she tossed the envelope on the bed she saw that something had been spilled on the surface of Max's night table. There were cobwebs high up where the walls met the ceiling. The windowsill was layered with dust. If she knocked down the cobwebs, the elusive but ubiquitous spiders would weave more. If she swept a cloth along the windowsill, the dust would merely flutter for a while in the air, then settle comfortably back where it felt it belonged.

Michelle sat heavily on the edge of the bed. This was no way for a living breathing person to be spending her time.

Ashes, the cat, stood up slowly, stretching, on one of the upholstered chairs at the far end of the long, wide bedroom. He looked over at Michelle and uttered a high squeak of a meow. She smiled as he leapt from the chair and stalked to the bed. She reached down to stroke him. He arched his neck and rubbed his big square head against the side of her knee. She stood, faced him, and patted her chest. "Come on, Ashes—jump. Kitty kitty kitty?" Ashes looked up at her reproachfully. He gave another squeaky meow and stretched the full length of his body up along her leg, his front paws reaching high and digging through her jeans and into the flesh just above her knee. She picked him up. "Oh, Ashes, you can't quite do it anymore, can you? No big jumps left, right? Never mind," she said, rubbing her chin against the top of his head, "you're a big strong old cat, got lots of smarts, you're making all the right decisions." She looked into his face, wide and blunt, grey like the rest of him. His eyes were large and green. "Save your strength for what matters," she told him. "Tricks don't matter." She put him down gently. He was twelve years old. It was only within the last few months that he'd begun refusing to leap from the floor straight up into her arms, or Max's, or, more likely, Lizzie's. He'd been Lizzie's cat more than anyone else's ever since they got him, when Lizzie was four.

When she turned resignedly to reach for the vacuum cleaner Michelle saw the manila envelope lying on the bed. She picked it up, intending to take it down the hall and drop it onto Max's desk. She hadn't noticed that it wasn't sealed. As she walked toward the door, holding the envelope by one corner, something slithered out and fell to the floor. Michelle picked it up.

It was a photograph, an eight-by-ten, black-and-white, head-and shoulders shot of a young woman. It was nobody Michelle had ever seen, a person who looked to be in her twenties, wearing a V-necked sweater which pointed directly at the just visible swelling of her breasts. The girl's dark hair was parted in the center and hung to her shoulders, where it curled under slightly. She had large eyes, a small nose, a full-lipped mouth. The fingers of one hand touched something which hung from a chain around her neck; Michelle couldn't make out what it was.

There were lots of reasons, she told herself carefully, why Max might have such a photograph.

Michelle put the picture on a small coffee table next to the chair recently vacated by the cat. She sat down and put the envelope in her lap and rested both hands on it, palms down, fingers spread. She was thinking about her throat, which was closing up, and about the rain, which was coming down harder now, snuffling at the bedroom windows like a voyeur who had abandoned stealth.

Her hands stuck briefly to the paper as she lifted them from the envelope. She picked it up and turned it upside down and watched the contents tumble into her lap. There were no more photographs. Just a lot of letters. She read them all. Even though there were more than a dozen of them, it didn't take her long. Michelle had always been a very fast reader. It came in handy, in a job which required her to sell books to booksellers.

It was extraordinary, what was happening to her. It all seemed to be physical. Her throat was tighter than ever; she felt it necessary to open her mouth a little in order to get enough breath. Her heart was pounding, pointlessly. Her hands were cold.

But her mind, she thought, was admirably calm and clear. It instructed her to put the letters and the photograph back into the envelope, so she did. It told her to put the envelope on Max's desk, as she had meant to do in the first place. So she began to stand up. She was astonished at how weighty her body had become, how difficult it was to get it moving. But she did it; she got up out of the chair. She thought about the cat hairs that were sure to be plastered all over her jeans, and was pleased that she was alert enough to make this observation. She turned herself toward the door and walked into the hall and opened the door to Max's den.

He had bought brown rice-paper blinds in Chinatown for his windows. He hadn't raised them that morning, and through them Michelle saw rain streaking the windowpanes, and the weak daylight that escaped into the room was twice filtered; the room felt damp, drab, stained by the brownness that seeped through the blinds.

She put the envelope right in the middle of the sheet of heavy glass that covered the surface of his oak desk. It was large and obvious, alone there except for a telephone, a tray stacked neatly with work-oriented papers, a large mug painted with a Chinese design and filled with pens and pencils.

Michelle looked around at bookcases and filing cabinets and a couple of easy chairs huddled under a floor lamp. When Max had to work on weekends he usually worked at home. But today he had a meeting at the office with one of his law partners. Michelle tried to imagine what would be happening right this minute if Max and his partner had been sitting in the easy chairs, immersed in the watery dimness here, when she walked in to toss the manila envelope onto his desk.

Of course he might have been lying about the meeting with his partner.

She went quietly from the room and gently closed the door. She stood in the hallway and took several deep breaths, sucking in vast quantities of air. She realized that her heart was still pounding, her hands were still cold, and that an irresistible wrath was building in her. She leaned heavily against the door to Max's office and clasped her hands tightly in front of her. She stared across the hall to the half-open door which led to Lizzie's room. Through it she saw on the opposite wall the edge of a window, flounced in yellow chintz, and next to it part of what she knew was a huge Tina Turner poster.

She did not want to be angry. She thought weakly about alternatives.

Her hands unclutched themselves and flew to her head. They pulled at her hair, dragged down across her cheeks. She looked left, then right. She saw Ashes sidling uneasily past her, heading for the stairs. And then she rushed to the bathroom at the end of the hall.

She thought she was going there to throw cold water on her face. But when she flung open the door it struck a towel rod on the wall and leapt back into her face. When it hit her, it demolished what remained of her self-control. She felt the unconstrained flooding of her rage, and welcomed it.

She hurled the door again and again, bouncing it against the rod until she heard wood splinter. She flew into the bathroom, threw open the medicine chest and deposited into the bathtub with great force everything which had to do with Max. A large bottle crashed against the porcelain and Pepto-Bismol splattered pink along one side of the tub. A tube of Preparation H split a seam when it landed and began oozing colorless goo. Michelle smashed various containers of after-shave lotion and men's cologne which sent glass splinters flying and instantly filled the bathroom with a suffocating conglomeration of fragrances.

Eye drops, nose drops, ear drops followed, their plastic containers bouncing harmlessly before becoming affixed to the sides and bottom of the tub by hemorrhoid ointment or upset-stomach medication.

She pushed open the small frosted window and the rain dinned abruptly louder and watched and peppered her hand with cold hard drops as she let fall into the dripping azaleas a wood-handled back brush, with natural bristles.

She snatched from the edge of the bathtub a bright blue duck which Lizzie had given Max as a joke, twisted off its head, and let it fall into the muck in the bottom of the bathtub.

She dropped his toothbrush into the toilet.

While the rain flicked eagerly through the open window she squatted in front of the cupboard under the sink and swept its contents onto the floor; among them were Max's special shampoo and hair conditioner. She wrenched off the tops, feverishly squeezed the contents onto the mess in the tub, and then tossed in the bottles.

When she left the bathroom she heard herself crying and shouting profanities.

She ran down the hall, intent upon removing from every room in the house all traces of her husband.

She tore into the bedroom, tripped over the vacuum cleaner, and fell headlong onto the carpeted floor. Her fury shot to new and dizzying heights. She grabbed the vacuum cleaner. Still weeping, still cursing, she stumbled along the hall toward the top of the stairs, the hose slapping against her knees, the carpet attachment banging her ankle. When the cord tautened behind her she threw her whole body behind a vehement snapping motion that ripped the plug loose from the bedroom wall.

As she reached the steps, the front door opened.

"Michelle?" called Max. "I'm home."

He looked up. She raised the vacuum cleaner canister above her head. "You son-of-a-bitch," she shouted, and with all her strength she pitched it down the stairs.

Max dropped his briefcase and dived out of the way.

The vacuum cleaner clattered three-quarters of the way down before the carpet attachment caught between two of the banister posts.

Max scrambled to his feet. His jacket was wet from the rain, and his hair glistened. He stared up at Michelle. "What the hell? What the hell's the matter with you?"

"I wish the goddamn thing had hit you," said Michelle, although actually she didn't. She was understanding for the first time why prisons were filled with people who had committed acts of domestic violence, and why afterwards, when it was too late, they were so tearfully repentant. It wouldn't be worth it, she thought, to spend the rest of my life locked up just for the joy of watching that vacuum cleaner bash his head in.

"Are you crazy?" said Max. "Have you gone crazy?"

She advanced down the stairs toward him and noticed with ferocious pleasure that he was involuntarily backing away from her.

"You son-of-a-bitch," she said. "You aren't so hot. Just look at you." She pointed imperiously at his stomach. "Just look at that. It's disgusting. You're overweight. You drink too much. You're lazy. You're selfish." She was four feet from him now, and he wasn't backing up anymore.

"What's this all about?" he said quietly.

"You're a sneaking, lying son-of-a-bitch. That's what it's all about." She turned away and hung onto the post at the end of the banister. There was a sharp pain in her left knee which she thought had been going on for a while, though she'd just noticed it. She was glad she hadn't put on any eye makeup that morning; it would be smeared all over her face by now. On the other hand she was humiliated not to be looking her best during this scene.

Max remained still, not saying anything, but Michelle knew his mind would be working furiously. She was damned if she'd stand there and wait until he'd figured it out for himself.

"Pretty terrific bedtime reading you've got there," she said, facing him again. She saw his sudden horror. "Do you wake up in the night and pore over it while I'm dreaming away beside you?"

"Michelle," said Max, reaching for her.

She pulled her arm away. "She's going to be greatly relieved. Now you don't have to have a talk with me. Now I already know. Now you can go get yourself damn well good and truly divorced."

"I don't want to get divorced."

"Fuck you, chum."

"I don't want a divorce. I don't love her. I love you, and Lizzie."

Michelle stared at him. He wasn't particularly good-looking. She had watched as lovely women met him for the first time, smiled politely, dismissed him. But his confidence was boundless. He snagged them with conversation, because he was attentive and clever and knew a lot about a lot of things. Soon they were looking at him differently, with faint surprised smiles, and eventually, when he judged that the time was right, he touched them, casually, socially, within perfectly acceptable boundaries; he would stroke a cheek, or put his pleasantly affectionate arm around a waist, or, feigning courtliness, lift polished fingertips and kiss them; and sometimes, when he felt it appropriate to be more aggressive, his hand would fleetingly cup a silk-sheathed buttock. Michelle had watched, had seen women respond with astonishing eagerness when he touched them. Not all of them. But many. He was not happy, when he'd met a woman he considered attractive, until he had made her want him.

His behavior was completely open and he had discussed it frankly with Michelle. It was, he said, an innocuous addiction. He implied that she should regard it as a compliment to her; this, however, was far too paradoxical for Michelle, who instead was embarrassed and alarmed by her husband's attentions to other women.

He had sworn over and over again that he never went to bed with them. She had twice blundered upon him kissing someone at a party, in a darkened hallway or a temporarily deserted kitchen, but she hadn't been above engaging in that kind of thing herself from time to time so it was easy enough to accept his explanations: intoxication, merriment, reckless impulse, even a reluctance to hurt somebody's feelings.

His protestations had seemed so sincere, his declarations of undiminished love for her so genuine, that Michelle had each time permitted him to soothe away her unease, and to reaffirm in bed his alleged commitment to monogamy.

On this day, however, she had proof.

"I love you," he said again.

"Bull shit," said Michelle, distinctly.

He slumped into a small, round-backed chair which sat in the foyer. Michelle's mother during a petit-point phase had fashioned its seat cover. "What can I say?" He raised his hands helplessly. "Yes, I had an affair with her. I didn't want you to know. It meant nothing. It's over."

"It's not over," said Michelle.

He shook his head. "Oh, yes it is. It's over."

"Somebody ought to tell her."

"I've told her." He stood and came very close to her. "Michelle, I'm sorry. I wish like hell it had never happened. I wish like hell that you'd never found out."

Michelle sat on the bottom step. She was unutterably weary and her knee was throbbing, in rhythm with the ceaseless rain. She thought about having a bath, and then remembered the mess in the tub. She began to cry.

Max sat next to her and put his arm around her shoulders. "Everything's going to be all right. Everything's going to be fine. You'll see." He began kissing her temple, her cheek.

She got up and moved away. "Everything's not going to be fine, Max. It's going to be a mess, and very painful, at least for me, and for Lizzie, and probably even for you, too." She wiped angrily at her eyes. "The only one not upset is going to be what's-her-name, your friend Gloria or whatever the hell her name is."

"Michelle, I'll burn the letters. Do you want me to do that? I'll be happy to. She doesn't mean a damn thing to me, Michelle."

"Max." She had, thank God, stopped crying, but she felt oddly clumsy, as though her hands and feet had become inexplicably enlarged. "She isn't the first one."

Max said nothing.

"I feel so stupid," said Michelle. "All these years, all your bullshit. I've been such an idiot." She rubbed her hands, trying to warm them. "I wish I hadn't had any kids. I knew I shouldn't have had any kids. Divorce is very bad for kids. Even sixteen-year-old kids."

"Michelle, I do not want a divorce. Will you please get that through your head?" He went to her quickly and grabbed her by the shoulders. "I don't want a divorce!"

She waited until he'd let go of her. "I do not give a flying fuck, Max, whether you want one or not," she said. "You're going to get one."

2

A few weeks later, on Good Friday, Casey Williams trudged through the parking lot at the bottom of Ocean Avenue, over the iceplant-smothered sand dune and onto what he considered the most beautiful beach in the world; an inimitable beach; Carmel beach, on Monterey Bay.

The riptide was treacherous and there were occasional shark warnings, so swimming here was not encouraged. But the sand was smooth and almost white, the bay was a perfect curve, and wind-twisted Monterey cypresses and live oak trees screened from view the magnificent houses, large and small, which looked down upon the bay from either side.

He walked with his hands in his pockets along the silken sand, and near the middle of the beach stopped and sat down against a log. The beach wasn't crowded; most of the Easter-time tourists, he thought, were probably spending the morning shopping.

The sky and the sea were so blue Casey thought he might die of it.

He had spent his adolescence on the Monterey Peninsula, where his father had taught high school music; or mathematics, whenever music had had to be cut as a "frill."

Now he sat here as a forty-two-year-old widower, a stranger to himself.

A group of teenagers were putting up a volleyball net a couple of hundred yards away. There were four girls and four boys, already tanned. Casey glanced down at his own white arms. He spread them along the top of the log and lifted his face to the springtime sky, letting the sounds of the waves, and the kids' laughter, and the barking of a dog somewhere down the beach fill up his mind. With his eyes closed he might have been back in Vancouver, where the same sea shouldered the land, plucked the same music from the shore.

Somewhere inside him there was a malignancy, which was the fact of Aline's death. It was a massive, ugly thing, difficult to carry around and enormously distracting. But whenever he tried to believe in its eventual disappearance from his body he was swept with terror, for he would truly be alone, then, without even grief as a companion, and the absence from his life of Aline, and music, and grief—this would surely kill him.

He sat there for a long time, watching the noisy, rambunctious volleyball game and the people who strolled, on holiday, up and down the beach, their faces turned to the sea. He saw the tide pull slowly out, dragging wet foamy fingers along the darkened sand.

Eventually he pulled himself to his feet and brushed at his pants, and as he turned to leave the beach his eyes burned with tears and he thought that he couldn't go back to Vancouver, he just couldn't do it, because she was there more than she was anywhere else, and he had to get away from her. As much as he had loved her, he had to get away from her, now that she was dead.

He managed to get to the parking lot, where he leaned heavily against the hood of somebody's Toyota—it had a Nebraska license plate and through the windows he could see maps and a box of potato chips and on the back seat a pile of towels and bathing suits.

He fumbled in the pocket of his short-sleeved shirt for his sunglasses and put them on. Three young children ran past him, whooping toward the beach, followed by a middle-aged man whose shorts exposed pale hairy legs, and a woman in a halter sundress which as she passed revealed a white *X* across her tanned back.

After a while Casey set off back to his father's house. He avoided the crowds of sightseers on Ocean Avenue by taking a parallel street up the hill, a narrow street where trees had the right of way and flowers spilled from the gardens of the houses he passed. He thought it would be pleasant to live here. He saw a house he particularly liked, small and low, with blossoming vines growing up a lattice on the side of the house and a yard ankle-deep in ivy; no lawns to mow, he thought as he walked slowly by, and he wondered if this house could be purchased.

He lowered himself onto the grass outside somebody's fence and leaned against it, clasping his knees.

He thought again about Vancouver. He knew he had been cheating his students and his choir, all forty-two voices, for the last three months. He had existed in a state of numbness, surrounded by his dead wife's belongings, incapable of making decisions, incapable of thought. He had gone through the motions of teaching, conducting, carrying on polite conversation—but there was a malignancy within him and an unbridgeable distance between him and other people.

The air was sweet. The sea was blue. The beach was transcendent. Maybe he should try to get a job in California. Maybe he should come home.

"A stroke." Donald Williams brushed stray grains of salt from the tablecloth. "I still can't believe it."

"Several of them, Pop," said Casey.

"I know, I know. You told me. But I don't think I knew that people as young as Aline could die from strokes."

"I don't think I did, either. I don't think she did, either."

"I wanted to go up for the funeral, you know."

"I know. It doesn't matter."

"I don't think she liked me much." He said this with an astonishment that lingered after twenty years.

"It wasn't that she didn't like you," said Casey. "She liked you fine. She didn't get to know you very well, that's all."

"You moved away, as soon as you got married."

"We'd been married for three years by then, Pop."

"Up to Canada," said Donald, as though he still couldn't get used to the idea.

"Yeah."

"So she never got to know me. Never got to know any of us."

Casey got up and started piling into stacks the dishes they'd used for lunch.

"Charles." Donald was the only person on earth who called Casey by his proper name. He did so out of love for his own father, after whom Casey had been named.

"What is it, Pop?"

"Did she suffer?"

Casey rested the palms of his hands heavily on the tabletop. "Oh, Pop, Christ, I don't know, I hope not."

"Were you with her when she died?"

"No. I'd gone home from the hospital to change my clothes."

His father covered Casey's hand with his own. "Your blitheness is gone, son. I hate to see you like this."

Casey shook his head. He picked up a pile of dishes and took them down the hall into the kitchen.

Connie was there, putting away leftover chicken, salt-and-pepper shakers, a quart of milk.

"Let me do the dishes," said Casey.

"No, I'll do them," she said with a smile. "You just have a nice chat with your dad. You're on vacation. Relax; take it easy."

She was thirteen years younger than his father, which made her fifty-seven. She had let her curly hair grow grey. She had grey eyes, too, which crinkled and almost disappeared when she laughed, and she was firm and trim in her dark red track suit; she went for long walks every afternoon.

Casey's eyes blurred as he looked at her, and he put his arms around her so she wouldn't see his tears. "The old man sure knows how to pick his women," he said, his cheek against her hair. "I'll say that much for him." He gave her a smacking kiss. She flipped the dish towel at him, smiling, and Casey went back down the hall to rejoin his father.

"I hear there's going to be a big celebration tomorrow," he

said, turning one of the dining room chairs around so he could straddle it.

Donald waved a dismissive hand, but his face broke into a grin. Casey had always loved his father's quick delight. He knew Donald was a complex, secretive man capable of incongruous rage and bitter prejudice. But his joy in people, in living, was a grand thing. It was what Casey thought about most, when he thought about his father. That, and his musicianship.

"The whole gang's turning out, I hear," said Casey.

"All except Paula off there in Italy getting her bottom pinched, and Grant, God knows where." Donald shook his head. "Don't know if we'll ever get every single one of you around this table at the same time ever again, Charles." He looked down the length of the massive dining room table, which seated twelve comfortably, fourteen in a pinch. "And there sure as hell won't be room for any of the grandchildren."

"You can park the grandchildren in the living room by the TV."

"Yeah," said Donald.

"Maybe at Christmas. Try for Christmas. Paula will be back by then, won't she? And maybe Grant can wangle some leave."

"Yeah," said Donald. But he didn't sound enthusiastic, and Casey looked at him curiously. "I'd just hoped everybody could make it for tomorrow, that's all," said his father. "It isn't every day a man turns seventy." He looked up at Casey, fear and disbelief for a moment vivid on his face. Then he laughed. He leaned forward and whispered across the table, "I am going to get me so goddamned pissed . . ."

They heard the back door open and close.

"There she goes," said Donald, distractedly. "Off on her hike."

"It keeps her in good shape. She looks great."

"She's a fine woman," said Donald earnestly. "Truly a fine, fine woman."

Casey grinned at him. "How's Mom? And Barbara?

"They're fine. Good. I get cards from them every Christmas. And for my birthday, too." He turned around and fumbled among the dozens of cards stacked on the sideboard behind him. "They're in here with the rest, somewhere. Here they are," he said, turning back to his son. "Birthday cards from both of them. I knew they were here somewhere." He handed them to Casey. "Each of my divorces," he said with satisfaction, "was a genuinely amiable thing."

"Amicable," said Casey automatically. The handwriting on the cards was immediately familiar. *Best wishes, always,* his mother had written. *Love,* said Barbara. Casey heard regularly from both of them but hadn't seen either of them for years. He thrust the cards back at his father. He had a sudden, searing sense of déjà vu.

"No, Charles," his father was saying. "Not 'amicable.' 'Amiable.' We felt nothing but amiability toward each other. Both times."

Donald settled back in his chair, his hands folded in his lap. His hair had once been red, his moustache auburn; now both were white and it was his face that looked red, except when he was tired.

"So what happened," said Casey, "if you were so amiable? How come you got divorced?"

"I don't know what to tell you," said his father solemnly, brushing at the tablecloth. "It's hard to explain these things." He looked up at Casey, exasperated. "I don't plainly remember, to tell you the truth. I guess we just got tired of each other."

"But you and Mom had three kids, Pop. And then you had another three with Barbara. And then you got divorced from her, too. Jesus."

"I love children," said Donald indignantly. "So did Irene and Barbara. You're the joy of my life, all of you. I hated it every time one of you left home." He played with the fringe of the tablecloth. His hands were spotted with brown, and the knuckles were large and swollen. He must have difficulty, now, playing the piano and his violin, thought Casey. "I would have had more," said Donald, "except that Connie figured six stepchildren were enough."

"I can't say I blame her," said Casey, dryly. He wandered over to the open window in the living room and looked down the hillside, rumpled with rooftops, scattered with treetops that looked like bottle-green pillows, to where the afternoon sun struck sparks from the sea.

"How come you and Aline never had children?" Donald called from the dining room table.

Casey rested his forehead against the window frame. He heard his father getting up. Soon Donald's arm was around his shoulder. "I'm sorry, Charles. That was thoughtless. I apologize."

"It's okay, Pop." There was an intolerable ache in his throat. He turned around and embraced his father. "I think I ought to tell you," he said over Donald's shoulder. "I won't be doing any singing tomorrow."

Donald pulled away and looked apprehensively into his son's face. "No singing? On my birthday? Not even 'Danny Boy'?"

"I can't sing anymore," said Casey. "I can't sing a note." He tried to laugh. "I haven't even been able to hum. Not a note. Not since she died."

Very late the next night, when the debris from Donald's riotous seventieth birthday celebration had been cleared away and the rest of the visiting family had boisterously departed, Casey lay sleepless on the Hide-A-Bed pulled out in what his father called his den. Some light came through the curtains from a streetlamp not far from the house, which sat close to the road.

Casey could make out the lumpy shape of his father's desk, on which sat an ancient Smith-Corona typewriter. The desk was cluttered with letters and newspapers. Donald subscribed to more than a dozen papers and was an inveterate writer of letters to the editor. He also corresponded regularly with people scattered across the continent, people his family had never met, some of them pen pals whom he'd never met himself.

In the corner was a music stand, and nearby a violin in its case. Bookshelves were stuffed with sheet music, and books of music, and books about music. On the floor next to Casey's bed stretched an old bear rug.

He lay on his back with his hands clasped behind his head. This part of the world, he reminded himself, was home to him. He liked to think about all these brothers and sisters and their assorted offspring living within easy driving distance of his father's house; except for Paula, who was temporarily absent on an art history scholarship in Florence, and Grant, a restless thirty-one-year-old who was bound to tire eventually of the merchant marine. Surely, Casey told himself, he could be soothed and healed by living once more among his family.

On the other hand, he was here right now, and he wasn't feeling particularly soothed or healed. Maybe they had expected to find him more recovered from his bereavement than he was. They certainly hadn't expected him not to be able to sing. Casey had felt like an invalid, or someone recently disfigured in a car accident. He had been treated politely, even tenderly, but with a cautious detachment that had depressed him.

He turned restlessly in bed. The malignancy was still there. He would take it with him wherever he went, that was clear.

He was certain, when he thought about it logically, that the great and painful weight of Aline's death would soon leave him. But it was also logical to expect that in some ways he was forever changed. Would he ever feel happy again? Perhaps, he thought hopefully, it was a good sign that this had even occurred to him. Perhaps merely in wanting to be happy lay the seed of his recovery.

He lay on his back again and thought tentatively about places in California where he might be able to get a job.

There was a tap on the door, and his father entered the room. "Charles? Are you awake?"

"Yes, Pop. Come in."

Donald closed the door softly behind him and sat in a wheezy chair next to the Hide-A-Bed. "Didn't get pissed after all," he said, and grunted.

"You had a good time, though, didn't you?"

"Oh my, yes. All the kids, the grandkids." He sighed.

"All the presents. The loot." Casey smiled in the darkness.

"Got me some real nice stuff," said Donald with satisfaction.

"Especially that VCR thing. I've been wanting one of those." He reached over and patted Casey's arm. "Thank you, son."

"You're welcome, Pop. I'm glad you like it."

Donald settled deeper into the chair, which made rude sounds as he did so. "I'm sorry you aren't staying longer, Charles."

Casey sat up and shoved the pillow behind his back. "I'm sorry, too. But I've got to get back. Finish the term. And sell the house." He had to do that, anyway, he told himself, whatever he decided about the future.

Donald sighed again, and didn't speak for several minutes. "I'd like it very much, son, if you'd consider moving back home." He quickly held up a hand. "Now, just listen to me for a minute. There's lots of colleges down here. You taught here once; you can do it again." His hand rested again on Casey's arm. "I'd be so happy if you were closer."

"Pop, I'm less than three hours away by plane. That's all. You make it sound like I'm in Alaska, or Connecticut, or somewhere. You ought to come up and visit. You and Connie." I should confide in him, he thought. Let him know that I'm thinking about it. He felt a growing excitement.

"I always thought of it as a temporary thing," said Donald. "And it struck me, when Aline died, you've been up there for seventeen years now. That has a ring of permanence about it, Charles. A ring of permanence."

He couldn't see his father's face; it was too dark. But sometimes the light caught his eyes. And his white hair, his white moustache, seemed to glow.

"I'm a Canadian citizen, now," said Casey abstractedly. "So was Aline. I told you that." His mind was working busily.

Donald waved citizenship aside. "You're still American, as far as I'm concerned."

Casey sat up straight and began to speak, but Donald interrupted.

"Leave that aside for now," he said quickly. "Just think about it, that's all I ask." He moved uneasily in the chair. "I've got to tell you some news before you go," he said. "Connie and I, we've decided to call it quits."

Casey fumbled at the lamp beside the bed. He turned it on and stared at his father, who blinked and held up his hand against the sudden brilliance. "What did you say?"

"Connie and I, we're packing it in. Getting a divorce."

"Why, for Christ's sake?" He told himself that his distress was disproportionate, his anger presumptuous.

"Shh! Lower your damn voice."

"Why? Just tell me why, damn you."

"It's been seventeen years," said Donald defensively. "I've been married three times. Once for fourteen years, the second time for nineteen years, and this time for seventeen years. I haven't had any damn hit-and-run marriages. I've invested everything I've got into every single damn one of them."

"But for Christ's sake, you're seventy years old!" The man is mad, thought Casey, trying to control his fury.

"What the hell's that got to do with it? You think there aren't any women out there looking around for a seventy-year-old man?" He snorted. "You don't know much, Charles. You ought to go to some of those old people's dances they've got. Damn places are crawling with single women." He sneaked a look at Casey. "I intend to provide for Connie, of course."

"Jesus Christ," said Casey. He turned away from his father.

"It's something I wanted to tell you in person, Charles. I could have waited, and written you a letter."

"Go to bed, you damned old fool. Get out of here."

He heard his father get up from the complaining chair, pull the cord on the lamp, and walk heavily to the door.

When the door had closed behind him Casey suddenly felt like laughing, so he did.

Then, "Fuck him," he muttered bitterly. He grabbed the first thing that came to hand and pitched it at the door.

He heard sudden murmurings from the room next door, where Donald and Connie slept.

In a moment his door opened. He heard the remnants of his travel alarm clock grate against the floor as they were pushed aside. Connie stuck her head in.

"He was a two-time loser, Casey," she said. "I knew what I was getting into."

He couldn't see her face, just her hair, a curly silver halo in the light from the hall.

Before he could speak she began to close the door, but she opened it again to add, thoughtfully, "I think I'll go to China. Your father's always been a tightwad when it came to vacations."

Then she was gone.

3

On a warm sunny day in May, Michelle parked in front of the house she had shared with her husband and walked unhesitatingly up the four concrete stairs flanked by rock gardens and along the walk which divided the front lawn. She didn't even have trouble with the steps leading to the verandah. It was only when she stood at the front door and reached automatically for the big brass knob that she actually registered her permanent separation from what had been her home. She didn't have keys to this house anymore; she had left them behind when she moved out less than two months ago. Yet she would feel like a badly dressed Avon lady, ringing the bell. She faltered, and then the door opened and Max was standing there.

"Hi."

"Hi," she said, and flushed, because he must have been watching for her and seen her indecision.

"You're right on time."

"It's one of the things I'm good at."

He opened the door wide and motioned for her to go inside.

She had entered this house dozens of times after being away days, or weeks. But this time was definitely different. The cozy familiarity of the place tightened her heart. When Ashes appeared from around the corner in the living room and rubbed against her leg she heard his loud purring and had to blink hard, her lashes beating back tears. She reached down to stroke him and scratch under his chin.

"You and Lizzie will take Ashes, of course," said Max.

Michelle didn't reply.

"You'll want this chair, too," said Max, pointing to the one for which her mother had embroidered the seat cover.

Michelle straightened up and nodded briskly.

"Let's start in the living room and work our way through," he said, leading the way.

There was an alcove filled with bookcases at one end of the room. It was Michelle's favorite part of the house. The window looked out onto the side garden, where hollyhocks and sunflowers grew six feet tall in the summer, and masses of tulips and daffodils appeared in the spring. The daffodils, she thought, would be finished now, but some of the late tulips should still be in bloom. She restrained herself from walking to the window to see.

"Take whatever you like," said Max, studying the left-hand corner of the top shelf of books. "Just make a pile of them somewhere on the floor. I'll see that they get packed up for you."

"Some of them are yours," said Michelle. "Your English texts, from college."

"Take whatever you like," he repeated. "The only books I want are upstairs in my den." He walked to the middle of the living room and made a sweeping gesture. "I don't want anything here. I want you to have it all."

"I don't want it all."

"I'm moving into an apartment, Michelle. What do you expect me to do with all this stuff? Two sofas, four chairs, six lamps for Christ's sake, six, count them, six."

His face had reddened. She saw that he had lost some weight.

"I told you," she said. "I'll take what's mine, and I'll take what Lizzie needs to make her feel comfortable and at home, but I won't take one damned stick more than I have to. If you don't want the rest of it, then sell it."

He came back to the alcove and sat in the chair by the window, looking out. "I had somebody clean up the yard," he said absently. "Do you think that's what got the place sold?"

Michelle swallowed several times. She was standing across the room from him, her hands clasped in front of her, a leather handbag looped over one shoulder. There was a notebook in her handbag. She intended to get it out any minute now, and start making lists of the things she wanted.

"So," he said, looking at her. "How are things?"

"Fine," she said. "Just fine."

She didn't like the way he was studying her. She felt that her hair was probably mussed. Maybe he didn't like it that she'd arrived in jeans and a sweatshirt. He was practically dressed up, in a green silk shirt and a pair of lightweight pants.

"You look good," he said, and again she felt herself flush, and cursed her pale complexion.

"Thank you," she said politely. She rummaged through her handbag and brought out the notebook and a pen.

Max observed this without comment. A moment later he pushed himself out of the chair and surveyed the living room once more.

"I think you'd better take one of the sofas," he said, "and two of the chairs, one of the coffee tables, two end tables, two table lamps, and a floor lamp. That will still leave me enough junk to furnish two apartments, and as far as I know, I'm only going to want one. Decide which ones you want and put little stickers on them or some damn thing, I don't care. You'll find some masking tape in the drawer of the kitchen desk." He turned to look at her. "But of course you know that, don't you."

"Yes," said Michelle, and followed him into the adjoining dining room.

"This suite used to be your mother's," he said.

Michelle nodded. Her parents had bought it in Winnipeg, cheap, thirty-five years ago. It had been very dark brown. All of twenty years later someone had told her mother that this was not the wood's natural color. So she'd spent the next six months stripping the table and its two leaves, the china cabinet, the buffet, and the eight chairs down to the original honey-gold oak.

Michelle's mother had moved after her husband's death in 1973 into a small house near the water in Richmond, a few miles south of Vancouver. At that time she had bought herself a drop-leaf dining table and some chairs and had given the old suite to Max and Michelle.

"Obviously I'm not going to keep it," said Max.

"No," said Michelle. "I can understand that you wouldn't want it."

"You've got room for it, haven't you?"

"Yes. Okay."

Next they went to the kitchen. "My apartment will probably have all this stuff," said Max. "A fridge and stove."

"Yes, but it won't have a toaster oven, or a blender, or a microwave, or an electric can opener, or a coffeemaker, or—"

"Stop it," said Max. He dropped into a chair at the kitchen table. He laced his fingers together and pulled back on them, cracking his knuckles. Michelle had always hated it when he did that. She hated it no less today, but she didn't say anything. "I don't want it, Michelle. None of it. Only my own personal belongings. That's all I want."

"That is exactly how I feel."

They sat in silence, looking around the kitchen, avoiding each other's eyes.

"The Salvation Army," she said finally, "will be happy to take whatever neither of us wants."

"Fuck the Salvation Army."

After a minute she sat down opposite him. "I don't like this either," she said.

"Then why are we doing it?" He looked directly into her eyes. "Why are we doing it? I'm unhappy, you're unhappy, Lizzie's unhappy. Tell me, Michelle. Exactly why are we doing this to each other?"

"I can't live with you anymore."

"Try. Give it another try. That's all I'm asking."

She was shaking her head. "I can't. I can't." She stood up. "I'll take the toaster oven and the blender. And the coffeemaker. You take the rest. You'll need the microwave." She leaned against the counter, blinking tears into the sink. The stainless steel was dull and grimy. Jesus, she thought, can't he even clean a sink?

She felt his hands on her shoulders and turned to rest her cheek against his shirt. She liked it that he was taller than she. It had been a trial, when she was in high school, being taller than most of the boys in her classes. Her arms went around him and he soothed her. Soon he'll kiss me, she thought, and then we'll probably end up in bed, and that would be a dreadful mistake.

"I'm ruining your shirt," she said, and pulled away. She dabbed at the small wet splotches with her hand. She had stopped crying.

He tried to pull her close again but she pressed her hands against his chest and shook her head. She smiled at him, though, letting him know how fond she was of him: she considered this a gift of some substance. She could have pretended contempt for him, or even hate.

Finally, he let her go.

They went into the family room next. There were more books, more furniture, another stereo, and a television set. It was agreed that she would pick out some books and take the television set—Max would keep the one in their bedroom—and the stereo, mostly for Lizzie, because there was another one in the living room for Max.

"Make sure you don't forget to take half the records," said Max as they went upstairs.

In the bedroom they sat in the two upholstered chairs and looked blankly at the king-size bed which almost filled the other end of the room. To Michelle it was as though they were in a theater, waiting for a play to begin.

"Tell me about your house," said Max, his gaze still on the bed.

"It's on Bellevue. Only a block from the seawalk."

"That's nice."

"Alexandra found it for me."

"I wish it were closer. So I could see Lizzie more often. I miss her."

"It's West Vancouver, Max, not the moon. It's just across the bridge."

"Two bridges," he said stubbornly. "I don't understand why you have to live all the way over there."

Sunlight streamed through the full-length windows behind them. Ashes wandered in and curled up in a ball on the carpet, in the middle of a pool of light.

"Unless," Max added, "it's because you want to get as far away from me as possible without actually moving out of the city."

He got up and walked the length of the room and threw himself onto the bed, one arm over his eyes. For a long time he stayed there, and Michelle stayed in her chair, and neither of them said anything. Then, "Michelle," he said, not moving.

"What is it?" Her hands held her bag in a sweaty grip.

"Come over here. Just for a minute."

She put her bag on the floor and went to him. "What is it?" she said again, looking down at him.

He took his arm away from his face and she saw tears in his eyes. She marveled that he would permit her to see them. Perhaps he didn't know they were there. Or perhaps he knew, and hoped to melt her with them. He tugged at her hand until she sat down next to him.

"I know I was a son-of-a-bitch. I know it. Lots of times I wanted to tell you. I didn't have the guts. I thought you'd leave me."

He seemed to be waiting for her to say something. She couldn't speak. She just nodded.

"I don't want you to leave me," he said. "I love you."

She managed to get out, "I know. But I have to. I can't stay. It would turn me into an awful person."

"Never." He sat up, leaning against the headboard.

She nodded energetically, determined not to weep. His eyes were dry now. "It would," she said. "I'd never be able to trust you. I'd think about it when I was away, I'd think about it when you went away, I'd even think about it when you were late coming home for dinner."

He pulled her into his arms so that her back was against his chest, his chin resting on the top of her head, his hands holding her just under her breasts. "Put your feet up on the bed. That's right. Now think about it. Just once more. I won't ask you again. It's such a mess, Michelle. Such a goddamned useless wasteful mess. Look around you. See what we've got here. A home, Michelle—with you and me and Lizzie and Ashes and nice things around us and pretty things growing outside and vacations once or twice a year."

She looked, and saw. And she saw the manila envelope sticking out from under the bed, on Max's side.

She felt his erection growing, pressing against the crack between her buttocks.

"Now that you know what was going on," he whispered into her ear, "it wouldn't happen again. I would know that you'd be thinking about it, wondering if it was happening again. And so it wouldn't. It would never happen again, Michelle. You're too precious to me. We could make it work. I know we could."

Michelle pulled slowly away from him and stood up. She reached down to stroke his cheek. "Ah, Max," she said lovingly. "You're such a bullshitter."

She went to the far end of the room and picked up her handbag.

"I'm thinking about buying a bookstore," she said. "With my share of the house money."

"It's a lousy idea, Michelle."

She hooked her bag over her shoulder. What does he know? she thought. "Thanks very much for the vote of confidence. Obviously I've got more faith in me than you have."

Max was sitting on the edge of the bed. "It's not a question of my having faith in you," he said wearily. "It's a matter of economic realities."

"You don't know anything about this store. You don't know

about its annual sales, goodwill, the opportunities for expansion." She faced him defiantly, her hands on her hips. "You don't even know anything about books, for God's sake. When was the last time you read anything that you didn't have to read because of your work?"

He sighed and shook his head. "Sorry."

Michelle looked around the bedroom. She'd like to take the large fern that hung next to the closet. And the cedar chest, packed with extra blankets and quilts. But she didn't want to say so.

"We haven't accomplished much," she said.

"When are you moving in?"

"Saturday."

Max looked up at her. "I'll look after it. I'll get a van loaded up and sent over there."

He walked with her to the front door. On the verandah he kissed her cheek and said, "Good luck, Michelle. If you ever need anything—anything at all—call me."

She nodded quickly, looking down, and noticed that the floor of the verandah needed painting again. But that would be somebody else's responsibility; some stranger's responsibility.

There was a clenching in her chest. With her head averted she reached out her hand to Max, but he didn't take it, and she looked up to see the front door closing behind him.

4

When Michelle left Max, she went straight to her friend Alexandra.

They had met in Grade One. Neither of them had any brothers or sisters: in this they were unlike most of the rest of the class, and it formed an immediate bond between them.

Alexandra was a small child with very long, very black hair which she wore in braids. On the first day of school she caused a stir by refusing to hang up her jacket or her sweater in the cloakroom. She wouldn't leave her lunchbox or her thermos out there, either. She selected a desk in the last row, by the window, and sat down and took off her jacket and her cardigan and draped them carefully over the back of the chair part of her desk. She put her lunchbox and her thermos on the floor beneath it. At first Michelle, who occupied the desk next to her, thought Alexandra was afraid somebody would steal her stuff if she left it in the cloakroom, and she asked her about this, feeling insulted.

"I just like to have my things with me, that's all," said Alexandra, and she had to say it over and over again, because every kid in the room wanted to know why she wouldn't leave anything in the cloakroom, and how come they couldn't keep their coats and sweaters and jackets hanging all over their desks, and their boots or rubbers underneath, the way Alexandra did.

The teacher, Miss Perkins, had spent the summer taking some

courses in child psychology. She decided that Alexandra's behavior reflected her unease about going out into the world on her own for the first time (she hadn't been to kindergarten, although she knew how to read because her parents had taught her). Miss Perkins explained to Alexandra's bemused mother that Alexandra was in effect transforming her desk into a nest into which she could burrow, and feel secure.

Weeks later, when she and Michelle had become best friends, Alexandra confessed that when she walked into the cloakroom on the first day of school she had found that she wasn't tall enough to reach the coat hooks, and that this discovery had so mortified her that she immediately decided okay—then she wouldn't use them.

A year later she could do it, although she had to stand on tiptoe, and from then on she used the cloakroom like everybody else.

During that year, Grade Two, Michelle was given a puppy, a golden cocker spaniel whom she called Pat, for no particular reason. She and Alexandra, who wasn't allowed to have a pet because her father didn't like animals, loved Pat and lavished attention upon him and tried without much success to teach him things like "roll over." They didn't bother trying to teach him to come when he was called. Usually he did come, because he loved them, too, and wanted to be with them. But one day when Michelle and Alexandra were in Grade Four he began playing with another dog in the middle of the street and Michelle, standing on the sidewalk, clutching the loaf of bread her mother had sent her to the store to buy, shrieked and shrieked at him to come but he didn't, maybe he didn't hear her because he was having so much fun, and the car just came straight along and slowly ran over him and slowly kept right on going.

It was like a nightmare. She thought the car must be empty, that it must be driving itself blind and deaf down the road, unable to see anything or hear her screaming or feel the bump.

Only Pat was hit, not the other dog. Michelle ran to him and touched him and even though he was warm and his eyes were open she could tell that he wasn't there anymore.

It was a Saturday so her father wasn't at work. He brought Pat home and dug a grave for him in the garden and both he and Michelle's mother were obviously sad that Pat was dead, and tried patiently and unsuccessfully to comfort Michelle.

Alexandra came right over and they had a funeral. Michelle would not have believed that anything that was not physically painful could hurt as much as Pat's dying hurt. She and Alexandra made a cross for the grave. They held hands and cried and Michelle saw that Alexandra was suffering, too, and in this, somehow, there was comfort.

They remained close friends for years. But they did different things with their lives. Michelle went to university; Alexandra went to art school. Michelle got married; Alexandra didn't. Michelle lived what she considered an interesting but predictable sort of life; she thought that Alexandra's was exciting and sophisticated. Eventually they grew apart, and by the time Michelle had catapulted herself out of her marriage they were talking on the phone perhaps once a month and meeting for lunch only a couple of times a year.

Yet Michelle went straight to Alexandra when she left Max.

She stayed in Alexandra's apartment for more than two months, and during this time they became once more very close.

Eventually Michelle found a house to rent which was only three blocks away from Alexandra.

The house had two bedrooms and a bathroom upstairs, a kitchen, living room, dining room, and bathroom on the main floor, and a room in the basement which Michelle had decided would serve as her office and a guest room, as well.

"Corinne can use it when she sleeps over," she told Lizzie, the weekend they moved in.

"Corinne sleeps in my bed when she sleeps over," said Lizzie. "Otherwise what's the point? How could we talk, with her down there and me upstairs?"

"Then Mother can use it," said Michelle. "It's a long drive from here to Richmond. I'm sure she's going to want to stay the night, sometimes, when she comes to visit."

Lizzie shrugged.

Michelle sat down wearily upon a box of books. It was late afternoon. The movers had arrived at eight in the morning with far more pieces of furniture than Michelle had wanted; she had thought she'd never find room for all of it, but it was amazing, she thought, looking around, how well it fitted. She imagined Max selecting these things for her, pieces of their shared past for her to take into her new life, and bent her head and rubbed the back of her neck so that Lizzie wouldn't see her sudden pain.

She told herself that Max undoubtedly wanted to start clean. He'd probably have a wonderful time buying a whole bunch of new things to live among, to show off to all his goddamn girlfriends.

"Mom," said Lizzie. "What are we doing here, anyway?"

Michelle looked up to see Lizzie wiping angrily at her cheeks. She stood, and put her arms around her daughter. "Don't," she said. "You're going to have me crying, too." She sat on the sofa and pulled Lizzie gently down next to her.

"I don't want to be here," said Lizzie.

"I know," said Michelle.

"It seems to me that I ought to have some say about where I'm going to live."

"Oh, Lizzie. Please. We've been over this and over it. I've explained it to you; your father's explained it to you. It's better that you live with me. It's not forever. You've just got one more year of high school. Then maybe you'll want to get an apartment of your own, near the university. But until then, Lizzie, really—it's better that you live with me."

"That's not necessarily my opinion," said Lizzie. "Not when you insist on moving all the way over to West Vancouver. Not when it means I get hauled out of my school, and away from all my friends. I don't see the point of it. Things are bad enough—" she said, and ran upstairs. Michelle heard her bedroom door close loudly.

Michelle leaned back into the sofa. She ached, from hefting

furniture around, and unpacking boxes, and there were still what seemed dozens of boxes yet to go through, and no food in the kitchen, they would have to go out . . .

She closed her eyes. The house felt alien. She didn't know its sighings and squeakings, what sounds the wind would make in the backyard trees, whether rainwater would collect in the driveway—and would it be warm, in winter?

"What will you tell Lizzie?" Max had said.

"What do you mean, what will *I* tell her? We'll tell her together," said Michelle.

"I mean—what reason will we give her?"

Michelle had looked at him coldly. "Incompatibility," she had said.

And that's what they'd done.

Max had been grateful.

But it hadn't been very successful.

Lizzie thought she had seen respect and affection between her parents throughout all of her life. Michelle's abandonment of Max astounded her. And when she was finally told about the divorce, Michelle watched her try desperately to make some sense of it, and fail.

She was still trying, Michelle knew.

Alexandra kept urging Michelle to tell Lizzie the truth. "She needs to know," she would say. "Stop treating her like a child, for God's sake. She's bewildered, and hurt, and you've got to lay it out for her, so she can begin to understand, and to accept it. All she knows now is that she's lost her father. And she blames you for it, because what else can she do?"

But Michelle told herself that Alexandra's advice in this instance was suspect. Alexandra had never been fond of Max.

Michelle got up slowly and started trudging up the stairs. If she and Lizzie had been closer, maybe she could have done it; told her the truth.

Sometimes Michelle wondered if she ought to have had any children. Sometimes she wondered if she oughtn't to have had at least one more.

She knocked softly on Lizzie's door, resting her forehead against the jamb. "Lizzie? Let's get cleaned up and go out and eat. Okay?"

There was caution between them. A prickliness. It had been there almost since Lizzie had begun to walk and talk.

"Lizzie? What do you say?"

There was no prickliness between Lizzie and her father. No distance. Michelle banged her head softly against the door jamb. Oh, Jesus, she thought, maybe she *would* be better off with Max, maybe she would.

The door opened. "Yeah," said Lizzie. "Okay." Michelle reached out to stroke her hair, but Lizzie drew back. "I've gotta get my purse," she said, picking it up from the end of her bed. "Okay," she said, unsmiling. "Let's go."

Two weeks later it was Lizzie's seventeenth birthday, and Alexandra was having a small dinner party for her, just the three of them and Lizzie's grandmother. Alexandra had offered to invite Corinne, too, but Lizzie had said no.

Michelle saw that Lizzie was trying very hard to be civil, since warmth eluded her; courteous, because affection was beyond her. She watched her walk straight to the long, high windows in the living room and pretend to enjoy the view.

Lizzie saw Alexandra as a participant in the breakup of her parents' marriage. She had denied this, when Michelle brought it up, because of course she knew that Alexandra hadn't had anything to do with Michelle leaving Max. Yet it was to Alexandra that Michelle had fled, and Michelle knew that in Lizzie's eyes, Alexandra was therefore at least partly to blame for the fact that Michelle had not returned.

Alexandra lived in a building which was separated from the ocean by only the seawalk and a rocky beach. And her apartment was on the seaward side, looking out across English Bay to where Point Grey jutted west. The campus of the University of British Columbia sprawled across the tip of Point Grey.

"Look," said Michelle. "That's where you'll be going, after next year." She put an arm around Lizzie's shoulders and squeezed. "It's beautiful here, isn't it," she said.

"Yes, beautiful," said Lizzie. To the west they could see along the shoreline of West Vancouver as far as Lighthouse Point, several miles away. Left, to the east, half of the Lions Gate bridge was visible, soaring north toward West Vancouver from Stanley Park.

"I'm glad the sun's shining on your birthday," said Michelle.

Lizzie shrugged, and Michelle removed her arm from her daughter's shoulders.

"The sun was shining the day we brought you home from the hospital, too," said Michelle, standing next to Lizzie, looking out the window. "You were so tiny. I'd never seen anything so tiny. We'd fixed up the sun porch for you. It had white curtains on all its windows. But mostly we left them open. A big acacia tree shaded the back of the house. We wanted you to be able to watch it from your crib."

"I don't think babies that small can see that far," said Lizzie stiffly.

Michelle smiled. "Maybe not. Anyway, we took you into the sun porch and put you in your crib. And there were roses everywhere. Little pink roses. They grew on the fence in the backyard. It was falling down from the weight of them. And Max had picked dozens and dozens of them, and shoved them into vases and peanut-butter jars—they were on your dresser, and on the table next to the rocking chair—all over the room. They were so pretty."

"You've told me all that before," said Lizzie.

"Of course I have," said Michelle, and bent slightly to kiss Lizzie's cheek. Then she gave her a hug and went to help Alexandra with dinner. "Can I get the rotten kid a Coke?" she asked.

"I'll do it," said Alexandra. She scooped ice into a glass and poured in Coke.

"The sound of that fizzing makes me all nostalgic," said Michelle. "Do you remember? Saturday mornings?"

Allie grinned and nodded. "First the library, then the bakery for two glazed doughnuts each, and finally the corner store for Coke."

"In green bottles," said Michelle.

Alexandra laughed, and Michelle watched her walk from the kitchen down the hall toward the living room. Alexandra moved like water, or the wind. She never made a movement that was graceless or unnecessary. She wasn't beautiful—but she had a serene elegance that was beautiful. She dressed well, too, thought Michelle enviously. Flamboyantly, but with good taste. Which was just as well, since her job was to look after the women's clothing displays in the biggest department store in the city.

Just as Allie returned to the kitchen Lizzie called out, "Do you mind if I put on a record?"

"Play anything you like," Alexandra called back, and in a few moments she and Michelle, working in the kitchen, heard the first cut from *Abbey Road.*

Then the doorbell rang, and Lizzie called, "It must be Grandma. I'll get it."

When Michelle got to the door Lizzie had lifted her grandmother right off her feet in a bear hug. Mrs. Jeffries got into a laughing fit and started wheezing. Lizzie patted her on the back and sat her down on the wide leather sofa, while Alexandra hurriedly poured a glass of sherry.

"Here, Mrs. J.," she said, handing her the glass. "Down the hatch and I'll get you another one."

Michelle grinned at her mother as she pounded her chest, sipped some sherry, put down the glass, and wiped her eyes, which were still full of laughter. "No thank you, Allie, this'll do me fine," she said, and gave Michelle a wink.

Eleanor Jeffries did a lot of things to keep active. She went to dances, and church, and bingo, and did volunteer work, and read a lot. She was staunch and resilient, thought Michelle, looking at her fondly, and her loyalties were unshakeable. "Is it another woman?" she'd said when Michelle told her about the divorce. "Several of them, it seems," said Michelle, trying to laugh. Her mother shook her head and took Michelle in her arms and patted her back while she cried.

At least I don't cry anymore, thought Michelle now, smiling at her mother.

At least I only cry when I'm alone, now, she corrected herself.

Dinner was boeuf bordelaise, pommes dauphine, and spinach salad, Lizzie's favorite things. She was allowed wine, because it was her birthday, although when after her third glass she wanted more, her mother demurred.

Lizzie leaned close and whispered in Michelle's ear, "It's pretty ridiculous, don't you think, that a person who's been on the Pill for nearly a year, just in case, shouldn't be able to have a fourth glass of wine." She sat back and giggled as her mother's face turned red.

"It's time for coffee," said Michelle firmly. "Coffee's what goes with birthday cakes."

Lizzie emitted an eerily childlike squeal followed by, "A cake! A cake! I get a cake!"

"Of course you get a cake," said Michelle sharply. "Don't we always have birthday cakes in this family?"

"Yeah, but it isn't exactly a family anymore, is it?" Lizzie looked blurrily around the table, as if in search of her father.

"Of course we're still a family," said her grandmother. "Don't ever let me hear you say such a thing, Elizabeth."

Lizzie looked at her in astonishment. "Did you hear what she called me?" she said to her mother. "She called me Elizabeth!" She turned to her grandmother, who was sitting next to her, and hugged her. "Elizabeth. I love it!"

"You've gotten taller. You've filled out. You're becoming a beautiful young woman," said her grandmother. "Elizabeth seems more fitting."

"She's right," said Alexandra, studying Lizzie. "You've turned into an Elizabeth, before our very eyes."

Michelle watched her daughter straighten almost imperceptibly in her chair. Lizzie's skin was smooth, her body was firm and shapely, her chestnut hair fell in a glittering frame around her face. Michelle saw Lizzie glance at her, smiling faintly, and knew that her daughter felt youth to be an advantage, and could have wept for her.

"I think," said Michelle when the dishes had been cleared away and the four of them were sitting in the living room, "I think I'm going to quit my job." Her mouth was a bit dry; their reactions were important to her.

"It's getting to be too much for you, is it, Michelle?" said her mother. "All that traveling around?" She had a rope of grey hair which she wore braided and swept into a complicated arrangement on the back of her head. Michelle watched as she removed a few loose hairpins and jabbed them more firmly into place. When her mother brushed out her hair it reached almost to her waist.

"Not exactly," said Michelle. "It's just that now that I'm on my own, I'd like to be working for me, instead of for someone else."

"What have you got in mind?" said Alexandra.

Michelle braced herself. She knew that she was already blushing, and cursed the fair skin that so often gave her away. "There's a little bookstore on Marine Drive," she said. "The owner wants to sell. I've been talking to my bank manager about it."

"You mean you want to buy it?" said Alexandra. "Go into business?"

"I think so, yeah. If I can arrange the financing. The house has been sold," she said, looking at each of them in turn. "I was going to put my share of the money into term deposits. I thought maybe I'd buy a house, once I'd had a chance to think about things, settle down a bit. But I like this idea much better. It's—it's kind of an investment in myself."

"It sounds crazy to me," said Lizzie.

"No, it sounds good," said Alexandra. "But are you sure it's the right time to do it, Michelle? Things aren't exactly booming around here."

"I think she should go right ahead, if it's what she wants," said Mrs. Jeffries. "I might even be able to help you a bit, Michelle, if you need it." She turned to Lizzie with a smile. "She wouldn't have to travel anymore. She'd be able to stay home, with you."

"We had that all worked out, Grandma," said Lizzie. "I was going to stay with Dad when she was out of town. I'm helping him look for an apartment. With two bedrooms. One's going to be for me."

"I won't do anything," said Michelle to Alexandra, a shade irritably, "if my bank manager advises against it."

"But why are you going it now?" said Lizzie.

Michelle looked at her in bewilderment. "What do you mean? I just told you."

"I mean, why do it now? Why now? Why not last year, or the year before, when it would have made a difference, when it would have done some good?" Lizzie's lower lip was quivering. She wiped the palms of her hands on her white linen dress-up pants.

"I don't know what you mean, Lizzie," said Michelle. She felt an urgent need to wrap her arms around her daughter and rock her back and forth. She stood up. But Lizzie raised her arms, palms out, like a policeman.

"Hey, Lizzie," said Alexandra.

"If you'd done it last year, you wouldn't have had to get divorced," said Lizzie. "It doesn't make a damn bit of difference now, it's too late, you've gone and done it, Daddy probably doesn't even want you back anymore."

Michelle sat down, and Lizzie lowered her arms. She seemed unaware of the tears rolling down her cheeks.

"Hey, wait a minute," said Alexandra softly. "You've got it all wrong, honey."

"You keep out of this," said Lizzie. "Don't you call me 'honey.' You don't know anything about this. It's none of your business."

"Elizabeth, control yourself," said Mrs. Jeffries in a tone she seldom used. Lizzie squeezed her eyes shut and clenched her fists and took a deep breath and then another one.

"My job had nothing to do with it," said Michelle. She had

picked up one of the throw cushions from the sofa and was clutching it to her stomach. "My job had nothing to do with it," she said, shaking her head.

Lizzie looked at her. "You stopped getting along together. That's what you said. But you got along just fine until you got that job."

Michelle opened her mouth, but no sounds came out. She saw that her mother was looking at Lizzie and trying without saying anything to get her to stop talking.

"I mean, listen," said Lizzie to Michelle. "One minute you're there and the next minute you're gone, off to Alexandra." She shook her head. "But it *couldn't* have happened like that. You couldn't just all of a sudden not care anymore, could you? About Dad? About me?" She lifted her hands and wiped at her cheeks.

"Of course I care about you!" said Michelle. "I care about your father, too. Of course I do."

"No, you don't!" said Lizzie. "You just got tired of us! You just want to live some other life! Well, I want my old life back, that's what I want. I want my old life back!"

"Oh, for Christ's sake," said Alexandra. She stood up. "I've had it with this. You want to know what happened?" she said to Lizzie.

"Allie, shut up," said Michelle.

"I'll tell you what happened. Your father fucked around," said Alexandra, looking at Lizzie with fury in her eyes. "He fucked around on your mother, you ungrateful child, as you must know if you've got a brain in your head, your father is a fucker-around, and that's why all this happened, and it has not just happened to you, either, kindly remember that, you sniveling little twit."

They were frozen in the moment, the four of them, each trying to absorb its impact and assess its damage. And then Michelle suddenly felt unutterably weary, the whole business seemed indescribably boring, and she thought about Max making love to the girl in the photograph, his face flushed, burried in her breasts, his lips sucking at her nipple, one hand fumbling at her crotch, the other clutched in her hair, and to her amazement, she began to laugh.

She couldn't stop for a long time, even though she saw clearly her mother's shock, and Alexandra's concern.

And Lizzie's contempt.

That's why I didn't tell her the truth, she thought, as her laughter began to die. I didn't want to see that look on her face.

5

Casey heard the busy *click-clicking* of the dog's paws along the tiled floor of the hallway and looked up wearily over his reading glasses.

There was a peremptory scratching at his half-open door and it opened wider. Casey leaned across his desk and saw a black woolly head and two shiny brown eyes. The eyes peered suspiciously around his office.

"You should get him to cut your toenails," said Casey to the dog, which ignored him and sidled around the door and into his office.

It was followed by a tall, overweight man with thinning black hair, a black moustache, and a large, gap-toothed grin. He taught composition and was Casey's closest friend on the faculty.

"All I have to say is 'Let's go see Casey,' " said Ed Bernstein, "and she jumps up and sets straight off down the hall." He sat down in a straight-backed institutional chair near the window. "She likes you," he said, watching the dog fondly as she sniffed her way around the office.

"Great," said Casey resignedly.

The dog, whose name was Corky, settled itself at Ed's feet and he reached down to give her a pat. Few people in the music department approved of the dog's constant presence in the building, but she never peed on the floors and hardly ever barked, and it happened that the dean of the fine arts faculty was an animal lover.

Ed reached over to push the door closed. "I've got an announcement to make," he said. "We've finally decided," he said. "We're going. I'm just about to make it official."

"Oh, shit, Ed," said Casey, tossing his glasses on the papers that cluttered his desk. "What are you doing to me?"

"I'm going home, Casey. Ohio's our home," said Ed. "It's our folks, mostly, I think," he said, staring down at the knees of his green-and-blue-plaid slacks. "They're on top of the world about it. We called them last night." He looked at Casey. "They're getting old, Casey. You know how it is. Your dad's got all those other kids living near him. Myra and I—" He shrugged. "We're all our folks have." He turned to look out the window, where a September sun shone benignly upon the campus of the University of British Columbia.

"Shit," said Casey.

"We're not going until May," said Ed. "And maybe we'll come back." He was still looking out the window. "You know. Later."

"Yeah. Sure." Casey got up and tried to pace around the office but the room was too small. Finally he sat on the edge of his desk, one foot swinging near the head of the small black dog, which looked up at it warily. "What am I going to do without you? I don't think I would ever have left the house again after Aline died, if it hadn't been for you and Myra." Ed and his wife had dragged Casey out to movies, made him go with them for walks along the beach, taken him to their house for dinner at least twice a week.

"You're going to be okay now," said Ed, trying a smile. "Besides," he added after a minute, "you're thinking about going home yourself, aren't you?"

Casey got up and sat behind the desk again. He picked up a pencil and drew a musical staff on the back of a memo from the chairman. "I was. I am. I don't know." He started scribbling notes on the staff. "Haven't even written any letters yet." He threw the pencil down. "Hey, look," he said to Ed. "Ohio State's a good department. If that's what you want to do, that's what you ought to do." He reached over and grabbed Ed's shoulder. "I'm happy for you, pal, whatever you do, wherever you go. You know that."

When Ed had left, Casey stood by the narrow, rectangular window and looked out at trees and shrubbery and lawns and at the Buchanan building, across the boulevarded mall, where students thronged the wide concrete steps. He wanted to get out of his office and walk around in a distant part of the campus, where agriculture was taught, or medicine, or the sciences; someplace where he was unlikely to encounter anyone he knew.

It occurred to him that he had made a certain amount of progress. Last term, it had been agony for him to make his way through the music building. He had had to let people say things to him and pat him on the shoulder and look sorrowful. He had appreciated their concern; but he had trouble identifying himself during these exchanges—which weren't really exchanges at all, since he said nothing, did nothing but bow his head and wait for them to be over. He felt, as people murmured at him, a distance, an incredulity, which he supposed now had been part of his months-long inability to accept, in the tissues of himself, the fact of Aline's death.

Finally, in desperation, he had begun assuming a worried, preoccupied expression and rushing through the halls almost at a gallop, refusing to stop or even slow down when colleagues or secretaries tried to get his attention. He would flap his arm at them, vaguely, implying important business elsewhere. When he reached the spacious lobby after the first time he did this he had felt pleased with himself. He'd found the trick. Just ignore them; look like you're busy thinking about something else; refuse to discuss it.

He picked up his jacket and left his office.

"How's it going?" said Barry Fox, whom he met on the stairs. He was a short, fair-haired man, director of the department's early-music ensemble. Unlike other members of the faculty, he always dressed for classes in sports jacket, tailored trousers, shirt and tie.

Casey stroked with exaggerated awe the sleeve of Barry's tan suede jacket. "I've got to get me some new clothes," he said, and Barry, laughing, shook off his hand. "I go around here looking like an unemployed accordionist," said Casey.

"You've got the tousled, absentminded look," said Barry as they reached the lobby. "It's very popular with the kids. Soothes them."

Yes, he had made a lot of progress, Casey told himself firmly, as he watched Barry go off down the hall to one of the studio rooms on the main floor. He could greet people easily, now, and even exchange smiling pleasantries.

But he still hadn't managed to start singing again.

Ohio, he thought, dismayed.

He pushed through the glass doors and went out into the sunshine to sit on a wooden bench at the edge of the large patio that fronted the music building. He watched students coming and going from the cafeteria in the basement of the old auditorium across the street.

He still hadn't sold his house. But he had at least put Aline's clothing into boxes and delivered it to the Salvation Army. He had sent her jewelry to her parents, and packed everything else into trunks which now sat in the basement. He had just recently gotten rid of her car, too, because the insurance was about to expire and he had to get it off the street. It had been ridiculous, anyway, one man with two cars. Living in a house that big was ridiculous, too. He ought to get cracking, call a real estate agent, start looking around for an apartment.

"Excuse me." The girl slid onto the bench next to him. "Do you remember me?"

She was dressed with considerable attention to quality, and probably style, as well—how the hell would he know?—in flat leather shoes, hose, a tan suede skirt, and an ivory-colored blouse that looked like silk. It had no collar, and the top two buttons were open. He noticed that the skirt had a slit up the side so that she could cross her legs without splitting the seam.

She was tanned, too. It must have been a good year for sunbathing. In fact he did seem to remember that the sun had shone more than usual.

She had long, blond hair which was parted in the middle and

fell straight to her shoulders. She didn't seem to be wearing any makeup. Except for her clothes, she looked to him like someone out of the sixties.

But he didn't remember her.

"I'm not surprised," she said with a smile. "You can't be expected to remember all your students."

"I'm sorry," he said with a smile.

He looked at his watch. He meant it to be an obvious gesture, preparing her for his imminent departure.

She stretched out her hand. "My name is Nancy Murray," she said.

Her fingernails were polished. On her right wrist she wore a thin gold watch. "Are you left-handed?" said Casey.

She nodded, her hand still outstretched. He took it.

"I was very sorry to hear that your wife died," she said. "I wanted to tell you as soon as I found out. But there never seemed to be an opportunity."

He nodded, aware of her perfume, which was faint but intriguing, and the firmness of her grip.

"I'm registered with you for voice this term," she said.

"Mezzo," Casey guessed.

"Right," she said, laughing. "I get my first lesson Tuesday." Slowly, she relaxed her clasp upon his hand. He held on until to go on doing so would have altered the situation considerably. Then he let go, feeling flustered.

She stood and adjusted a large leather handbag over her shoulder. "I'll see you Tuesday afternoon, then," she said, and walked away.

Early that evening, right after dinner, he changed into a sweatsuit Aline had given him. It was dark green, which she had said looked good with his eyes. He'd worn it several times, when he had to wash one of the cars, or put in some resentful hours in the garden.

But she'd gotten it for him in the hope that it would encourage him to get more exercise. He told her that if it was his heart she was worried about she had no need, since it was well known that conducting strengthened the heart. "It's all that waving about of the hands," he'd said.

He looked into the mirror and thought it pretty fucking ironic that Aline, always concerned with diet, never missing her twenty laps a day in the university pool, was the one to have died.

At forty.

He sat on the edge of the bed and wondered what he was doing.

Finally he got up and went downstairs, patting his belly. "Gotta do something about this," he muttered to himself. "Gotta lose ten pounds. Minimum."

He opened the front door and looked outside. Nobody in sight. He went up the sidewalk, turned right and walked briskly to the corner, turned right again. Then, out of view of his neighbors, he began, cautiously, to jog.

6

It was now October, and still Casey could not sing.

His sister, Margaret, the only other singer in his family, called regularly from Los Angeles to keep track of his progress. She kept telling him that this, too, would pass. And he tried to believe her.

He had even subjected himself to a complete checkup, only to be told that there was absolutely nothing physically wrong with him. It was a psychological problem, and it ought to disappear on its own, in time.

But it might not disappear soon enough to save his career. He was at the moment useless as a voice teacher, and as a conductor. He knew it, his students knew it, the whole department knew it.

It had been suggested to him that he get psychiatric help, a notion that filled him with horror, yet one which he was having to seriously consider.

He kept trying, alone at home, at the piano which he had always thought of as Aline's because she had played it so much better than he. He didn't even really *want* to sing, at least he didn't think he did; but he knew that he had to, if he wanted to keep his job.

It was as though something in his throat had died; there was a deadness, a heaviness there which prevented him from opening it wide enough to sing.

He was close to panic when, by the end of the fourth week of the new term, it was clear that he was no better off than he'd been last year.

When his second-to-last student left the small teaching studio one dreary Tuesday afternoon, Casey kicked aside the music stand and hit the soundproof wall a few times with his fist. He was contemplating knocking his head against it when the door opened and Nancy Murray came in.

"Let's get to work," he said. "No time for pleasantries. Show me what you've done since last time."

He sat down at the piano and began banging out scales. She got herself organized, opened her mouth, and began to sing. He listened for half a minute. She was dreadful. As bad now as the first time he'd heard her, three sessions ago. If he'd been present at her audition he knew damn well she would never have been admitted into the program, let alone one of his classes.

"Stop," he said.

She stopped.

He stood up and paced the floor. "That's awful," he said finally. "Terrible. You sound terrible. Do you know that?"

She looked chagrined, but hardly broken.

"For God's sake, woman, you've got to open your mouth," he said, practically shouting. "Otherwise not a goddamn thing is going to come out." He was furious, and a part of him strongly disapproved, because he had learned a long time ago that rage seldom worked as a teaching tool. When it did, it was only because a decision had been made to use it, and then it was of course feigned rage, not the real thing.

Casey was possessed by the real thing.

"Try this one," he said. *"Me-may-moh—mah-moo,"* he said. "Open it." He poked at her throat. "Open it." He pushed his finger at her lips. "Open up and try it again."

She opened her mouth wide. *"Me-ee ma-ay mo-oh mah-ah moo,"* she offered. She sounded like a stricken calf. It was too much.

"Me-ee ma-ay mo-oh mah-ah mo," bellowed Casey.

He looked at her, astounded. He touched his throat. He did it again: *"Me-ee ma-ay mo-oh mah-ah moo."* His smile, he knew, was dazzling. "Shit," he said. He went over to Nancy Murray and picked her up and swung her around. She yelped, and he put her down. He stood back and with a hand theatrically on his chest sang a few bars of "Danny Boy." Then, breathless, he grinned at her. "You think I'm crazy," he said confidently, "but I'm not."

"Well, there's certainly something peculiar going on," she said, irritated.

"I'm sorry I was so rough on you. You don't deserve it. You haven't been making progress because I haven't been helping you. But now, I can." He saw the beginnings of a hopeful smile on her face and added quickly, "I don't know how much I can help you. It's hard to tell," he said delicately, "just what kind of a voice you have, how much we'll be able to do with it."

She nodded soberly.

"But we'll do the best we can. Okay?"

"Okay."

"And now," he said, "that's it for today. I'll see you next week. Same time, same place." He beamed at her. His joy was too large and tumultuous to be contained in a room so small.

"That's it? We've hardly done anything!" she wailed.

She was really extremely attractive, he thought benevolently. Today she was wearing dark brown leather pants that squeaked enticingly when she walked, and a big soft brown and caramel sweater that made him think about the size of her breasts. He shook his head admiringly.

"It's my throat," he said. "A sore throat. I've had it for months. But I'm sure, I'm positive, that it'll be completely better by next week." He opened the door and gestured her in a gentlemanly fashion out into the hall.

He realized when he'd bounded up the two flights of stairs and down the hall to his office that it had begun to rain. From his window he saw kids unleashing umbrellas, huddling under backpacks, holding newspapers above their heads as they hurried for shelter, or to a bus stop, or toward one of the distant student parking lots.

Casey threw on his raincoat and quickly left his office. He

could hardly wait to get home and sing. He'd start with easy stuff; he had a lot of work ahead of him to get his voice back into shape.

He ran through the pouring rain to the faculty parking lot only a block away, trying to decide whether he should accompany himself first on the piano or the guitar. He'd pick one of his sister's favorites and sing it over the phone to her. He anticipated with great pleasure Margaret's relief and delight.

When he got to his car he heard someone yelling. He turned around.

"Hey! Wait! Please wait!"

He squinted through the rain and saw Nancy bolting toward him, her coat collar turned up, her arms full of books. "Could you possibly give me a ride," she said breathlessly when she'd reached him, "to the bus stop? My friend didn't show up. It's her day to drive, but she hasn't shown up."

He opened the passenger door and helped her in. Her long blond hair was drenched, and her eyelashes were stuck together by the rain.

She said she lived only a few blocks from the campus gates, so he offered to drive her home.

When he pulled up in front of the house in which she rented a basement apartment, she asked him to come in for coffee.

He shook his head, smiling at her.

She leaned closer to him, put her hand on his thigh, and asked him again. She was looking steadily into his face and seemed extraordinarily confident.

Casey felt his eyes widen. He also felt himself starting to get hard. He shook his head again, but this time he wasn't smiling.

"Casey," she said, her hand still on his thigh, her eyes still on his face. "May I call you that? Casey?"

Casey just looked at her.

"Well, Casey, then," she said. "Casey, I don't know how old you are, but I myself am past the age of consent. You're a very attractive man."

He was much harder, now. He tried to ease his discomfort by adjusting his position. She saw this, and slowly straightened, causing her breasts to thrust against her sweater. Sweet Jesus, thought Casey, offended by her obviousness. But his penis swelled still more, and his balls ached.

"Listen, Nancy. I don't sleep with students. It's kind of an unwritten law."

"Ah, but so many people do. That's why it's a law that's remained unwritten." She held out her hand to him. "Come on. Have a cup of coffee, anyway. It's cold, and you're wet. You ought to come in and dry off. Otherwise your sore throat might get worse."

She gathered her books together and got out of the car. He followed her along a walk at the side of the house to a private entrance in the back. He had nothing to feel guilty about, he told himself; but he was relieved to be able to go in and out of her apartment without being seen. Of course his car was sitting right out in front of the house, but it was unlikely that anyone would recognize it, it was just an ordinary American car, a small one, two doors, four cylinders, good mileage, he'd been hearing funny noises lately, though, must get it into the garage. . . . Jesus Christ, he thought, what the hell am I doing? But by then he was inside.

She put some coffee on, which relieved his mind somewhat, but then she disappeared into another room and came out wearing nothing, absolutely nothing at all. He gaped at the sight of her, honey-colored skin except where she'd worn a bikini, breasts so large and firm and high his hands reached for them like a dying man reaches for water, dark blond hair between her legs profuse and crinkly, he was so grateful, he almost wept with gratitude when she unzipped his pants and then the only pain he felt there was the pain of needing to be inside her.

"I knew it," she said later, lying next to him on a bed fitted with a singularly lumpy mattress.

"You knew what," he said, his hand on her soft flat belly.

"I knew you'd be good. I could tell the first time I met you, when you didn't want to let go of my hand."

"We can't do this again, you know, Nancy," he said.

"Maybe we will and maybe we won't," she said. "Next time let's smoke a little grass first. Make it last longer."

"There won't be a next time," he said, looking up at the stained ceiling. "Why are you living here, anyway? Anybody who wears the clothes you wear can afford something better than this."

"It's this or live at home. I prefer not to live at home."

He sat up and looked down at her. "How old are you?"

"I told you," she said. "I'm an adult."

"An adult. What year are you in? Second, isn't it? That makes you probably nineteen."

"Right. An adult."

"Jesus Christ," said Casey in a whisper. He got off the bed and started getting dressed.

She followed him to the door, naked, and helped him into his raincoat. Then she took his hands and put them on her breasts.

"See?" she said. "My nipples are all hard." She touched his crotch, rubbed gently at his penis. "We could do it again." She took a step back, smiling. "Don't worry, Professor. I'll never tell a soul. I like having secrets."

"I can't do this again, Nancy." He opened the door and stepped out into the rain. "I loved it. You're gorgeous and sexy and I loved it. But I can't do it again."

But he did.

And when it ended, he found another girl. Or she found him.

And then there was another one.

And another.

And another.

7

"You're going *out?*" said Lizzie, incredulous. "With a *man?*"

"I've got to start doing it someday," Michelle said grimly. "I might as well do it now. He could be the only man who ever asks me out."

"I think it's absolutely disgusting," said Lizzie. "You've been out of my father's house for barely six months—"

"Seven," said Michelle into the mirror. "And it was *our* house."

"What difference does it make, seven, six, haven't you got any shame, any sense of decency?"

Michelle turned and looked thoughtfully at her daughter. Lizzie's face was red, her eyes flashed, her hands were fists. "How is your dad?" she said. "You see him a lot. Talk to him on the phone. How is he, anyway?"

"He's lonely," said Lizzie, with passion. "Terribly lonely. He misses us. He says so every time I talk to him."

"I saw him the other day," said Michelle, turning back to the mirror. "Downtown. Having lunch at the Pan Pacific. With some girl. They were holding hands on the tabletop."

"Can you blame him?" said Lizzie, and began to cry.

"No," said Michelle. "And I don't blame me, either."

Lizzie stormed away and Michelle closed her bedroom door

and leaned wearily against it. She wished she could crawl into bed with a large brandy and a good book. She let herself slide down the door until she was sitting on the floor with her knees up.

She wondered often if it had been a good idea to insist that Lizzie live with her. Lizzie herself continued to maintain stubbornly that she'd be a lot better off with her father—because Max needed someone to look after him was how she'd put it when she and Michelle had discussed the situation for the fifty-second time.

Oh but Lizzie needed someone to look after her, too, thought Michelle in despair, and she could do that better than Max could, she knew it, she knew it.

She sat on the carpeted floor of her bedroom, her bathrobe scrunched up behind her, and remembered holding Lizzie's hand tight while her terrified daughter got an immunization shot . . . and chasing away with uncontained wrath a little boy who had harrassed Lizzie all the way from the schoolyard to her front steps; helping her put pictures in a photograph album; showing her how to clean her new white shoes; looking for the mouse. . . .

She had trudged up and down the lane behind their house, hand-in-hand with a weeping, five-year-old Lizzie, searching for that mouse. It was a pink mouse made of felt, about eight inches long, which disappeared somewhere between the house of Lizzie's friend Brenda and Lizzie's own house, two blocks away. The small creature was called simply "Mouse," and it was Lizzie's favorite possession. Michelle and Lizzie looked and looked and they couldn't find it. Michelle hadn't even considered this possibility. It had been unquestionably established that Mouse had been lost within a two-block stretch of back alley; surely it was simply a matter of patiently searching the lane, inch by inch, over and over again, if necessary. Which they did. Finally Michelle sent Lizzie indoors because it was cold and dark, and with a flashlight she scoured the alley alone, again and yet again, and still she couldn't find the damn mouse.

When finally she gave up she went inside and with tears in her eyes said that the mouse was gone forever. Lizzie had flung her arms around Michelle's neck and comforted her.

Michelle couldn't remember the last time Lizzie had hugged her.

It was Max, she reminded herself now, to whom Lizzie had talked when she was trying to decide what to be when she grew up. And she went to Max, too, when she was trying to figure out how she could kind of like a boy in her class when she still hated boys in general as much as ever. And she always modeled her new clothes for her father, and if he wasn't enthusiastic about them, then neither was Lizzie.

Michelle pushed herself clumsily off the floor. She stood in her bedroom and tried to think about what she ought to wear.

A suit, maybe. Businesslike. Nothing provocative. She didn't want to give this guy any ideas.

He was a sales rep, and she was pretty sure he was just lonely and had no intention of coming on to her. He wore a very ostentatious wedding ring, after all.

She laughed out loud, then. Max had worn a wedding ring, too.

The next day she had lunch with her mother.

"The first thing I noticed when he picked me up, Ma," she said, over an omelet at Jonathan's on Granville Island, "was that he was no longer wearing it. The wedding ring."

"It's very discouraging," said Mrs. Jeffries, "the kinds of people there are in the world."

"Actually, he's pretty nice," said Michelle with a sigh. "That's what's so depressing. We had a pleasant time. Went to a very nice restaurant, ate good food, drank good wine, enjoyed each other's company."

"And then what?" said Mrs. Jeffries, buttering half a roll.

"And then I said, 'How come you took your wedding ring off? What kind of an evening did you think this was going to be?' "

"Michelle," said her mother, slowly, admiringly. "However did you find the nerve?"

"We were parked in my driveway and he was slobbering all over my neck at the time," said Michelle. She took a bite of her omelet, sipped from her glass of wine.

"Oh, dear," said her mother.

"He pulled away right smartly," said Michelle, grinning. "And then Lizzie, bless her heart, opened the front door and stood there in the porch light, her hair in rollers, wearing that old bathrobe that I loathe. So I didn't have any trouble getting out of the car." She put down her fork. "It isn't as though I don't want to have sex, Ma."

Mrs. Jeffries looked uneasily around the restaurant.

"But I don't want to have it with just anyone."

"No, of course not, dear."

"Well, sometimes I think I *could* have it with just anyone."

"Oh, no, I don't think you mean that, Michelle," said Mrs. Jeffries vaguely, patting the edges of her mouth with her napkin.

Michelle leaned across the table toward her. "Ma, do you think I'll ever fall in love with anybody again?"

Her mother put her napkin on the table. "I don't know. Is it very important to you, do you think?"

"It would have been easier if he'd died," said Michelle. She fished in her handbag for tissue. "Oh, God, Ma, I don't want to cry in public, I hardly ever cry about it anymore."

"One thing's the same," said Mrs. Jeffries, "whether they die or you leave them. You have to make yourself a brand new life." She looked out the window at a sailboat plying its way up False Creek. "You're going to be lonely."

Michelle dabbed quickly at her eyes, blew her nose, and shoved the tissue back in her purse. "I know," she said.

"You think you're lonely now," said her mother. "But it will be worse when Lizzie goes off to university." She turned to look at Michelle. "Sometimes," she said calmly, "I'm so lonely that I ache with it, and it's hard for me to tell whether I'm just lonely or genuinely ill."

Michelle put a hand over her mother's. "Ma."

Mrs. Jeffries withdrew her hand, slowly, so as not to seem

rude. "Just sometimes, Michelle. Usually I'm very content. But I thought I ought to warn you. Because you've never lived by yourself, and it might not have occurred to you."

"I'm going to miss Alexandra," said Michelle woodenly. "I know that, all right."

"You will have a job," said Mrs. Jeffries. "A business of your own. I'm glad you're going to do that. It will help a lot." She reached down to retrieve her handbag from the floor. Then she looked her daughter in the eye. "It will help a lot more, Michelle," she said, "believe it or not, than going out for dinner with men who leave their wedding rings in their hotel rooms."

"Yes, Ma," said Michelle humbly. "You're right."

8

"We should have had a party for you," said Michelle. She poured herself more brandy, and refilled Alexandra's glass, too. "Your last night in Vancouver, it ought to be more—it ought to be momentous, somehow."

"I had a party. At work," said Alexandra. She took a drink. "I have no desire to do anything momentous, my dear. There's nobody I really care about here except my parents and you. I left my parents when I left home. So they don't count. Only you count." She turned to Michelle, who was curled up in the opposite corner of the couch, and patted her bare ankle. "This is where I want to be. It's exactly where I want to be, my last night here."

She had been offered a job in New York which even Michelle agreed she couldn't turn down. She was to start work Monday, October 24. She had made a quick trip to New York to find an apartment and had already sold her furniture. Since then she had been staying with Michelle and Lizzie.

Michelle got up to put on more music. She looked for her favorite tape, the one that had belonged to Max and had gotten into Michelle's boxes by mistake—or else Max had put it there on purpose because he knew how much she liked it. She admitted that this was possible. "The Four Seasons" was on one side of the tape. On the other were six selections whose titles Michelle could never remember, but which she loved.

"Who are they, anyway, these people Lizzie plays," Michelle grumbled, rummaging. She finally found "The Four Seasons" and put it on.

"You and Lizzie seem to be getting along better these days," said Alexandra, as Michelle got back on the sofa.

"Do you think so? I hope you're right. She's still upset about the name business, though."

Michelle had decided to abandon her married name and go back to using Jeffries. Lizzie disapproved of this violently.

"I worry about her," said Michelle. "She still spends more time with Corinne than with any of the kids she's met here."

"She's loyal. Besides, she hasn't had enough time here to make good friends yet."

"It seems she's always rushing off for the weekend, either to Corinne's house or Max's," Michelle complained. Tonight, it was Corinne's.

"Come on, Michelle," said Alexandra, lightly slapping her leg. "Shape up." She refilled their glasses. "Drink. I may get bombed tonight. I don't want to do it alone."

"I don't like getting bombed," said Michelle. She drank some more brandy. "I get sick when I get bombed."

"Don't drink that much, for God's sake," said Alexandra, alarmed. "I hate it when people throw up."

Michelle stretched out on the sofa and rested her bare feet in Alexandra's lap.

"You haven't got anything to feel guilty about, you know," said Allie, stroking her instep. "Sure you're working hard—you have to. But you don't go away anymore, now that you've got the bookstore. Lizzie knows where to find you when she needs you."

"I don't understand," said Michelle thoughtfully, "why I should have such trouble being a mother, when I love my own mother so much and feel so comfortable with her."

"You and Lizzie are different people," said Alexandra. "She's prickly. You're not. She adores her father, and she blames you because she doesn't have him anymore. Or at least she doesn't have the two of you together anymore. Of course she knows the divorce was his fault, not yours, but she can't admit that because she wants him to be perfect. Now, you lost your father, too. But he died. That was a legitimate loss. And you were able to share it with your mother . . . and listen to me, you'd think I was an avid reader of *Psychology Today*."

Michelle looked at Alexandra and felt a great swelling of love for her.

"You are an extraordinary friend," she said, and smiled as she saw the surprise on Allie's face. "You have managed to avoid both husband and children, as you always said you would, yet you go on giving me good and patient advice about troubles that don't interest you in the slightest."

"They wouldn't interest me if they were anybody else's troubles," said Alexandra. "They interest me because they're yours."

She swept to her feet in one of those liquid, sensual moves that Michelle loved and envied. "Now I think it's time we ate something," she said. "Is Chinese okay with you? Shall I phone in the order?"

While they waited, they drank more brandy and reminisced about high school, which made them laugh a great deal. They talked about people they'd known, boyfriends they'd had, ambitions realized and ambitions still fallow: they refused to admit that any of them might be dead.

"The Four Seasons" came to an end. Michelle turned the tape over and they listened to Mozart, and Haydn, and Albinoni.

When the Chinese food arrived Michelle set it out on the coffee table while Alexandra went to the kitchen for the bottle of red wine she'd bought that afternoon.

Michelle shooed Ashes away from the food spread out on the coffee table. Alexandra lit every candle Michelle owned and placed them on the coffee table, on the end tables beside the sofa, on the mantelpiece; then she turned out the lights. She flourished the wine bottle in the air and threw back her head and laughed. "What a wonderful night this is!" she said, as though she were singing it.

By the time they had eaten and finished the bottle of wine it was eleven o'clock. "Still early," said Alexandra with relief. "It's thirteen whole hours before my plane leaves."

"Are you scared?" said Michelle.

Alexandra thought about it. "No," she said firmly. "Nervous. Excited. But not scared."

She found their brandy snifters and filled them.

Michelle put a scratchy old record on the stereo and settled back on the sofa with Alexandra.

"Chances are . . ." sang Johnny Mathis.

"Oh my goodness," said Alexandra with a smile. "That does make me nostalgic. Or something."

"I remember you and Denny dancing to this song," said Michelle. "It was quite disgusting," she said, laughing.

"Don't talk to me about disgusting," said Alexandra. "When you danced a slow dance with Tommy Hogan it would have been impossible to pry the two of you apart."

"I had my first orgasm with Tommy Hogan," said Michelle.

"I'm not at all surprised. Not on the dance floor, I hope."

"Of course not on the dance floor."

"Good."

Michelle picked up her brandy glass from the coffee table. "I didn't actually sleep with him, Allie."

"Good heavens, I should hope not. You were only seventeen."

Michelle gave her a wry glance.

"Well, things were different then," said Alexandra gently.

"Think of what we missed," said Michelle. She put down her glass and banged her fist on the arm of the sofa. "Just think of all we missed. Do you know that I didn't actually have full-fledged coitus with anybody until I got engaged to Max?"

Alexandra burst out laughing. "Coitus?"

"Sex. Intercourse. Orgasm. You know what I mean."

"Well, more to the point." said Allie, "—if you don't mind my asking you a personal question, that is—how's your sex life right now?"

Michelle looked at her incredulously—and then laughed.

"Ah," said Alexandra, nodding sagely. "I see."

"I've had some dates, though," said Michelle. "I had one just the other day. I met him at the restaurant so I wouldn't have to let him drive me home but he grabbed me in the parking lot after dinner. Do you know what he said to me, Alexandra?" She sat up straight, indignant.

"I haven't the faintest idea. It could be damn near anything."

"He breathed in my ear and then he said, 'Tough or tender, baby? Which way do you like it?' "

"Good God," said Alexandra. "I am truly shocked."

"Can you imagine? Christ." Michelle slumped back down into the sofa.

Alexandra reached to stroke her knee. "They aren't all like that, Michelle. Really."

"Oh, Allie." Michelle looked at her in despair. "I'm afraid that I'll never ever meet anybody I want to sleep with who also wants to sleep with me."

"Of course you will," said Alexandra. She put an arm around Michelle's shoulders. "Of course you will."

"Oh God, I knew it," said Michelle. "I'm getting boozy, stupid, totally stupid, that's me. But the thing is, Allie, I'm afraid. That's what it is," she said, nodding to herself. "I'm afraid of sex with anybody who isn't Max. Also I'm afraid I've done the wrong thing, giving up my job. I'm not nearly as brave as you. It was a perfectly good job. What made me think having my own business would be any better? What do I know about running a business, anyway?" She felt Alexandra hugging her more tightly, and tried to laugh. "Sometimes I am absolutely certain that I'll never have sex with anybody again in my entire life," she said, "and that my business will be a total failure, and I'll end up with absolutely nothing and absolutely nobody." She heard herself begin to sob and cursed herself for having drunk too much. She didn't want Alexandra to remember her this way, sloshed and self-pitying, but she didn't seem able to do anything about it, so she lay back on the sofa and let herself weep.

Alexandra knelt on the floor and brushed the tears from Michelle's face, first with her fingers, then with her gentle mouth. Michelle thought she was saying something, too, but at first she couldn't hear her. She felt Allie's lips on her cheeks, her temples, her forehead; she reached up and held Allie's head between her hands and saw the tears in Alexandra's eyes and remembered that this time tomorrow, Allie would be gone. She pressed Allie's face to her chest, and felt tears against the skin that was bare where her open-necked shirt allowed it. She squeezed her eyes tightly closed and tried to pretend that Alexandra wasn't leaving. "Don't go," she said. "Please don't go."

"I won't, I won't, not yet," said Allie, and Michelle felt Allie's lips against her throat, and then her shirt was being unbuttoned, her front-fastening bra undone, and Allie's mouth was enveloping her right nipple. Allie's hand was kneading her left breast.

Michelle froze. She gripped Alexandra's hair, and Alexandra stopped moving, though her mouth and her hand remained on Michelle's breasts.

"Are we drunk?" Michelle whispered.

Alexandra moved her head slightly, so that her cheek was pressed firmly against Michelle's flesh. "Maybe."

Michelle tried to think. Neither she nor Alexandra moved. "I don't do this kind of thing, Allie. You know I don't."

"It won't hurt you to try it. Just once."

"Why?"

"Because I love you. Because I want to.'

Alexandra's face came near and nearer and she watched Allie's lips as they parted, and felt her own mouth open, and saw Allie's mouth disappear beneath her own.

It was so soft. For a moment it was like kissing the mouth of a child. And then Allie's tongue was in her mouth, circling, touching the top of her mouth and the sides, brushing her tongue; Michelle closed her eyes and tasted Alexandra, and felt her body pressed tight against Alexandra's; felt her vagina swell and open, thought that her clitoris would explode at the slightest touch of this woman's fingers, or this woman's tongue.

Alexandra broke away. Her cheeks were red and her eyes were

blazing. "First I'll do it to you," she said. "Then you do it to me. Okay?"

Michelle nodded.

Alexandra undid the button on the waistband of Michelle's jeans and pushed them down, and her panties, too; she thrust Michelle's shirt aside and with her hands on Michelle's breasts she buried her face in Michelle's belly, kissing the flesh there, biting her gently. Michelle grabbed Allie's hands and pressed them more firmly upon her breasts; Allie took her nipples and rolled them between her fingers and then lay full length upon her, and Michelle fumbled between them to pull up Alexandra's sweater, and without breaking their kiss she pushed Allie's breasts free of her bra and took them in her hands. "Oh, yes," said Allie into her mouth; "oh, yes."

Michelle ran her hands down to Alexandra's waist and undid the front of her jeans. She pulled her face from Allie's. "We might as well take our clothes off," she said.

Alexandra stood up. Her breasts were exposed above her bunched-up bra. Her hair was mussed. Her cheeks looked feverish. She pulled off her sweater and removed her bra. She stepped out of her jeans and hooked her fingers over the lacy top of her hip-hugger panties and pulled them down, too, and kicked them aside.

"You're beautiful," said Michelle.

"So are you," said Allie, and she knelt at Michelle's side. "Take off your shirt," she said, "and your jeans," and Michelle did, and Alexandra pulled off Michelle's panties. Still kneeling, she kissed Michelle's face, light fleeting kisses, and Michelle felt her hand on her thigh. Michelle spread her thighs as wide as the sofa would allow.

"Touch me," said Michelle. Her eyes were closed, her hands were clenched. She silently urged Alexandra on—and she was reminded of lying with Tommy Hogan in the hot helpless passion of virginal adolescence. She felt Alexandra's finger penetrate her, felt Alexandra's palm rubbing her clitoris, she writhed on the sofa, she rose higher and higher, and finally, thankfully, she came.

She lay panting and sweating, while Alexandra's hand smoothed the wet hair from her forehead.

After a while she sat up. Alexandra was sitting cross-legged on the carpet beside the sofa. Her breasts hung slightly, but she had no stretch marks, no extra flesh around her waist. Michelle held out a hand to her and Alexandra took it and pressed it to her cheek.

"How was it?" said Alexandra. "Was it all right?"

She hesitated. "Oh, yes, Allie," she said.

Alexandra looked at her warily.

"It was, Allie. Really."

Alexandra studied the brandy in her glass.

"Come on," said Michelle. "Now it's your turn. Lie down," she said firmly. She reached for her glass of brandy and drained it. "I think I must be very drunk, Alexandra."

Alexandra stayed where she was, staring at the floor. Michelle got up from the sofa. She put an arm around Allie's shoulders, and her other hand on Allie's breast. Alexandra shuddered.

"Get up," said Michelle. "Go lie on the sofa."

Alexandra got up. She rose from the floor in one delicious movement, and stretched herself upon the sofa, arms above her head, one knee slightly raised. She looked into Michelle's face, and Michelle saw her excitement.

And then they heard the front door open and close.

They moved as though driven by an electric shock. Within seconds they were grabbing at their clothes. But they weren't nearly fast enough.

Lizzie stood in the doorway. She looked around, bewildered, for a moment. "Why all the candles?" she said. Then she seemed to register the unconventionality of her mother and her mother's best friend shielding naked bodies from her.

"I thought you were sleeping over at Corinne's," said Michelle.

At the same moment, Lizzie said, "Corinne's grandparents are visiting."

Long seconds passed. Lizzie opened her mouth as if to speak, then closed it. Michelle looked at her pleadingly, her red plaid shirt clutched to her chest. Lizzie opened her mouth again. "I don't understand," she said pleasantly. Then, "I think I'm going to be sick." She clamped her hand over her mouth and fled, not to the bathroom, but to the front door. Michelle heard it slam behind her.

She turned to Alexandra. "Where's she going? What will I do?"

Alexandra, white-faced, said firmly, "You're going to get dressed. I think she'll go to Max."

"Oh, God," said Michelle, stumbling into her jeans. "Where are my shoes? They're upstairs. I have to go after her."

"I'll go after her," said Allie, pulling her sweater over her head. "You stay here, in case she comes home. Call Max." She wriggled into her jeans, grabbed her bag, and started for the door.

"Oh, God," said Michelle, crying.

"Michelle," said Allie, and Michelle looked at her through her tears. "Christ, Michelle," Allie said quietly. "I'm sorry."

Michelle felt a sickness inside her. She wanted only two things. She wanted Lizzie safe. And she wanted Alexandra gone. "I know," she said. "I'm sorry, too."

Alexandra hurried out the door.

Half an hour later Michelle was sitting motionless in the darkened living room when the phone rang.

"What the hell happened?" said Max.

Alexandra came through the front door. Michelle waved her away and huddled over the phone. "Is Lizzie there?" she said to Max.

"Yeah, she's here. What the hell happened, anyway?"

"Is she all right?"

"She's okay. Crying. Upset. But she's okay." He hesitated. "She says she doesn't want to go back there. Ever. What happened, Michelle?"

Michelle wiped at her cheeks and stood up straight. "Thanks for calling, Max. Good night." She hung up as he was trying to speak.

"Is everything okay?" said Allie, who was still standing in the doorway from the kitchen.

"Oh, sure," said Michelle, expressionless. "Everything's just fine." She headed slowly for the stairs. "Don't clean up down here," she said over her shoulder to Alexandra. "I'll look after it in the morning."

When she got to her bedroom door she heard Alexandra say "Good night." But she couldn't answer her.

Part Two

9

When Michelle had been on her own for almost three and a half years, she got herself a dog from the S.P.C.A. It was a female German shepherd more golden than most, whose eyes were outlined dramatically in black; but who when Michelle took her home weighed about half what she ought to have weighed, shivered a lot, and made no sounds whatsoever.

Michelle decided to name her George.

She fed the dog generously, was patient but firm about housebreaking her, talked to her, brushed her, spent a great deal of time with her. She even took her to the store every day. Soon George stopped flinching whenever Michelle came near. She even began tentatively licking Michelle's hand, now and then. But she remained silent.

Michelle, worried, called the vet, and was told that she was already doing everything that could be done. God only knew, said the vet, what the animal had suffered before it ended up with the S.P.C.A.

Early one workday morning when she'd had the dog for about six months Michelle let her out into the backyard, as usual, and turned on the coffeepot, as usual, and as usual padded sleepily into the bathroom to put on her makeup. Her eyelashes were in the grip of a device meant to curl them when she became aware of an unfamiliar sound. She freed her lashes and stood still, frowning, thinking. Then she dropped the curler into the sink and rushed to the sliding glass doors that led from her dining room into the backyard.

In the middle of the yard stood her dog, legs stiff, ears cocked, "barking her fool head off," as Michelle proudly told her mother later.

Michelle shrieked, ran outside, and threw her arms around George, who licked her face and with great enthusiasm resumed barking.

That day Michelle phoned around and arranged to take George to obedience class.

George loved obedience class. Every vestige of fear and shyness seemed to have fled with her first bark, and she took enormous pleasure in the other dogs, in the people, and in learning.

Only once did she seriously embarrass her owner. Michelle lost track one day of how many hours had passed since George had been outside, and was perambulating the dog briskly around the ring, a wary eye on the skittish Dalmatian in front of her, when she felt a pull on the leash and looked down to see George leaving a trail of wetness on the rubber matting.

"Paper towels on the table!" came the triumphant cry from the instructor. "Everybody please take note; make *very sure* your dog has relieved himself properly before every class!"

A man whose dog was a middle-aged black miniature poodle appeared at Michelle's elbow as, red-faced and simmering, she stooped and began mopping up the elongated puddle.

"I'll help," he said, attempting to wrest the paper towels from her grip.

"Don't bother," said Michelle, restraining herself from informing him and the class at large that this hardly ever happened anymore and when it did, it was her fault, not the dog's. "It's done," she said, getting to her feet. She dumped the paper towels in a wastepaper basket next to the table and dragged a mortified George back into the ring.

"*Down* your dogs!" screeched the instructor.

"*Down*," said Michelle, fixing her eyes threateningly on

George's, and George humbly lay down.

She fled to her car as soon as the class was over, and was shoving George into the backseat when someone called out, "Don't beat her when you get her home."

She turned quickly and saw the man and the poodle approaching. The man was grinning.

"I beg your pardon?" she said.

"A small joke," he explained, and stepped back as Michelle yanked on George's leash, preventing the dog from carrying out a jovial attack upon his person. "I thought you might be angry with her," he said. From behind him the small poodle, whose name was Corky, growled ominously at George.

"Not that angry," said Michelle. "I wouldn't dream of hitting her. She's a very good dog. That wasn't her fault, in there. I—" She snapped her mouth shut. Unnecessary explaining was one of the things she wished to eliminate from her life.

George was now sniffing delicately around the man's feet, working her way closer to Corky. The poodle's growls became louder.

"Sit, George," said Michelle. *"Sit!"* she hollered, pushing on the shepherd's haunches.

"Stay," said Michelle fiercely.

The dog stayed. Michelle felt a rush of pride.

"Why do you call her 'George'?" said the man curiously. He was about her own age, reasonably slim and not unattractive, and he had an easy manner which Michelle enjoyed.

"She's spayed," said Michelle. "And I happen to like the name 'George.' "

"Ah. Well. That makes sense," said the man.

Michelle told George to heel and marched her back around to the side of the car. The dog sat patiently while Michelle opened the door. "Okay," said Michelle, and George jumped into the backseat. "It was my father's name, as a matter of fact," said Michelle as she slammed the door shut.

"I see," said the man thoughtfully. He opened the passenger door of his car, which was parked next to Michelle's, picked up the poodle, and tossed her inside. He stood next to his car and watched as Michelle drove off, giving him a wave.

"Just fixing my eyes, George," said Michelle three months later. It was a Wednesday evening in April. Michelle glanced at George in the bathroom mirror. "Got to look good for the last class, right?"

Putting on makeup was a habit, like sweeping the driveway. As she maneuvered mascara onto her lashes she suddenly grinned, getting a black splotch on the skin below her eyebrow, remembering Lizzie's friend, Corinne.

Corinne had come for a sleep-over one Saturday, years ago, long before the divorce, when the girls were about thirteen. They had sat cross-legged in front of the fireplace inspecting their faces in hand mirrors that served no purpose but to magnify every flaw. They peered at themselves with an intensity that caused Michelle, hiding behind that day's edition of the Vancouver *Sun*, to shudder and feel vaguely nauseated.

"Never, never, ever leave the house without your makeup on, Lizzie," Corinne had said.

How come?" said Lizzie, studying her nose, which she thought was too large.

Michelle knew that, although she wasn't participating in the conversation, the girls were aware of her presence. She also knew that if Max had been home that night, Corinne and Lizzie would have conducted their self-scrutiny in the privacy of Lizzie's bedroom. She liked the thought that they were freely permitting her a glimpse into their uncertainties; it meant, she thought, that they trusted her.

"Because," said Corinne, with confidence, "you just never, ever know. My sister's got this friend, her mother sent her to the SuperValu for toilet paper . . ."

Lizzie snickered.

". . . this is true," said Corinne, "I swear it. So she changed out of her gross sweats . . ."

Both girls were giggling, now, hands alternately clapped over their mouths or fluttering helplessly in the air.

". . . and she went to all the trouble of doing her eyes and slapping on blusher . . ."

They toppled on their backs onto the floor, clutching the mirrors to their stomachs.

". . . and combing her hair and all like that, and sure enough, the guy who packed her toilet paper into a bag ended up asking her out!"

They screamed with laughter, and Lizzie's legs flung themselves into the air and made vigorous bicycling motions.

Michelle saw herself in the mirror, smiling.

The dog got up, stretched, and yawned.

"You just never, ever know, George," said Michelle.

George scratched impatiently at the bathroom door.

"Okay, okay," said Michelle as George began to bark. She got rid of the splotch of mascara, put away her makeup, and she and George went to the laundry room for the dog's leash, which hung from a hook beside the back door.

"*Sit,*" she said sternly as George in her joy leapt first at the door and then at Michelle. "*Sit!*" she hollered. "How do you expect to pass, for God's sake? Is it your plan to humiliate me or what?" Finally the dog sat, and Michelle attached the leash to her collar and heeled her out to the car.

Churches were among the few places in Vancouver willing to rent their halls to the Canadian Kennel Club. There had been stern warnings on the evening of the first class that nobody must ever allow his dog to relieve itself upon church property. But when she left the hall that rainy evening in January Michelle had noticed dead branches all along the base of the cedar hedge surrounding the churchyard; a lot of dogs, she figured, had peed upon that hedge during the four years the church had permitted obedience classes to be held there. She had made up her mind that George wouldn't be one of them. Of course George didn't pee on hedges, anyway, being female.

Michelle had enjoyed the classes, though not as much as George had. She hadn't worked her dog as much as she should have, so George was still insufficiently trained in some areas. She was a good "stayer," though, and that was the most important thing, since Michelle was still taking her to work, and had to be able to trust her to remain in one spot when instructed to do so.

The group comprised fifteen people and their dogs, although they didn't all show up every week. It had been a pleasant experience, thought Michelle, unloading George in the parking lot of the church, to watch each of the dogs, including her own, gradually improve over the eight weeks. Tonight they were meeting for the last time, to go through the exercises once more and officially "pass" the beginners' class.

Or, thought Michelle uneasily, to fail it.

"*Heel*," she told George firmly, and marched toward the door.

She walked into the hall.

And froze.

There must have been a hundred people there, and at least as many dogs.

A large Canadian Kennel Club banner had been strung above the stage at the far end. Others were tacked onto the walls: "Have a PET, Not a PEST," and "TRAIN Your Dogs."

Three rings separated by sawhorses had been set up in the middle of the large rectangular room, each formed from wide strips of rubber matting, and rows of chairs three deep flanked the walls.

Michelle hardly recognized their instructor, who was clad this evening in a skirt, blouse, and high-heeled shoes instead of her usual shapeless pants and sweatshirt. She was rushing around with a pen and a large clipboard, engaging in urgent conversation with several official-looking people Michelle had never before laid eyes upon.

She made her way to a desk near the entrance. "What's going on?" she said to the smiling woman behind it.

"Oh, it's going to be a busy night," said the woman. "Three beginners' classes, two novice, and a few utility dogs." She noticed George. "Is your dog participating?"

Michelle gestured uneasily into the hall. "I didn't expect all this hoopla. It's intimidating."

The woman laughed. "She must be a beginner," she said, nodding at George, who was shaking with excitement.

"Oh, yes. We're both beginners."

The woman gave her a square piece of paper with a number writ large and black upon it, and an elastic band. "Please put this on your left arm," she said. "And I need your name." She wrote on a list, "Number 43, Jeffries, Shepherd," and smiled reassuringly. "Just find yourself a seat over there by the far ring, and wait until your number is called."

Michelle, wrestling with a disconcertingly exuberant George, made her way past knees and dogs and sat down. She nodded to a few people from her class. She thought they all looked nervous, which made her feel slightly better. She pushed down hard on George's haunches, forcing the dog to sit. "*Stay*," she said loudly, above the baying of a hound somewhere behind her.

"I didn't come here to be part of a spectacle," muttered the woman next to her. She was holding on her lap a Pomeranian whose hair for the occasion had been swept back and tied with a red ribbon.

Michelle nodded absentmindedly. She had noticed, neatly arranged upon a table, a collection of ribbons and cups awaiting bestowal upon successful dogs. Her heart sank in her chest. She glanced guiltily down at George.

From all sides came the sounds of excited, anxious, or irritated animals under varying degrees of control. Their howlings, barkings, yappings, and whimperings created a cacophony unlike anything she had ever heard. George, who was very friendly, had upon her face a look of delight and incredulity. She, like Michelle, had never before seen so many dogs gathered together; such a thing George had never even dared dream of. Michelle took a firmer grip on the leash.

Michelle saw at the entrance to the room the man with the black miniature poodle. She watched as he stood stock still and looked around, aghast. For a moment she thought he was going to turn tail and leave, but he was captured by the woman with the arm tags. They had a brief conversation, in which he might have been pleading sudden illness or another engagement, and then the woman laughed, patted his arm, and thrust a tag and an elastic band at him. He looked over the sea of people and dogs, aiming his despairing gaze to follow the woman's pointing finger, and saw Michelle.

He made his way down the length of the room toward her, pulling frequently at the leash to which his reluctant dog was attached.

George rejoiced at the arrival of the poodle, who immediately sat in front of the man, between his legs, without being told. She then greeted George distractedly and turned her solemn gaze upon the multitude of dogs surrounding them.

"I didn't expect all this," said the man.

"George, *sit*," said Michelle. "Neither did I."

"You look nervous."

"So do you."

"Me? Nervous? Hell, no."

"Attention, please, ladies and gentlemen," said a woman loudly from the center of the ring nearest them. "We're about to get under way."

"Shit," said the man.

Michelle grinned and was suddenly glad he was there, although she didn't even know his name.

George passed, and so did Corky. Corky did better than just pass; she got a third-place ribbon. Since several dogs actually failed, Michelle's relief far outweighed her envy.

It took a long time for the hall to empty. Some of the dogs were by then very irritable indeed, and care had to be taken to keep them apart from competitors to whom they had taken a particularly strong dislike.

Michelle and the man with the poodle were quickly separated, but when she finally reached the parking lot she found him leaning against her car.

"Congratulations," she said, smiling. "Where's Corky?"

"In the back of the wagon, flaked out."

Michelle deposited George in the car and went around to the driver's side, where the man was apparently waiting to open the door for her.

"That was something, wasn't it?" he said, bemused. "I guess she's smarter than she looks."

"Of course she's smart," said Michelle. "She's a poodle."

"I'm looking after her for a friend," he said. "What's your name, anyway?"

"Michelle Jeffries. You mean, she isn't yours? And you're taking her to obedience class?"

"Actually, he gave her to me. When he moved away. Said I needed a responsibility." He held out his hand. "I'm Casey Williams."

"Hi," she said, shaking his hand. "Are you going to take Corky on to the advanced class in the fall?"

"Hell, no," he said fervently.

The parking lot was emptying.

"If you don't enjoy all this," said Michelle, "why on earth did you do it?"

He rested his hip on the fender of her car. "Somebody told me it would help us get better acquainted. She missed her owners. I was worried about her."

"She certainly seems fond of you."

"Yeah? Do you think so?"

"Yes. Really. She wouldn't have done so well in there if she didn't like you. That's the only reason they do anything. To please us." She began to open the car door. He put his hand over hers, which startled her. It felt warm and firm and foreign. From behind the window George began to growl, a deep, rumbling sound.

"Who are you, anyway?" he said.

All the heat in Michelle's body seemed concentrated in her left hand. "I run a bookstore."

"I teach. At U.B.C. Music. Are you married?"

"No, I'm not married, not anymore." She was about to add

something like, "Kindly remove your hand, so that I can get myself home," when he did so, and took a couple of steps away from her car.

"Me either," he said. "A bookstore. That's good. I like bookstores. Where?"

"West Vancouver," said Michelle. "Dundarave. Listen, I've got to go." She opened the car door and got in.

"One day," he said, "I'll come and see you in your bookstore."

"Fine," said Michelle, and smiled politely before she backed out and drove away.

She expected never to see him again.

10

Michelle's bookstore was small, wider than it was deep, and there was a large window that let in a lot of light. Behind it were three rooms—a tiny bathroom, a cubicle of an office, and a storage room. It was a corner building and there was a window in the office, too, looking out onto the side street.

Across the alley were the parking lot and back entrance of an animal clinic which also housed a dog groomer. Every so often Michelle delivered George there in the morning for a bath and picked her up at the end of the day. She tried to schedule this to coincide with her infrequent author book signings, since if the author was popular and personable enough there was sometimes a small crowd, and George was boisterously fond of crowds.

It was a sunny Monday morning in June, and she was alone in the store. Business was slow, but Michelle tried not to worry too much about this. She depended largely upon regular customers whom she'd been collecting slowly over the almost four years she'd had the shop, and Monday mornings were not the times these people were likely to show up.

She had swept the place, cleaned the windows inside and out, dusted and rearranged the displays, unpacked and shelved some books, paid some bills and done some budgeting. She was now sitting on a stool behind the counter, her legs crossed, one foot tapping space, filing her nails but absorbed in work.

She had a bunch of small metal boxes filled with index cards, one for each of her regular customers. Each time someone new bought a book from her shop Michelle tried to get his or her name and address, so that she could send off a postcard similar to those mailed out by libraries, letting the customer know whenever she had in stock a book of the sort she thought he would enjoy. She was now trying mentally to match the books she had just shelved with the people in her boxes.

This was not obvious, however, to Casey Williams, who saw when he came through the door a woman engrossed in giving herself a manicure. She lifted her head when the bell above the door rang, announcing his presence, and smiled at him.

It was her smile which had caught him, at the first dog class. (It was always a small thing which snagged his interest. He then fed this initial attraction with further observations, and sometimes it grew large and lusty and sometimes, to his regret, it didn't.) This woman's smile was wider than the reach of her eyebrows, despite the fact that her eyes were set quite far apart. It was the biggest smile he'd ever seen. He wondered how huge it got when she was not merely being polite but was overjoyed, or delighted, or even merely pleased.

He stood in the doorway. She was looking at him curiously, and he was forced to admit that she hadn't recognized him.

"The dog class," he said.

"Oh, my goodness, of course," said Michelle, putting aside her nail file with no apparent discomfiture at having been caught, a businesswoman, idling away her valuable time. She smiled again. Casey was fascinated. Her mouth didn't really look all that wide, when she wasn't smiling.

George's head poked around the corner of the counter. She advanced upon Casey eagerly. He came all the way into the store and let the door close behind him; he was afraid the dog would make a run for the street.

"Hi, George," he said, and got down on his haunches, stretching out his hand.

George sniffed his hand, wagged her tail, then sauntered back behind the counter and settled down at Michelle's feet.

"I said I'd come to see you," said Casey, standing. "And here I am."

"So you are," said Michelle, politely.

Casey put his hands in his pockets. "I like bookstores. I can't walk past one. Have to go in and have a look around."

"Browse away," said Michelle.

He began wandering about, and eventually pulled a pair of reading glasses from his shirt pocket and put them on. He picked a book from a shelf, read the inside of the dust jacket, looked at the cover, turned it over and looked at the back. Finally he leafed through the dedication and title pages and read the first few paragraphs. Then he put it back and went on to another one.

Michelle scrutinized him cautiously as he roamed around her store. He wore grey corduroy pants, clean but not ironed, and a blue-and-grey-checked shirt with the sleeves rolled up to just below his elbows. His hair was brown, going grey, and she guessed that he wore it cut short mostly to keep it under control; it was very wavy, another couple of inches and it would spring into tight curls—rather like his dog's, she thought, and wanted to grin. He was slim but round-bellied. His face, bent over yet another book, was absorbed behind his glasses. He had an early-summer tan. She couldn't see what color his eyes were. She liked the jut of his chin, and the way his lips remained slightly parted as he pored over the book in his hand.

Suddenly he looked up at her and grinned. She felt a plummeting in her stomach, and saw that his eyes were green.

"Know anything about this one?" he said, holding up the book. It was called *Good Dog, Bad Dog.*

"Yes," she said. "It's very good. I've got a copy myself."

"Maybe it would be a useful substitute for the classes," he said, flipping through the pages. "What do you think?" He took off his glasses, to see her clearly.

"It's very good," she repeated. She ought to climb down from her stool and join him there among the books, take *Good Dog, Bad Dog* from his hand and turn to the index, show him all the things the book might teach him. But she remained on her perch. She uncrossed her legs and hooked her sandaled feet behind the stool's buttom rung, anchoring herself there.

He looked disappointed. "Oh, well," he said, and replaced the book on the shelf. Michelle found herself becoming agitated as his eyes moved around the store; she felt him begin to think about wandering back out onto the street.

She couldn't remember what he had said he did for a living; if she had been able to recall that, she might have steered him toward some books that would interest him professionally.

"How's your dog?" she offered, finally.

He was putting his glasses back into his pocket. "Corky? Oh, good, she's good. Misses the classes, I think." Hands in his pockets, he walked rather aimlessly to the door. "Every Wednesday night, believe it or not, she trots back and forth between me and the place where I keep her leash."

"Aren't you still working her?" said Michelle. He shook his head.

"You've given her expectations," she said, exasperated. "You can't just shrug your shoulders and forget all about it. She loved those classes. How's she supposed to know they're all over, that's it, kid, back to the kitchen for you?"

"The kitchen?" said Casey, at the door.

"Well, wherever," said Michelle.

He stood with his hand on the doorknob, evidently mulling this over.

"Not exactly a crowd in here this morning," he said.

Michelle didn't consider this worthy of a response.

"Do you ever hang out a sign that says, 'Back in Fifteen Minutes'?" said Casey.

"I don't have a sign that says 'Back in Fifteen Minutes.' "

"*Hmm.*" He began to open the door.

"I've got one that says 'Gone for Coffee,' " said Michelle, striving for casualness. "I put that out sometimes. When things are slow, and I'm all caught up on my paperwork."

"What do you do about the phone? Of course, it doesn't seem to ring much."

"When I'm alone in here," said Michelle coldly, "which only happens, by the way, on Mondays, I've got a machine that I turn on."

"Let's go for coffee, then," he said with an enthusiastic smile, as though suggesting an exciting, possibly hazardous activity.

(Michelle suddenly imagined Alexandra standing nearby, invisible, observing him. "He's a hugger," she heard Allie whisper in her ear. "He loves to hug, I'll bet.")

Michelle realized that he had moved and was quite close to her now, leaning against the counter behind which she sat.

("He's probably a sweet toucher, too, Michelle," Alexandra murmured; "a real sweetheart in bed, don't you think?")

Michelle saw that his smile had faded. He added, seriously, "I've got nothing better to do."

Casey realized as this phrase left his mouth that it probably wasn't the best thing he could have said. But he kept himself quiet and watched her tenderly as she tried to decide whether or not to be offended.

11

"How about some ice cream instead?" he said when they were out on the street.

"What? Ice cream? Why?"

"There's a good place in the next block. I noticed it when I parked." He was walking quickly. Michelle had to stride to keep up with him. "Unless you don't like ice cream."

"I like it fine. But I thought we were going for coffee."

He stopped abruptly in front of a florist's shop four doors away from Michelle's store. "You're right," he said, looking in the window. "It's just such a nice day. Are those real?" he asked, pointing to a display of silk roses, pink and red.

"No. Fake. But good fake."

"There's no such thing as good fake." He turned from the window and grabbed her arm. "Okay. Let's get going," he said, turning her around and propelling her in the opposite direction. "Where's the nearest coffee place?"

"I've changed my mind," said Michelle, slightly dizzy. "I think I'd like some ice cream, after all."

"Good," he said, and quickly turned them around again.

"I wonder, though," said Michelle, "if we have to go quite so fast."

He dropped her arm as though she'd told him she had a communicable disease, and slowed to a loiter. "I'm sorry," he said. "I'm afflicted with terminal restlessness."

"You didn't seem restless in the shop."

"Oh, it doesn't affect me when I'm absorbed."

"Ah," said Michelle, feeling weary and middle-aged.

He got a double scoop of chocolate almond, and she got a small black cherry.

They walked up to the corner and turned south toward Dundarave beach, several blocks away down the hill. A female cyclist passed them, limbs tanned golden, wearing sneakers and yellow shorts and a white T-shirt, with a yellow bandanna tied around her hair. As Casey stopped to watch her pass, Michelle was reminded of the bicycle on which she had ridden to school as a ten-year-old. It had straight-up-and-down handlebars, and no speeds at all. She liked to take her feet off the pedals when going downhill, with her hands in the air, even though whenever she had to slow down or try to stop, because of a car intruding from a side street, or somebody's pet deciding to cross the road, her ankles got banged and bruised as her feet sought the spinning pedals which, when pressed backward, braked the bike.

"I can't stay away from the shop very long," she said. His pace had quickened again, and although she was a tall, long-legged woman, she wasn't a natural rusher and resented the way she was automatically hurrying to keep up with him. "Not long enough to get all the way down to the beach and back, that's for sure."

He stopped, his face crinkled with anxiety. "I'm sorry," he said, and waved his cone in the air. "I'm not thoughtful, among other things." Dark brown ice cream dripped upon the front of his shirt.

Michelle reached over and moved his ice cream cone into an upright position. "Have you got a Kleenex or something?" she said, pointing to the splotch on his slightly protruding belly.

He looked down. He brushed at his shirt with his free hand, then bent his head slightly and ran his tongue around the mound of chocolate almond perched sloppily on top of the cone. She watched as his tongue, ice-cream-laden, disappeared into his mouth and emerged to run itself across his lips, first the top one, then the bottom.

"Face it, madam," he said, sticky-mouthed, "you are having ice cream and a nice trot along the sidewalks of West Vancouver with a jerk."

She wanted to clean his mouth with her own.

She bent to her black cherry ice cream. "I think we'd better turn around now. Let's just stroll back, okay? So we can enjoy the walk. Because you're right, it's a lovely day."

Casey believed people ought to accept others as they were. He was usually more than willing to do this, himself. But he also believed that people ought to make serious attempts to alter those unimportant things about them which caused other people exasperation. There were many things about himself which if eliminated, even simply modified, would make life less frustrating for him and more comfortable for everyone who knew him.

He was thinking about this as Michelle spoke, and didn't hear her, and so it wasn't until he turned, intending to make a friendly and considerate remark of some kind, that he realized she was no longer walking beside him.

He whirled around and saw her perhaps half a block behind him, leaning against a fence, licking at her ice cream cone. Her hair, ruffled by the breeze from the ocean, was a color something like cinnamon, he decided. There was a little grey in it, but not much. Her arms looked pale, and so did her legs beneath the denim skirt she wore. He remembered that when he'd been walking or standing next to her she'd been nearly as tall as he. And she was wearing flat-heeled shoes, too.

He rushed down the sidewalk toward her, holding his ice cream cone out to one side so that it wouldn't drip on him again. When he got close enough he saw that she was exasperated, all right.

"What the hell is it with you?" she said. "Are you always like this, or is it just a bad day?"

"I'm always like this." He tossed his cone into the tall grass next to the fence. "Sorry."

"Don't apologize," said Michelle. "I just wanted to understand what was going on." She began heading back up toward Marine Drive, West Vancouver's main street, and he found himself following, being careful not to stride absentmindedly ahead of her.

She popped the last bit of sugar cone into her mouth and chewed. "It was a good idea," she said. "Ice cream, instead of coffee."

"I get restless sitting at a table with nothing to do," Casey explained.

They turned the corner and walked slowly toward Michelle's shop. "That's why you're reasonably fit, I guess," she said. "Do you run or play tennis or something? That sort of thing's supposed to be good for hyperactive people, isn't it?"

"I'm not hyperactive," said Casey, indignant. "I'm just uncoordinated."

"What an unfortunate combination," said Michelle. "An excess of energy, and no grace."

"No grace? How the hell do you know I've got no grace? I've got plenty of grace."

He whirled away from her and swept up the sidewalk, arms outstretched like a ballet dancer's, giving an occasional backward kick and endangering as he did so several passersby, who leapt into shop doorways or between parked cars to avoid his flying feet: it was an artful comic display.

Michelle, who was less easily embarrassed than she once had been, watched him critically. Eventually he stopped and collapsed against the glass front of the drugstore on the corner.

When she reached him she said, smiling, "You're right. Plenty of grace. Is that what you do to stay in shape?"

He panted, hands loose at his sides, waiting to catch his breath. It occurred to him to confide that he'd given up jogging for a superabundance of sex with very young women, but he thought better of it.

Still breathing heavily, he leaned close and looked intently at her smile. It was indeed wider than the span across her forehead of her eyebrows. He shook his head wonderingly.

Michelle saw a reddened face, damp and animated, delicately

but unmistakeably lined, and vivid green eyes, and white teeth; one of the top front ones crossed very slightly over its neighbor. There was a cleft in his chain. She felt his warm breath on her face. She wondered about the dip at the bottom of his back, and whether his thighs and buttocks were firm, or flabby. It seemed inappropriate to be speculating about the buttocks of a man whose name she couldn't even remember. She stepped back, away from him.

"What's your name, again?" she said.

"Casey Williams. That's the third time you've asked, I think."

"Only the second. And what's your work? How come you're wandering around West Vancouver on this workaday Monday morning? You don't live here, do you?"

" 'Two different worlds,' " he sang, and immediately she remembered that he taught music. " 'We live in two different worlds.' " He began to walk on, and she followed. He slowed down for her, wishing she realized how genuinely difficult this was for him. "You're a businesswoman. I'm a musician. Actually," he said reproachfully, "I've told you this before, too. I teach at U.B.C."

"Yes," said Michelle. "I remember now." He heard no apology in her voice. "And school's out, of course."

"Yeah."

They were back at the bookstore. He waited while she unlocked the door and greeted George, who had been sitting worriedly in the window next to a stack of another coffee-table book about Andrew and Fergie.

Michelle removed the sign from the inside of the door and stationed herself behind the counter. He assumed she was waiting, politely, for him to leave. But she hadn't yet thanked him for the ice cream. Perhaps she didn't want him to go yet.

"Thanks for the cone," she said, and plastered that smile upon her face again.

He noticed some freckles across her nose, and on her cheeks. "Do you tan?" he said.

She shook her head. "Never. I've given up trying. Almost.

Sometimes I put on some of that stuff that tans without sunshine and for a day or two I go around feeling terribly sexy. But eventually I have to have a shower, and it's too much trouble to go through it all again."

He wanted to tell her that pale skin and freckles and cinnamon-colored hair could be very sexy indeed. But he didn't know yet whether that was a good idea. He hadn't had time to decide whether he wanted to see her again.

She was observing him with patience.

He wondered how she behaved when she was feeling terribly sexy.

What the hell, he thought.

"Do you ever go to concerts?" he asked.

"Maybe once or twice a year."

There was a bulletin board near the door. He saw notices for poetry readings, posters for several theaters. He wondered if she put up posters twice a year for the performances of his choir. He reminded himself to ask the choir manager if her bookstore was on the list.

"Would you like to go hear the symphony? They're performing in a tent—"

"In Vanier Park, I know. But I don't think it's started yet. Otherwise I'd have something up on my board."

"*Hmm*," he said to the floor.

"I think it's in a couple of weeks," she said.

"Right. I think you're right." He looked up. "Well?"

"You're asking me to go with you?"

"Yeah."

"But you don't know when," she said, patiently.

Shoulders raised, he threw out his arms, in the manner of Pierre Trudeau. "I'll call them."

"Okay," she said. "You call them. Then phone me, and tell me when the performances are, and I'll let you know if I'm free."

"Yeah, well, of course that's what I ought to do, all right."

"If it's too much trouble . . ." said Michelle, and he looked at her quickly, and saw again her amazing smile.

"I remember your name," he said, "but I'd better get your number," and he fumbled in his shirt pocket, behind the reading glasses, for a small notebook with a pen attached.

12

A*lso, I've met a man.*

She was sitting at her dining room table, and stopped writing to look out the wall of windows into the backyard. The high wooden fence dividing her property from the neighbors' beyond it had a flower bed running along its entire length which in the spring was full of daffodils and tulips. She thought she'd probably overdone the daffodils and tulips. She preferred the pot full of salvia which hung from a branch of the large cedar tree in the middle of the yard. She loved the ferocity which which it flamed, red against the grey-green background of the cedar boughs.

Michelle picked up her pen and continued with her letter. *I don't know much about him. I don't even know if I like him. He seems kind of sweet. And I found myself wondering about his body.*

There's something pathetic about this, she thought.

She got up and went to the kitchen to make coffee. She didn't like Sundays much. She'd never liked them much, even as a child, when they meant Sunday school and dinners with grandparents whose presence made her mother tense and unhappy because they disapproved of her father.

As the water dripped through the coffee into the pot Michelle rested her chin on her fists and her elbows on the kitchen counter and looked up through the window at the sky, fuzzy with almost invisible clouds. The mountains would be indistinct today, vague dark-blue splotches against the white sky, and Vancouver Island would be invisible, so that the ocean would appear to stretch into a blurry infinity. She thought about putting George on the leash and going to the seawalk, so that she could look at the mountains and the sea.

She ran a restless hand through her bangs and wondered if it had been a mistake to let her hair grow so long. It touched her shoulders now, thick and heavy. Maybe she ought to get a permanent.

She took her coffee back into the dining room and resumed her letter-writing.

Have I ever told you about my lust attacks? she said to Alexandra. *I don't think I have. They come suddenly, from right out of the blue, when I'm not thinking about sex at all. They seem to have two phases. In the first phase, I just become wonderfully aware of myself.*

Her limbs would feel extraordinarily supple; her neck, longer; her entire self, balanced with exquisite precision upon her pelvis. She would become pleasurably absorbed in her own body. She would stroke it, slowly, marveling at the curve of her shoulders, the roundness of her belly, the firmness of her buttocks. She would hold her slackening breasts in her hands and find them beautiful. She would finger the dark pink nipples until they became stiff and tender, and resembled the engorged heads of miniature penises; she would admire the pale brown halos which encircled them, and the timorous blue veins which here and there in the fruit-flesh of her breasts revealed themselves. The insides of her thighs were as flawlessly soft as the petals of a rose, she would think—ivory, with the faintest tint of apricot.

Phase Two, she told Alexandra, *is an unusually strong awareness of men.*

She didn't at these times want to hop into the sack with every man who caught her eye, exactly; because it was never an entire man who caught it. She was made breathless by a shirt open to reveal a patch of chest hair, or crisp white shirt cuffs resting upon square brown hands; stupefied by a curl stuck to a sweaty forehead, or a firm ass encased in a tight pair of trousers. Long-lashed eyes beneath a high forehead, a sudden grin revealing straight white teeth, broad shoulders under a T-shirt, the outline of strong-muscled calves hidden by light summer pants—these things made her whimper and mutter to herself, under her breath, where no one could hear, while delight spread itself through her body and her crotch throbbed with unreasonable expectations.

I've been having them for years, she wrote, *these lust attacks. I can't remember when they began. They were a lot less frustrating while I was married, because even though he screwed around Max was always ready and willing. Always.*

She could recall making orgiastic love, then, to specific parts of his male anatomy, ignoring the whole in favor of one or more of its parts. Sometimes it was the scrotum-penis combination, but just as often it was his silky-haired underarms, or the vulnerable curve of his throat, or the place where his back gave way to the glorious slope of his ass.

I haven't had any lovers since Max, she told Alexandra. *So my lust attacks, when they come, are extremely welcome. They make me feel completely alive again. Even though I never do anything about them, lacking the opportunity.*

She knew what Alexandra would have said about that. "What a waste, Michelle," she would have said, slowly avoiding contempt by a hair. "What a goddamned waste."

Michelle thought about the man she'd met. The music teacher with the poodle.

Of course I know what your advice would be, she wrote to Allie. *But why the hell would I listen to you, after all the trouble you've caused me?*

She drank some more coffee and sat back, flicking the pen against the edge of the table. It was a way to spend a Sunday afternoon, anyway. Maybe it was cleansing. Maybe it was healthy. She clung to the idea that it was healthy. And truthfully, she often did feel better after these sessions with notepaper, pen, and an absent friend.

On Wednesday, she wrote, *we're supposed to go to a concert. The music teacher and I.*

She thought about this man who had wandered into her life and somehow caused her to become interested in his specific body.

I'd gotten to the point, Allie, where I didn't even speculate anymore about whether I'd actually go to bed with someone I liked the looks of. Because if they're the right age, they're not available. Or they don't have to settle for somebody over forty.

Unless there's something wrong with them, she thought suddenly. That's what it was, all right. There was something wrong with him, this music teacher.

Maybe I should go to an exotic beach, she wrote, *and pretend I'm rich. Maybe I could get some young guys that way. Maybe it would be good for me. What do you think?*

Allie would probably insist on going with her.

You'd gather them all up for yourself, selfish bitch that you are, and croon to them, and show them just what to do, if they didn't already know it, which they probably wouldn't, and afterwards you'd graciously show them the door, and re-oil yourself with suntan lotion and stroll straight back out onto the sand, ready for Round Two.

Men and women, both, she added to herself, but she didn't write this down. Truly, she had no prejudices about that. No resentment. No guilt. None.

Michelle got up to open the sliding glass doors that led into the backyard. She thought there was a fragrance in the air of willow leaves, and sunlight, and nostalgia.

After a while she went back to her letter.

I continue, of course, to have little communication with Lizzie. (Note how disapproving I sound—"uptight," Lizzie would say, or at least she would have said so once. Perhaps her vocabulary has changed.) Max keeps me posted. She's doing well, he says. He also says I should call her, arrange to see her more often. My mother says the same thing.

She shook her head impatiently and took hold of her pen more firmly, as if it were the pen, and not she, which had gone astray.

I know, I know. It's just that it still hurts, it's still so goddamn humiliating, and you don't have to tell me that I shouldn't be humiliated because I know that, I believe that. But it doesn't help. I've never ever felt such contempt, from anyone. Why the hell should I put myself through that again? For what? At least Max, whom I hardly ever talk to and practically never see, is a civilized person, something which his daughter does not appear to be. Though I'm sure if we ever got drunk together he'd finally ask me all about it, and I'd probably tell him, and he'd want to know every detail, every single one, it would probably turn him on.

She began thinking about the details, and felt her face grow hot, like the salvia in the pot hanging from her cedar tree. She was upset now, her hands were trembling, and she had to blink and swallow to fight back tears.

She put down the pen and held her face in her hands for a moment, until she had become calm again.

I might not have had any lovers since Max, she wrote, *but I've had plenty of dates. Remember the bank manager I told you about? He wore something around his middle, I suppose to keep his stomach flat. But the poor man; he sat positively rigid in his chair—I guess the thing, whatever it was, had sharp edges that stuck into him if he relaxed.*

Now I mean it's terrible to remember a person because of something like that. He was a very interesting man. Very kind. Shy, but able to carry on a decent conversation. Yet whenever I think of him all that comes into my mind is the fact that he wore a girdle.

She drank some coffee, which had gotten cold, and pushed the cup away from her.

I've even found some of them attractive.

I wonder why I haven't been to bed with any of them?

Maybe I'm just a coward.

Or maybe I don't want to care enough.

She just signed her name, when she had decided not to write anymore. Affectionate good-byes weren't necessary, with Allie. They had known each other too long.

Besides, Michelle knew she wouldn't mail the letter.

She never mailed any of the letters she wrote to Alexandra.

13

"It's going to be pissing rain out there any minute," said Casey. He turned from the living room window, a Scotch and water in his hand. "The rain on the roof of that damned tent's going to drown them out. What a damnfool idea, orchestral music in a tent."

"It's a terrific idea when the weather's good," said Barry Fox mildly. He was wearing a pair of navy sweatpants with a white stripe down the legs and a matching short-sleeved shirt. His racquetball gear was stuffed into a bag he'd left in the hall. He frequently stopped by after a game to tell Casey how good all this athletic activity made him feel.

Casey sat in an easy chair opposite his friend. "I hate going to things like this when I can't hear the music properly."

"Why are you going, then?" said Barry. He had a serenity Casey envied, and a warmth which Casey loved, and from which he had occasionally drawn strength.

Casey rattled the ice in his glass.

"Well?" said Barry. "Why are you going?"

"I promised to take this person," said Casey, vaguely. "This woman."

Barry studied him with interest.

Casey consulted his watch. "I have to pick up the tickets at seven forty-five, it's a half-hour drive to West Van—that's where she lives—and another half hour back, give her fifteen minutes in case she's congenitally late—I've still got half an hour." He put down his glass and looked around the living room. "This place is a mess. Thank God the cleaning lady comes tomorrow."

"You're not only ready on time," said Barry, "you're actually early. I'm impressed."

"Do you think I look okay?" Casey spread his arms and looked down at himself.

"You look fine to me. Can I have another drink?"

"Oh, Christ, I'm sorry, Barry." He took the glass Barry held out to him and went to the kitchen for ice.

"Who is this woman?" said Barry as Casey handed him his drink.

"She runs a bookstore. I think she owns it. She's got a dog—" He suddenly sprang to his feet. "Where's Corky?"

"You put her out in the backyard, I think. When I got here."

Casey reached for his Scotch. "I've got to start taking that dog out for walks again. I've given her expectations, with those damned classes."

Barry leaned forward. "This is actually a woman you're going out with, is it?"

Casey sat down. "Of course it's a woman."

"An adult woman?"

Casey said nothing.

"A grown-up woman?"

Casey continued to say nothing.

"You know what I'm getting at. Ed told me he talked to you about it before he left."

Casey made an impatient gesture. "Don't tell me about Ed; the son-of-a-bitch went off to Ohio and left me with his damned dog."

"You like the dog. The dog likes you. That's not what we're talking about here."

Casey looked at his watch. "We don't have time to talk about anything, Barry. I've got to get going." He stood up.

"You've got almost half an hour," said Barry calmly. "Sit down. Let me get it over with."

Casey sat down.

"You're getting a reputation. Hell, man, you've already got one."

Casey, hostile, stared at the floor, his heel beating time to an inaudible score.

"Hey, Casey. Look. I'm glad it's made you happy. Really."

Casey glanced up at him. Barry looked drawn and worried. Casey shifted resentfully in his chair.

"But you've got to take it easy," said Barry. "You've been rampaging through the nubile young things out there for, what—three years now. People are talking. It's not good."

"Those young women," said Casey with dignity, looking Barry in the eye, "are of age."

"I know they're of age. But they're students. You don't fuck students."

For the first time Casey was forced to admit that Barry's disapproval must be based on genuine concern, rather than envy. It wasn't like him to use words like "fuck."

"Don't screw yourself up, Casey. Maybe you don't care about losing your job—"

"I'm not going to lose my job," said Casey irritably.

"Hey, listen, don't give me that," said Barry. "Where have you been hiding, man? Don't kid yourself." He was agitated and frustrated. "How do you think the budget-cutters would react if they found out you were in that kind of trouble? They'd chop you without a second thought, and replace you with somebody a whole lot cheaper."

"In what kind of trouble?" said Casey, angry. "I'm not in any trouble, Barry, and I don't plan to be." He stood up. "And now, if we've finished discussing my personal life, I've got to feed the dog and get going."

"Wait a minute," said Barry, holding up a hand. "Sit down. I've got more to say. Professionally."

Casey sat. "Make it quick."

"You haven't been doing as many recitals as you used to."

Casey shrugged. "I do my share."

"I've got an idea for you. It'll give you a nice change of pace. Get your mind off your—"

"Don't say it," said Casey sharply, "or I swear I'll throw you out of my house."

"—and back onto music," Barry went on calmly, "where it belongs. Here's my idea. I'll lend you the ensemble, if you'll do the Bach *Magnificat* in the fall. We'll share a concert."

"Yeah?"

"My fiddles and winds, your choir. I'll do some Vivaldi in the first half. Then your *Magnificat.* What do you say?"

"I'd still need a good trumpet player," said Casey.

"Hire one of the symphony's. You'll have to pay him out of your own pocket, though. Think about it," said Barry, standing up. At the door he said, "Just let me know before you take off for the summer."

"Yeah," said Casey. "Yes. I'm letting you know. Now." He grabbed Barry by the shoulders. "Yes," he said, a grin all over his face.

The phone rang as Michelle was getting ready. She picked it up on the bedroom extension, clothed only in her underwear. Her face and hair were done; she just had to put on shoes and step into a sundress. Except that she'd noticed since she'd gotten home from work that clouds were gathering sullenly in the west, threatening to hurl themselves across the sky.

"Hi, dear," said her mother.

"Mother, hi," said Michelle.

"Did I catch you at a bad time?"

"No, I'm going out, but I've got a few minutes. What is it?"

"Nothing in particular, dear. Just wanted to check in and see how everything is. Are you selling a lot of books?"

Oh, God, thought Michelle. How long has it been since I called her?

"Oh, it's not bad, Mom, not bad," she said, trying to inject into her voice a confidence about her financial situation which she did not feel. "Everybody's stocking up on paperbacks to take down to the beach or out on the boat or wherever." She reached out with one bare foot to scrabble her sandals toward her but the cord linking telephone and receiver wasn't quite long enough. The phone slipped from her bedside table and clattered to the floor. Michelle picked it up quickly. "Mom? Are you still there?"

"Still here."

"Sorry, I managed to drop the phone." She sat on the edge of the bed in her bra and panties. She cricked her neck to look almost fearfully out the window, but the sky was obliterated by the branches of the cedar tree. "What's the weather like in Richmond?"

"Clouding over. But don't worry. I'm sure it's nothing serious. Michelle, are you busy on Sunday?"

"Sunday? No, I don't think so. Why?"

"I'd like you to come for lunch. There's a friend I want you to meet."

Michelle belatedly registered her mother's distracted tone. And realized that she hadn't even asked who Michelle was getting ready to go out with.

"A friend?" she said curiously. "What friend? Who?"

"You don't know him, dear," said her mother. "Otherwise I wouldn't have said I want you to meet him, would I?"

"Him?" said Michelle.

"His name is Van Hudson. I think you'll like him."

"I'm sure I will, Mom, if you do. How long has this been going on? Where did you meet him?"

"I'm going to ask Lizzie, too," said Mrs. Jeffries. "And I don't want any arguments from you. I haven't seen that child for weeks, or you, either, and I want you both here, together, for once." She sounded unusually heated.

"Sure," said Michelle, after a minute. "It's your party. What time? Can I bring something?"

"It's not a party, Michelle. Just lunch. Come at noon. And don't bring anything except yourself."

When she'd hung up the phone Michelle rushed to the second bedroom, across the hall, to look out at the weather. It was getting cloudier. She decided to scrap the sundress and put on a summer suit, which meant pantyhose, too. She hated wearing pantyhose.

As she rummaged through a drawer looking for a pair of hose without dabs of clear nail polish all over them, she remembered that her suit was at the cleaner's. "Shit," she said to George, who was watching hopefully from the floor beside the bed. Michelle's face was getting hot; she could almost feel her makeup starting to wilt, and the evening hadn't even begun.

Casey had been right. The rain drumming on the roof of the huge striped tent made concentration on the music impossible. By intermission time, a full-fledged thunderstorm was under way. The audience, milling around in the makeshift foyer, was generally pleased, since the crack of lightning and the crash of thunder were not all that common in Vancouver; they were even more exciting under the fragile protection of a tent.

Casey maneuvered Michelle to a spot near one of the entrances and rushed off to get a couple of gin and tonics. When he pushed his way back through the crowd to rejoin her, he noticed a pallor on her face and thought it was the peculiar effect of the light bouncing off the ceiling of the tent. He handed her a drink and then heard someone call his name.

"It's been *ages!*" she crooned, and his face was smothered in a perfumed mass of blond hair. She gave him a quick, close hug and shone her face up to him.

"Gloria, this is Michelle," said Casey, in some confusion; he had temporarily forgotten both of their last names. "Michelle, Gloria."

Michelle extended her hand. "Michelle Jeffries," she said. "How do you do?"

"Gloria Harding," said the blonde, smiling politely.

Her hair's tinted, thought Michelle, and lightning struck overhead and thunder crashed and Michelle ducked her head and tried not to think about it.

The blonde was murmuring to Casey, who was responding

casually, but warmly. When once more there was only the pounding of the rain to be heard from above, Michelle looked up to see the girl—for she was, truly, very young—cuddled comfortably close to Casey, who was alternately smiling down at her and looking seriously over at Michelle, who was plastered against the side of the bleachers, to which the audience was beginning to return.

She was beautiful, there was no getting around it, thought Michelle, with that pile of deftly streaked hair, and that tipped-up little nose, and that golden skin, and those turquoise eyes. She was talking to Casey about some choir which he apparently conducted; she must be a singer, thought Michelle, and there was more lightning, more thunder.

"Excuse me," said Michelle, with careful courtesy. She put the plastic glass containing her untouched gin and tonic on the edge of one of the bleachers. "I'm sorry to spoil your evening," she said to Casey, "but I'm afraid I'm going to have to leave."

"Leave?" he said, bewildered. "Now?"

"Are you sick?" said the blonde, curiously.

More lightning cracked the sky and this time the thunder came right on top of it. Michelle cried out, and instinctively hunched her shoulders and threw her hands over her head.

"What is it?" said Casey, his hand on her arm. "What's the matter with you?"

"Oh, shit, I can't stand it, it's the only thing in the world I'm afraid of!" Her husky alto voice had shot into the upper reaches of the soprano range.

"But—" Casey began. He looked closely into her face. Then without another word he took off his jacket and draped it around her shoulders and together they raced out of the tent and across the wide sweep of lawn to his car.

"I'm sorry," she said for the sixteenth time. "I feel like such an idiot."

They were sitting in her living room drinking hot toddies made by Casey. Michelle was curled up on the sofa, with George on the floor at her feet. She had changed into jeans and a sweatshirt, and her face was scrubbed and her hair was almost dry. Casey's jacket was suspended from a hanger above the kitchen stove, at a safe distance from the burners, all four of which Michelle had turned on to speed the drying process. His shirt and pants were wet, too, but she had nothing for him to put on while they dried so he had built a fire in the fireplace and was huddled on the floor in front of it.

Casey had expected her to make what was to him the obvious suggestion that he take off all his clothes and have a hot shower and wrap himself in a blanket or something while his clothes dried. Apparently this hadn't occurred to her. He ought to leave, he thought. Her inconsiderateness had made him disgruntled. He had legitimate reasons for feeling sorry for himself, he thought, as he sat there shivering and time passed and it became clear that the storm had utterly destroyed whatever sexual curiosity she might have had about him.

"Don't apologize, I told you," he said. "Everybody's afraid of something." He looked moodily into his glass, which was almost empty. Since she was a kind of invalid, at the moment, he guessed it was up to him to refill it, if he wanted another hot toddy. He decided he didn't.

"What are you afraid of?" she said.

"Failure," said Casey, with a nice touch of the dramatic. "Impotence. Death."

"No no no," said Michelle, laughing. "Not that sort of thing. Phobia-type things."

Casey gazed into the fire. "Moths," he said, reluctantly. "I'm terrified of moths." He turned his head to grin at her. "Never admitted that to anybody in my life before, I think. Except my wife." He looked back at the fire. "She's dead, by the way."

"I'm very sorry to hear that," said Michelle, formally.

"What about your husband?"

"We're divorced. He's a lawyer."

"Here?"

"In Vancouver, yes."

"Do you have any kids?"

"One. A daughter. She's studying business administration." She added dryly, "I'm the one who ought to be studying business administration."

"Oh, yeah?" he said, and turned from the fire to face her. "It's pretty tough running a business, I guess."

"Sometimes," said Michelle. "Do you have any? Children, I mean."

"No, I don't."

She looked pale and exhausted.

"The storm's over," said Casey quietly. "It's just plain rain, now. The gentle kind."

"I feel so stupid," she said, shaking her head. "If I'd known it was coming, I would have warned you."

"If you'd known it was coming you could forget your bookstore and go to work as a weatherman." He went into the kitchen to get his jacket and turn off the stove.

"Thanks for being so nice," said Michelle when he reappeared. "I'm sorry you got wet."

"It's nothing." Casey approached the sofa. George licked his hand enthusiastically when he stroked her and rubbed the back of her neck. Then he leaned down and kissed Michelle's cheek, which was very soft, and smelled of soap, or cleansing cream—something pleasant, anyway. George gave a deep growl, and Casey laughed. "I'm going home, now," he said, and put two fingers under Michelle's chin and tilted her head this way and that. "You're a very lovely lady. How would you like to go for a drive on Saturday?"

"I'd like that," said Michelle, looking steadily into his eyes.

Casey left, feeling pleased with himself; expansive, even. That was a situation he could have taken powerful advantage of. But he hadn't. He'd been a good person. Friendly, even affectionate; but respectful.

Smart.

14

It was Saturday afternoon, and they were standing in the middle of a dusty, rectangular room whose floor was made of wide wooden boards.

"It's my hideaway," said Casey.

At the far end was a sofa piled with small cushions and covered with a bedspread constructed from dozens of pieces of colored fabrics, irregularly shaped, some solid colors, some patterned; Michelle could see a triangle of dark blue with little yellow umbrellas stenciled on it, and a big piece striped green and orange, and a circle of brown, and a chunk of light purple which seemed to be appliquéd with butterflies.

"My mother made that spread thing," said Casey, shoving his hands in his pockets. "It was on my bed when I was a kid." He laughed and shrugged.

Above the sofa was a small window with a narrow bamboo blind rolled all the way up to the top, and through the glass, which had dust film on one side, dried streaks of rain on the other, Michelle saw a medium-sized fruit tree, maybe an apple.

Against one of the long walls was a desk and chair, with a brass kerosene lamp on top of the desk, and next to this, a torn leather chair, and then a tall old bookcase crammed with paperbacks.

Michelle went over to the bookcase and ran curious eyes along its shelves. They contained an eclectic selection of novels, Jane Austen and Patrick White in there along with Stephen King and Robert Ludlum, Graham Greene and Iris Murdoch, Malamud, Richler, Steinbeck, Updike.

Casey stood some distance away, not watching her, as she looked at the books. He had become suddenly silent.

At the front end of the room were some kitchen cupboards and a sink with a pump in it instead of faucets, and something which looked to Michelle's incredulous eyes like a wood-burning stove. From above the sink another window looked out onto a small yard of high tangled weeds with a silvery-grey picket fence almost obliterated by the thick prickly canes of wild rosebushes.

In the wall opposite the desk and the bookshelves was a door which Casey opened so she could look in at a narrow bedroom containing a double-size brass bed. There was another bookcase, too, this one low, and filled with dozens of copies of *National Geographic* magazines and still more paperbacks. A stereo and two small speakers sat on top of the bookcase, and a stack of records filled a wooden box next to it. This room also had two small windows, one facing the front yard, the other, the back.

"No bathroom, I guess," said Michelle, to whom the omniscient presence of another woman in the cabin was exceedingly strong. She felt a lot of curiosity aimed at her, from somewhere.

"There's a two-holer out back."

"It's unusual, these days, not to have electricity and hot and cold running water. Even in a cabin. It's not as though you were exactly out of the reach of civilization." She disliked herself for sounding critical, even disdainful. It's nothing to me, she told herself, how he spends his spare time.

"I kind of like it," he said.

Michelle stood in the middle of the room with her hands clasped in front of her. She felt taller than usual, and ungainly.

"You should have told me where we were going on this drive," she said, thinking not only about the discomfiting presence of his deceased wife but also about the lengthy walk along the pebble shore, and the struggle up a steep, overgrown, hillside trail with blackberry bushes reaching for her throat and nettles caressing her ankles. "I would have worn my jeans, and my sneakers."

He looked her up and down, thoughtfully. "Yeah. I should have. But I wouldn't have been able to look at your legs, then."

Instantly, the dead woman vanished.

Michelle was aware that sunlight from the open door was shining directly upon her. She felt naked. Warm air seemed to sweep upward from the smooth wooden floor to stroke her calves, the insides of her knees, her thighs; for a moment she was sure she'd forgotten to put on any panties.

This was it, then. The time was now, here in the strong July sun, not a thunderstorm in sight to screw things up. She stole a glance at the sofa at the end of the room; she knew they wouldn't be using the brass bed. She stood weak and docile on broad wooden planks and waited, the sun's hot gaze upon her.

Casey was quite close to her, and she thought he was looking at her.

Michelle's hands were cold, despite the sun; she would touch him first through his clothing, spread her cold hands wide on his shoulders, run them slowly along the muscles of his back, and by the time the two of them were skin to skin he would have caused the heat in the center of her to spread and spread until even the tips of her fingers were glowing and she could place them, then, soft upon his face and all the other parts of him and he would feel no coldness in her, anywhere.

Michelle waited. It was intolerable, this waiting; her skirt and blouse chafed skin unbearably sensitive, as though fever had struck. When he touched her, relief would become passion, they would become absorbed in passion—such a lovely, lovely thing, to be absorbed in passion, and a male body, and one's own.

She felt him near, determining precisely how to go about it: Should he take her by the shoulders and bring her close to him and kiss her mouth? Or should he begin with an arm around her waist? Or perhaps just take her hand . . .

She waited, patient, unmoving, letting him decide, while her blouse rested thoughtlessly upon erect and aching nipples.

"Besides," said Casey, "I didn't know I was going to bring you here until after we'd started to drive."

She tried to think of the moment in which he had made up his mind. Maybe when the breeze from the open window of the car had flung her skirt up to her thighs; she had had to pull it down and tuck it securely beneath her. Or maybe when she had leaned over to adjust his sunglasses, which were falling down the slope of his nose; her breast beneath her thin cotton blouse had rested briefly, then, upon his arm. Or maybe it happened when she laughed at something he told her about one of his choir rehearsals; he seemed to enjoy making her laugh.

"We'd better get going, I guess," said Casey.

Dumbfounded, she realized that he was standing uneasily at the front door.

"Right," she said, and preceded him quickly into the yard.

Furious, she fought her way through the weeds and stalked through the broken gate in the rose-smothered fence and trekked across the dusty one-track road and into the bush on the other side.

"Hey, wait a minute," she heard him call, but she struck out through shoulder-high underbrush.

Her sandals slipped on some moss-covered rocks. Her hands grabbed involuntarily at saplings, then salmonberry bushes, but they couldn't or wouldn't slow her plunging and she ended up colliding with a thick-trunked fir tree, and there she rested, shaken and panting, as Casey made his way cautiously down the slope toward her: she caught glimpses of his hair, his face, his brown T-shirt as he approached, bits of him visible for a moment through the foliage, then gone, then again visible, and finally right there in front of her.

He put both hands on the tree trunk, one on either side of her head, and leaned there, looking at her. He was out of breath and obviously irritated. "The trail's way over there," he said, jerking his head to the left. "You should have waited for me."

Twice, she thought, enraged, twice in one week I have gone running away from something, and this fool has been forced to pursue me.

Somebody was tittering in her ear; Lizzie, or Alexandra, or maybe Casey's dead wife.

A few strands of curling hair clung to his damp forehead. His face was brown; his eyes, she noticed, seemed to get greener as his tan deepened. He was very close, leaning over her. It was quiet in the woods, except for their breathing, which was now less labored, more cautious.

Yet it was not quiet at all, Michelle realized after a minute—she heard scurryings, and warblings, and rustlings. There had been a time—it didn't feel like all that long ago—when she had thought she was as comfortable in the woods as the squirrels and snakes and birds and bugs who lived there. No more. Now these creatures were foreign to her. She was an uneasy intruder. The melancholy this created in her now, in another time, was absurd, but real.

She pushed herself away from the tree. Casey dropped his hands and stepped quickly back. Probably so he wouldn't have to touch me, thought Michelle bitterly, brushing leaves and dirt from her skirt. My God, she thought, looking up at him, maybe he's gay. The man's gay, despite his dead spouse.

"Okay," she said finally, tired out, wanting only to get home, "lead the way."

She followed him back up the steep slope. Soon he grabbed her hand to haul her out of the clutches of some blackberry bushes, and when that had been accomplished he didn't let go but gripped her hand more firmly, helping her over fallen logs, guiding her around tree stumps, leading her through the tangled underbrush.

"I would be perfectly capable of a hike like this," she said, "if I were properly dressed for it." Her pride demanded that she make this clear; actually, she didn't feel like talking to him at all, even though she had experienced a new rush of sexual expectation—not mere hope, but actual expectation—when he took her hand. She couldn't make up her mind whether she was in the middle of a lust attack or an infatuation. Either way, there wasn't much of a future in it.

"Oh, yeah?" he said.

"Yeah. I spent a lot of time in the bush when I was a kid."

He stopped and pointed to some white flowers growing low to the ground. "What are those, then?"

"Trilliums," said Michelle promptly.

"Wrong," said Casey. He struggled through a final barrier of salmonberry bushes and out onto the road, pulling her behind him.

"What are they, then?" she said testily.

"How the hell should I know? You're the one who spent the time in the bush." He let go of her hand and went a hundred yards up the road and pointed down the hill. "Here's the trail. Follow me, and watch your step."

"Why did we come here, anyway?" she said. He held a low-hanging branch until she grasped it, so it wouldn't whip back and strike her.

"You didn't like it, did you?" said Casey, glancing back to be sure she was following without difficulty. "I didn't know whether you would or not. That kind of thing doesn't appeal to a lot of people—no bathroom, no water faucets, no television."

The sound of the sea began to blend with the whine of mosquitoes, the scuffling of their feet along the fern-bordered trail, the whirring of birds' wings above them. When they emerged onto the narrow, rocky beach Michelle had to narrow her eyes against the sun glittering upon the limitless sea.

"Those were your wife's books, weren't they?" she said as they began walking along the beach. "That was your wife's entire cabin, in fact, wasn't it?" She shook her head. "I think you should have asked me if I wanted to go there. Really, I feel very uncomfortable about this. Peering around at another person's things, another person's place. It was probably very important to her, very private." The heat thrummed in her head. She would have liked to take off her sandals and wade in the cool shallow water close to shore.

"My wife was a singer," said Casey. His eyes crinkled against the sun when he looked at her.

Michelle thought about this. She stumbled on a rock and he caught her arm to steady her. She pulled away, irritably. "So what, she was a singer? Aren't singers entitled to privacy, the same as the rest of us?"

"I'm a singer, too," he said "How can a dead person want privacy?" He looked interested, waiting for her reply.

"Well, for God's sake," said Michelle, throwing up her hands. "You're missing the point. Let's hurry up. My face is burning. I have to get home to feed my dog." She walked faster.

"We should have brought the dogs with us," he said. "We could have let them run on the beach. We could have stopped at a McDonald's and bought them hamburgers."

Michelle didn't reply. She walked more quickly. Apparently it was only on city sidewalks that he found it necessary to streak along like a perpetually alarmed person, or a fugitive.

"I bought the place after she died, as a matter of fact," said Casey, a few steps behind her. Michelle slowed her pace, almost imperceptibly. "I just thought you might get a kick out of it. The pump, and the wood stove, and the kerosene lamp and all that."

She was walking much more slowly, now, and he was beside her. She felt like a fool, but she wasn't thinking about that, she was thinking that they could have used the brass bed after all. Except that it was clear he didn't want her, didn't find her attractive enough.

They were now heading up a sandy incline toward his car, their backs to the sea, and the sun.

"I'm glad you brought me," she said finally. "Really. It's a lovely place."

He opened the passenger door and rolled down the window. "It's going to be hot as hell in there until we get going, get a breeze." He held the door open wide while she climbed in.

"I never thought of it," he said as they drove away, "or I would have told you that Aline never went there." He gave her a quick glance. "She's been dead for four and a half years, you know. There aren't any shrines."

They drove through the town of White Rock in silence, and slowly, because of the traffic and the hordes of people crossing the street, heading for the wide, sandy public beach on the left or the fish-and-chip places on the right.

"Smile at me," said Casey, when they had to come to a full stop to avoid hitting a group of bronzed, bikini-clad teenagers. Michelle, startled, nevertheless managed a smile. He nodded in evident satisfaction, and drove on.

They followed the main street out of town and up a hill, and when they got to the top Michelle turned around to look at Boundary Bay spread out beneath them, Washington's San Juan Islands in the distance. "It's so beautiful," she said. "I'd like to come again."

"I've never brought a woman up here before," said Casey after a minute. "When we got there, I wanted to make love to you. But I didn't know how you'd react. I haven't had much experience, lately, with . . . women like you."

She was going to ask what kind of woman he thought she was, but then he turned to look at her, and the intensity in his face sent something warm and weakening rushing through her body, and she wasn't able to say anything at all. She wished she could make a wildly provocative gesture; she wanted to cup her hands around her breasts, offering them to him, she wanted to slowly lift her skirt and snuggle her hands between her legs, enticing him. But she couldn't even continue to look into his eyes; she looked away and said, "Watch the road, will you? You're making me nervous." She sounded nervous, too, her voice had risen, and she tripped over the words.

They traveled through the summer afternoon toward West Vancouver, and didn't talk much, although it was a long drive. Michelle, aware of every movement he made, also felt his constraint in her presence, and it dismayed her.

She kept changing her mind.

But when he pulled into her driveway, she did it.

"Come inside," she said.

He got out of the car before she finished speaking, and went around to open the door for her. She smiled and shook her head at his outstretched hand and got out without assistance.

She walked ahead of him, her eyes on her front door, and heard and felt him following.

15

She hated the thought of awkward preliminaries, not knowing how to begin, trying to anticipate the first advances and respond to them instinctively. She wanted to dispense with all the opening moves, just strip off her clothes quickly and efficiently while he did the same and then pull back the bedspread and lie down with him and get right to it.

It didn't help that before either of them could do anything she had to cope with George's delirious greetings and put her outside in the fenced backyard with a piece of rawhide to chew on.

Michelle closed the back door and went through the laundry room and the kitchen back toward the living room, all the time hating her self-consciousness and wondering if desire had expired or what. It was broad daylight, not yet evening; hardly the best time, she thought, for the first sexual encounter with a stranger.

What the hell to say, what to do? Should she sit in a chair or on the couch, should she offer him coffee or a drink? She could hardly drag him upstairs just like that. Some people she knew were capable of that but not she; not Michelle.

Oh, Christ you're an adult woman, she thought in despair, hesitating in the kitchen. Just march right in there and smile at him and if he doesn't do anything then after a while go sit in his goddamned lap or something.

She flung open the door and saw him standing in the middle

of the living room, his eyes fixed on her, as though he'd been watching her through the door.

She walked right into his arms, it seemed, although she took only two steps to accomplish this so he must have walked right into hers, too.

There were sheer curtains on the windows and as he reached to kiss her she assured herself that nobody could see anything through them, from the street.

His lips were warm and smooth. They enveloped her mouth while his hands on her back pressed her so hard against him that her breasts hurt. Without taking his mouth from hers he let go of her and began undoing her blouse, which buttoned up the front.

Oh, thank God I didn't wear a bra, thought Michelle; it was so much tidier this way.

He was on top and he was too heavy to let himself fall upon her, but he didn't want to withdraw from her yet, to create a precipitate spewing of semen all over her, all over the carpet. So he let himself rest gently upon her, his weight supported on his hands which were on the floor on either side of her. Then he lay on his side, hooking his left leg over her right hip so that she turned a bit to face him.

Her eyes were closed and he studied her thoroughly, looked her over very carefully. She was certainly not young. Her skin was flushed to the color of a ripe peach. Her cinnamon hair was splayed away from her face; he smoothed it back from her forehead. She was always brushing at her bangs with her hands as though they might grow suddenly long and obscure her vision. There was grey in her hair and tiny blood vessels were visible in her sun-sensitive cheeks; her neck was lined, her breasts sagged, and although she was a slim woman there was extra weight around her waist.

Yet he thought her beautiful. He traced with a finger the shallow channels from her nostrils to the edges of her mouth, and touched the skin around her eyes, which was as soft as powder; tracings as delicate as spiders' webs were etched there. Amazingly, he thought her beautiful.

She opened her eyes and he saw that they were hazel; dark brown pupils, with irises that looked moss green. She ran them across his face, from temple to temple, from forehead to chin, and then down along his body. He suffered this—it was only fair—and tried to smile, but her face was inscrutable; he became uneasy, and wished he could without appearing rude roll away and quickly dress himself.

Michelle was beginning to feel cool, almost chilly, and she, too, wanted to put her clothes back on. She wanted some distance between them, she wanted no longer to be physically joined to him; the weight of his leg upon her hip was causing the rough carpet to dig into the softness of her buttock.

His eyes were extremely green, and bright, and warm. His face was brown, in fact his whole body was brown, except for a small area which just covered his buttocks and genitals, and this was not exactly white, but certainly very pale compared with the rest of him. She wondered if he sashayed around the campus a lot wearing nothing but a bikini. She thought that in a bikini, his protruding belly must be more noticeable than ever. But then so must be his hard thick thighs, and muscled calves, and strong shoulders and upper arms. He was covered, she noticed, with a sheen of hair, seductively unobtrusive, bleached gold by the sun.

He leaned down to kiss her temple and smooth her eyebrow with his tongue. "I loved that."

Michelle didn't say anything.

He watched her face. "How about you?"

"Me, too," she said.

"Then how come you're not smiling?" He looked at her for a moment longer. She didn't seem happy at all. "I know it wasn't perfect," he said.

"It was fine," said Michelle. "Really." Her flush deepened, and she shifted away from him.

"You must be getting uncomfortable," he said. "I think I'd better remove myself." He did so, and reached for his jockey shorts, which were lying on the floor near the sofa, and slid into them. "Don't move. I'll be right back."

Michelle lay on her back with her hands under her head. When he returned he was carrying a small hand towel from the bathroom. She reached for it but he pushed her hand away and wiped gently at the semen smears on her thighs and belly. Then he tucked the towel between her legs and sat back, looking at her body.

Michelle felt shockingly naked. Early evening sunlight slanted through the sheer curtains and struck across her abdomen. "I've got stretch marks," she said, as though making a confession.

He leaned down to put his lips on them, silver streaks through the whiteness of her belly flesh. "It looks like somebody's been weeping over you." he said, "and his tears have marked your skin."

She looked at him kindly. "That's a very pretty thing to say." She pushed herself upright and he held out her blouse, and helped her put it on.

"Ah, it's such a shame to cover yourself," he said, slowly doing up the buttons. "But you're right, it's time we got dressed, and had something to eat. Shall we go out? Or can we make sandwiches in your kitchen?"

He sliced the bread and put butter on half the slices and mayonnaise on the other. Michelle sliced tomatoes and cucumber and cheese. They took the sandwiches and a pot of coffee into the dining room and ate and watched through the big window George in the backyard, chasing birds or digging holes or lying in the middle of the grass, surveying her kingdom with an imperious air.

"Why did you buy that cabin?" asked Michelle.

"White Rock reminds me a bit of California. That's where I come from. That's why I got it, I think." He wiped some tomato juice from his chin with a paper napkin, and Michelle offered him another sandwich. She thought she wanted him to leave, but she wasn't absolutely sure.

"How did your wife die?"

"She had a stroke."

"Oh, my God. Was it sudden?"

"Yeah."

"Did you love her very much?"

Casey put down his sandwich. "Yes, I did. Very much." He took her hand and spread her fingers. It was quite a small hand, for a tall woman, and there were freckles all over the back of it, which had worked their way up the fingers as far as the first knuckle. "What about you? How come you got divorced?"

"My husband was having affairs with other women. So I said I wanted a divorce."

"And your daughter didn't come live with you?"

She took back her hand and poured them more coffee. "At first, she did. Then she decided she'd rather live with Max. And now she has an apartment of her own." There was a tension around her mouth that he hadn't see before.

He stretched, and grinned at her. "I like you."

Michelle smiled back, though cautiously. "I like you, too."

"I think we should see each other again."

"I think I'd probably like that."

She got up and began clearing the table, but he took the plates from her hands and pulled her down into his lap. "There's nothing to be afraid of, Michelle."

"What on earth makes you think I'm afraid of anything?"

"You're stiff, and wary. All your lubricity is gone." He put his hands on her breasts, through her thin blouse, and felt her shiver. "Oh, good," he said. "I'm wrong," and he nuzzled her through the blouse until she began stroking the back of his neck, and he felt her ease against him, pliable and frightening; then she stiffened and pulled away.

"That's enough," she said firmly; laughing, though. She got up and smoothed her hair.

He looked up at her, his hands around her waist. "What shall we do tomorrow?"

"Tomorrow I'm having lunch with my mother."

"I'll pick you in the afternoon, and take you out for dinner." He ran his hands down her buttocks. "We just need to practice together, that's all. Can't expect it to be bang-on perfect the very first time."

"It was fine. I told you."

"You held back, did you know that? You didn't want to, but you did." He pulled her into his lap again, pushing up her skirt so that she could straddle him. "Maybe we'll try it this way, sitting down. Or maybe in the shower. Or with you on top," he said, grinning, "my cock flailing you on to ecstasy."

"For heaven's sake," said Michelle.

He kissed her, and her lips were swollen. They didn't open to him but he tasted their soft undersides and thought about tasting his own juices there, and hers, along with mayonnaise and tomato and the slippery sheen of butter.

"Don't rush things," said Michelle into his mouth.

He pulled away from her. "There's no time to lose," he said. "We've got to cram in all we can in the next couple of weeks, because after that I'm going away for a month."

"Where are you going?" She was certainly not upset, maybe not even disappointed. Casey felt relief, but he was also somewhat hurt.

"New York and San Francisco," he said. "To listen to some terrific music."

She nodded, and got up. This time he got up, too, and helped her take the dirty dishes to the kitchen.

"Then I'm going to come back and make some of my own."

She looked at him questioningly.

"I'm going to do the Bach *Magnificat*," he said. "In November. With the choir. Do you know it?"

"I think I've heard it," said Michelle.

"It's great stuff. I love it. Needs a small orchestra—I've got the university's Baroque Ensemble. Maybe you'll come and hear it. What do you think?"

"Maybe I will," said Michelle politely.

"Will you be going on vacation sometime this summer?" he asked.

"I'm not sure yet," said Michelle, who knew she wouldn't be able to afford a holiday. "I haven't decided."

The sun was much lower, now, and George was scratching at

the back door and barking. Michelle saw Casey out and agreed to be ready at four the next afternoon. She watched him back out onto the street, wave, and drive away before she let the dog in.

She fought, weakly, all evening, a flourishing joy, and finally went to bed and gave herself up to it, and dreamed that she went to heaven and saw there her father, and Ashes the cat, and all sorts of people and animals she had known, and heaven was a green and warm and fragrant place filled with sunlight and flowering things, just as she had imagined it as a child, and she looked around at the smiling faces surrounding her and in her delight moved first to stroke Ashes' grey fur, which was restored by death to a splendid youthful gleaming, but though she reached again and again she could not feel her cat beneath her fingertips, and one of the people in the loving assemblage gathered to welcome her said, "It's true, it's the only flaw; we cannot touch one another."

16

When Michelle got up the next morning the sun was shining, so she took her coffee out into the backyard, still wearing her bathrobe, and sat down on the grass. She felt deliciously languid in her body, but her brain was skittish; really, she didn't want to spend any time with her brain this morning.

She wished she had something new and summery to wear to her mother's house for lunch. I must go shopping, she thought, and wondered if there would be time between lunch with her mother and Lizzie and dinner with Casey Williams to go somewhere and buy something. It even occurred to her that maybe Lizzie would go with her. I ought to be able to expect that of her, she told herself resentfully. I ought to be able to expect the same daughterly things of Lizzie that my mother enjoys from me.

But resentment faded rapidly, and the familiar Lizzie pain rushed in to replace it.

She turned the coffee mug around in her hands. It was English china, with roses all over it, and if she held it up into the sunlight she could almost see through it.

She was pretty sure that she hadn't even called him by his name, yet. She frowned a little, trying to remember if she'd perhaps said it while they were making love. No. She was sure not. She hadn't said a word.

George, who had been dutifully circling the yard, keeping guard, finally decided that all was well. She flopped down on the grass next to Michelle and rested her nose on Michelle's foot.

Was it true, Michelle wondered, drinking her coffee, that she'd held back? She determined to be analytical and honest with herself. She told her brain to relax, what could hurt her, sitting there warm and quiet in the sunshine?

She decided that yes, it was true. She'd felt awkward and at risk while she and Casey Williams made love; she'd felt on trial. And she had held back. Was there any reason to believe it might be different the next time, if there were a next time? She certainly found him attractive. She had very much enjoyed the sensation of her body next to his.

But it was true that she hadn't been able to abandon herself in what they were doing.

She put down her coffee mug and leaned back on her hands, stretching her legs out in front of her and thereby dislodging George's nose. The dog got up and looked at her expectantly.

"I'm not even dressed yet," said Michelle. "How can I take you for a walk? Wait awhile."

She wondered how a person might arrange to stop holding back. First of all—obviously—she'd have to decide that that's what she wanted to do. *Was* it what she wanted to do?

"I do like him quite a lot," she told the dog.

She intended to think about all this some more—but suddenly, like being visited by a dream, or a half-remembered fragrance, or a piercing moment of déjà-vu she had a dizzying sense of time passing, life changing, things threatening, and she felt an urgent need to spin around, turn back, to fiercely retrieve and clutch to her breast something undefined, insubstantial—but absolutely essential.

She arrived at her mother's house before Lizzie did. Mrs. Jeffries led her to the living room instead of the kitchen, where they usually sat at the round table and drank coffee and watched people pass by outside. Michelle sat down as instructed in a worn stuffed chair in the corner. Her mother disappeared for a moment and came back bearing a large tray on which sat a bottle of sherry and four glasses.

"I don't see any reason why we should wait for him," she said, setting the tray on a coffee table, scratched and scarred but polished, which she'd had for as long as Michelle could remember; Michelle moved out of the way a low bowl of roses which she knew came from one of the prolific bushes in her mother's backyard.

Just then they heard a knock at the door and Lizzie opened it and shouted, "Hello!" and Mrs. Jeffries hurried to usher her into the living room.

"Hi, Mom," said Lizzie offhandedly a moment later.

Michelle smiled. "You're looking great," she said. "All that curly hair. It suits you."

"Thanks," said Lizzie, sitting on the sofa. She was wearing white slacks and a loose black top with a shallow neckline and cap sleeves, and she'd put on shoes with two-inch heels.

"Where *is* the man?" said Mrs. Jeffries.

"Mother, he's not late," said Michelle. "It isn't noon yet."

"He's usually here half an hour before he's supposed to be," said her mother, pouring sherry.

"He's probably nervous about meeting your family," said Lizzie.

"What's for lunch?" said Michelle.

"Fish," said Mrs. Jeffries. "Salmon."

Michelle had expected this. Her mother was fond of taking long, brisk walks along the dikes to nearby Steveston, where the several fingers of the Fraser River seeped and swelled into the sea, and fishermen sold crab and cod and salmon and sometimes even tuna from wide wooden jetties which groaned and squeaked as they were lapped by salt water and nudged by the fishboats. Her mother was a hard bargainer, as Michelle knew from having sometimes accompanied her on these walks, but the fishermen seemed to like her, probably because she almost always bought something.

Michelle wondered if her mother would like Casey Williams. Should she ever meet him. Which of course was unlikely.

She wondered if Casey Williams had ever been to Steveston. Surely he had. Yet not necessarily. It probably depended on how much he liked seafood. She had no idea whether he liked seafood.

"I simply do not know where he can be," said her mother.

"Sit down, Mom, for God's sake," said Michelle. "Tell us about him."

Mrs. Jeffries sat down reluctantly, on a wooden-backed chair whose seat was petit-pointed. "I met him at a bingo game down at the church," she said stiffly. "Then he turned up at one of the dances in the hall. We go for walks together. Sometimes out to dinner." She glanced up quickly. "He's trying to get me to go bicycling," she said.

Lizzie giggled, and her grandmother gave her a sharp look. "It was just your tone of voice, Grandma," Lizzie said apologetically.

"He's a widower," her grandmother announced, folding her hands in her lap. "I might have known his wife. I can't remember. She died sixteen months ago, of a heart attack."

"He's a free man, then," said Michelle, and blushed, saw Lizzie's curious glance.

"He was an electrical engineer," said Mrs. Jeffries, "before he retired."

"I'm sure he's very nice, Grandma," said Lizzie.

"This salmon is great," said Van Hudson. "Absolutely delicious."

He was extremely large. The small house in which Michelle's mother lived had shrunk the moment he walked into it. He was about six feet two or three, Michelle figured. He couldn't be described as fat, but there was certainly a lot of him. He looked as if he must have played a violent sport of some kind when he was younger. She thought he was about seventy, a couple of years older than her mother. He had a balding head and large, slightly protruberant blue eyes and a mouthful of straight teeth which Michelle inspected closely whenever she got the chance; she hadn't yet been able to decide whether they were real.

He treated her mother with a gentle courtesy with Michelle

found touching. He got up to pull out her chair every time she sat down. He picked up her napkin whenever it fell to the floor, which was often; her skirt was made of a shiny, obviously slippery fabric. He had brought a bottle of white wine and made sure that it was chilled, and then poured it himself into glasses he got out of the cupboard without having first to ask where they were.

Michelle looked curiously at Van Hudson. Had he ever grabbed her mother and made mad passionate love to her? On the floor? Or even on a bed? She sneaked a glance at her mother, trying to decide whether she looked like she'd had mad passionate love made to her recently.

"I hear you go to U.B.C., Elizabeth," said Van Hudson, reaching for the salt shaker.

"I knew I didn't put enough spices in," muttered Michelle's mother, but Van patted her hand and she subsided.

"Yes," said Lizzie. "I do. Just finished my third year."

"And you're taking business, your grandmother tells me."

"That's right."

"You must have gotten your interest in business from your mother," he said with a smile.

"Good God, I don't think so," said Michelle, startled. "It's books that interest me, I'm afraid. Not business."

"My goodness," said her mother. "I haven't made any dessert."

"We don't need dessert, Grandma," said Lizzie.

But Mrs. Jeffries ignored her, and left the table to fetch fruit and cheese.

"Well," she said, as she put the platters on the table, "I might as well make my announcement, before I get the coffee." She looked determinedly at Michelle. "It seems that we're going to get married, Van and I."

It was an oddly ponderous moment, and Michelle, briefly, didn't know what to do with it. She considered weeping, for her dead father. Then she decided that applause was far more appropriate, in recognition of her mother's joy. But it was difficult to applaud, because her mother looked so damned grim.

"Congratulations," she said finally, smiling broadly and stretching out her hand to Van Hudson. She turned from him to her mother and gave her a gentle hug and kissed her forehead. "Congratulations, Mom," she said.

"Yes," said Lizzie, with a quiver in her voice. "Congratulations." She smiled at them both, but Michelle could tell that this was an effort for her. "When's the wedding?"

Her grandmother looked at Van Hudson. "Well, we haven't actually settled that yet."

Van laughed. "I say tomorrow. She says we've got to wait awhile, make some decisions, arrange things properly." He raised his hands in defeat, beaming. "So it'll probably be sometime in the fall."

"I think it's wonderful, Mom," said Michelle. Yet even though she knew she was being childish, she wished her mother had told her privately. At the round table in the kitchen, with the sun shining on them as they bent confidingly toward each other, with nobody else in the house, nobody at all.

She saw Lizzie dabbing at her eyes with her napkin. She knew that Lizzie liked sometimes to flee to her grandmother for the comfort, the companionship, or the attention that she couldn't or wouldn't accept from her parents. Was Lizzie now panicking, thinking that in the future she would have no refuge here?

And would there be no refuge here for Michelle, either, anymore?

They decided to have coffee in the living room.

Her mother and Van Hudson sat on the sofa. Michelle went back to the worn old armchair and Lizzie sat in a chair by the window, near the door.

When a lull occurred in the conversation Lizzie said politely, "You're looking very pretty today, Mother. That jumpsuit looks good on you; it's just the right color green. And I like your hair like that. You've always worn it so short. I like it long."

"Thank you, Lizzie," said Michelle. "Actually I've been thinking of getting a perm. What do you think?" We sound just like any old mother and daughter, she thought happily, although she knew it wouldn't last.

"Who do you want to look good for?" said Lizzie with a grin.

Michelle felt her face grow beet red, and tried to hide behind her hair.

Lizzie looked at her in astonishment. "You're blushing, Mother. Are you dating someone? Someone special?"

Michelle threw a pleading look at Mrs. Jeffries, but she and Van Hudson were murmuring to each other, oblivious for the moment to anybody else.

"You can tell me, Mom," said Lizzie, with a nervous laugh. "I'm your daughter, after all."

Michelle crossed her legs and picked up her coffee cup. She sipped, put the cup back in its saucer. "I don't think," she said uneasily, "that you could actually say that I'm dating someone. No."

" 'But?' " said Lizzie.

"But I've met someone," said Michelle, "who seems quite interesting."

She heard herself, and was incredulous. "Quite interesting," she had said. My God, she thought, and felt his hands slide from her buttocks up her back, and shivered.

"Tell me about this person," said her daughter. "Where did you meet?" Michelle saw that she was fidgeting in her chair, her body twitching like a bird in a cage, as though it longed to be anywhere, anywhere, but where it was.

"We met at an obedience class," she said.

Lizzie laughed heartily.

"I mean it," said Michelle. "An obedience class for dogs. I took George, and he took his little black poodle. And we met."

"He's got a little black poodle?" said Lizzie, and she laughed again.

"What's so funny, anyway?" said Michelle, exasperated.

"Oh, Mother, I don't know, I guess it's all this stuff about animals. Tell me something else about him."

"I may never see him again, you know," said Michelle, and

Lizzie smiled knowingly. "He teaches," said Michelle. "At U.B.C."

"Oh, God," said Lizzie, and made a face. She got up to kneel on the floor next to the coffee table, and buried her face in the roses. Mrs. Jeffries turned from Van Hudson and put her hand on Lizzie's hair, and Lizzie looked up and they smiled at each other.

"He teaches music," said Michelle, putting her coffee cup on the floor next to her chair. "His wife died of a stroke. About four years ago, I think."

Lizzie looked down at the roses, and leaned forward as if to see them better. After a long moment she put her hands flat on the coffee table and slowly pushed herself up onto her feet. "Christ, I'm dizzy or something," she said absently. "What does he look like, anyway?"

"Oh, he's not much taller than I am, he's got curly hair, going grey, and green eyes."

"Mother," said Lizzie. She turned, as if uncertain where she'd left her chair.

Michelle stood up. "Good heavens, Lizzie. You're not well." She went to her daughter and took her by the arm.

"No, please."

"Elizabeth?" said Mrs. Jeffries, alarmed. "Was it the fish?"

Lizzie managed a laugh. "No, please. It wasn't the fish. I'm fine. I promise."

"I'm going to get you some Eno's," said Mrs. Jeffries, but before she could get up, Lizzie pulled away from Michelle and sat next to her grandmother on the sofa.

"Hey, listen, it's nothing," she said. "Really. I just got a little funny feeling there for a minute. Too much sun yesterday, that's all it was." She looked at them both, her mother and her grandmother, and Michelle saw that her smile was painted upon her face, and was afraid to know what lay behind the glitter in her eyes.

17

Casey sat on the edge of his hotel room bed and looked into the long narrow mirror attached to the closet door. He was not happy. He usually loved San Francisco, but not this year. There was a heat wave. The hills were bare and brown.

He said to his reflection, carefully, watching his lips form the words, "I think I miss the evergreen trees."

Honey-colored legs, spread wide and crooked at the knee, stirred on the bed behind him, and he felt a hand on the small of his back.

"That must be it," he said, nodding at himself.

The hand pulled his polo shirt out of his pants and pressed itself against his skin. He lay down, hands behind his head, staring up at the cracked ceiling. "I think it's too hot," he said, when the girl raised herself onto one arm and ran her other hand beneath his shirt.

She sighed and let herself flop down on her back beside him. "Let's go find a bar," she said. "An air-conditioned bar."

Casey reached with his right hand and found the top of her bikini panties. He burrowed his fingers into the warmth and dampness of her crotch.

"It's too hot," she said, and giggled.

"Maybe not," said Casey, raising himself above her.

Her name was Linda Thornton. She was in his conducting and

advanced voice classes. He had been seeing her since January, and in March they had discovered that they would be in San Francisco at the same time for a few days in August. Casey, not knowing how long this relationship might last, hadn't made any promises then, but when the term ended in April and they were still sleeping together they had arranged to meet. She had moved in with him when he arrived from New York two days earlier, and she was scheduled to fly back to Vancouver tomorrow, with the two friends with whom she was traveling.

He was not enjoying her company much. He half-heartedly attributed this to the fact that the air-conditioning unit in his hotel room had broken down.

They felt now like rubber creatures, he thought, as they slicked and thwacked against each other, in the throes of sweaty sex.

When they had finished, Linda went as usual straight into the bathroom to shower. Casey was sprawled flat and naked on the bed, emptied, drained, his head aching. He listened to the water running and longed for a cool drink, a sea breeze, a glimpse of a snow-covered mountain; or better still, his shady cabin and the stony beach below it.

He looked down at himself and saw glistening skin, and a belly which gravity had spread and flattened until it looked like a huge, thick pancake with hair on it.

When he heard the shower being turned off he sat up against the pillows. He pulled up one leg and tried to rest his elbow casually on his knee but the slipperiness of his skin made this impossible. He contented himself with tensing his stomach muscles.

Soon she came out of the bathroom, rubbing at her dark hair with a towel, and for a moment he couldn't breathe, looking at her, golden skin taut over a shape so perfect it made him want to gnaw and nibble and suck her all over; he felt his sleepy penis quiver. She threw the towel onto the bed and shook her head vigorously, flicking droplets of cool water all over him. He reached for her but she laughed and flapped him away.

"Get away, you dirty old man. Get in there and shower, and then take me someplace cool for a long, cool drink."

She bent to pick up her panties from the floor, leaned over to get a sundress from the back of the chair. He groaned, watching her move, and she looked at him over her shoulder and giggled again.

He went into the bathroom and stood under the shower, eyes closed, arms hanging limp at his sides, his face lifted gratefully to the water, and he wondered in what ways this day might be different if it were Michelle getting dressed out there in his bedroom, instead of Linda. When he and Linda weren't making love he didn't have a great deal to talk to her about. This was usually okay, because Linda had lots of things to say that required no response from him. But sometimes Casey felt like talking, and then although she fixed her eyes attentively upon his face, he figured that she was uneasy, not really listening, and maybe even a little bored.

He decided not to think about this.

He heard the phone ring while he was toweling himself dry, and stuck his head around the bathroom door but Linda was already hanging up. She scribbled a message on the notepad by the phone. "It was your father," she said. "Very formal, isn't he? 'Just tell him, please,' " she read, " 'that I returned his call.' " She handed him the piece of notepaper.

"I believe," said Casey thoughtfully, staring down at Donald's message, "that I'd better make this call in private." He smiled at her. "Would you mind waiting for me downstairs in the bar? It'll only take a couple of minutes."

She ran a finger along his jawbone, and his flesh felt weak and tremulous. He sometimes made love to her quite roughly, wanting to leave permanently upon her flawless skin his handprints, the marks of his teeth. When she touched him life and energy for an instant fled from him, and when if flooded back into his nerves, his blood, he felt a rush of relief which became ruthlessness, as though their grappling were not for pleasure, but survival.

She picked up her straw handbag and sauntered from the room.

Casey finished drying himself and climbed into his clothes. Then he placed the call to his father.

"How are you, Pop?" he said.

"Are you planning to come down here, or not?"

"Yeah, of course. Do I ever come this far without going to see you?"

"Who was that who answered the phone? The maid?"

Casey sighed. "No, Pop. It wasn't the maid. It was a friend of mine."

"A friend, huh? She sounded pretty young to me. How old is she, anyway?"

"What does it matter how old she is?"

"Is she there right now?"

"No, Pop. She's waiting for me downstairs."

There was a heavy silence on the other end of the line. Then, "I'm worrying about you, Charles," said Donald.

"You're worrying about me how, exactly?"

"You're carrying on with kids. Don't you think that ought to worry me? It sure ought to worry *you*."

"She's not a kid, Pop. She's an adult."

Donald was silent again.

"I've called you," he said finally, "what, maybe a dozen times at your house up there in Vancouver in the last couple of years, and four of those times some young sweetie thing answered your phone. What kind of goings-on is that, for a man of your age, a respectable man, a university professor, for God's sake? And now I phone you in a hotel room, a public hotel, in San Francisco, for God's sake, and who answers but another one. What the hell's going on, Charles? What's going on in your life, anyway?"

Casey sat down. He felt very tired, "Ah, Pop," he said. "I don't know what's going on. I really don't."

He heard his father sigh. "What're your plans?" said Donald. "How long are you going to be up there?"

"She's going back tomorrow. I thought I'd rent a car and drive to Carmel as soon as I put her in a cab to the airport. If that's all right with you."

"I was afraid you might be planning to bring her along," said his father.

Casey laughed. "No, Pop. It never even occurred to me."

"You get yourself down here tomorrow, then," said Donald grimly. "We'd better have ourselves a talk, you and I."

Casey jerked the phone from his ear as the dial tone sounded. "Shit," he muttered, furious.

18

"I don't have much in the house in the way of food," said Donald, standing in the doorway. It was late afternoon of the following day. "I thought we'd go out to eat."

"Fine with me," said Casey, lifting his bags from the car.

Donald came down the steps and along the walk. "First, though, we'll have us a drink," he said, picking up the larger of Casey's two suitcases. "And maybe you want to take a shower. It's another hot one." He trudged back toward the house, Casey following. Donald was wearing a short-sleeved shirt and a pair of baggy tan shorts that reached down to his knees. On his bare feet were brown leather sandals. His legs were white, and fuzzed with pale grey hair.

When Casey had showered and changed, they went out to the backyard and settled into plastic and aluminum chaise longues. "Mesh," said Donald, squirming to get comfortable. "Lets the air through."

"Uh-huh," said Casey, and took a long swig of his gin and tonic. "That tastes good."

The house faced west, and the backyard was now in shade. There was a bedraggled rose garden on the left, running the length of the fence that separated Donald's house from his neighbor's. A long, high hedge had been planted by the neighbor on the other side. Except for the rose garden, which had been Connie's province, the backyard was all lawn. A tall acacia tree grew at the end of the yard, near the back fence.

The grass was parched and brown. Close to the house it was almost worn away; patches of bare earth had appeared around the old, weathered picnic table planted a few yards from where Casey and Donald were sitting.

"One good thing about a heat wave," said Donald. "The grass stops growing."

"It looks like it's dead," said Casey.

Donald had canted the chaise back almost as far as it would go. He was holding his glass in both hands. His knees were slightly bent, his feet were splayed, and his eyes were closed. "It's not dead," he said. "One good rain, it'll turn green again."

"I guess."

"I water the roses, now and then."

"Uh-huh."

"Don't bother with all that spraying and pruning."

"I can see that."

"They thrive on it. Neglect. You should have seen them, a couple of months ago. Loaded with flowers. Loaded."

"Uh-huh. I didn't know you cared so much about roses."

"I don't." Donald opened his eyes. "Tell me about this life you're living."

Casey took another drink and swirled the rapidly melting ice around in his glass. "I teach. I conduct. I work on my voice."

"You sold that house yet?"

"No. I decided not to. Well, I didn't actually decide, I guess. I just got used to it again. After a while I didn't mind it, without Aline. It seemed like too much trouble to move, then."

Donald put his glass on the small patio table that sat between his chair and Casey's. He adjusted the chaise to a more upright position. His manner spoke of an intention now to discuss serious matters.

"Do you ever hear from Connie?" said Casey hastily, to ward him off.

"She's living in Florida now. Went there when she got back from her trip to China."

"I know," said Casey gently. "You told me. And she writes to me now and then."

"Oh, does she now," said Donald, and reached for his drink.

"She sounds happy. Busy."

"Got herself a man, I've no doubt," said Donald gloomily. "Good-looking woman like that. Hardly more than sixty." He didn't move his head, but his eyes darted to Casey's face and away with the speed and furtiveness of a pair of lizards.

"I wouldn't know," said Casey. "How about you? I thought there were hordes of eligible ladies out there praying for your release from matrimony. But every summer I come to visit and you're still on the loose."

Donald threw him an injured look. "I did some miscalculating there," he said delicately. "Had a lady in mind. Then after Connie and I split up, and I got to know her some . . ." He sighed, and reached to scratch his ankle, where one of the straps of his sandal was chafing his skin.

"What the hell did you think was wrong with Connie, anyway?" Casey finished his drink and set his glass down hard on the little table, which wobbled in panic.

"Nothing was wrong with her," said Donald tiredly. "I just figured it was time, that's all. These things have a limited life span." He nodded, sagely. "You'd have found that out for yourself, in time, if Aline had lived. I woke up one day and I'd been married to Connie for seventeen years. Just two short of my record. And I'd gotten to know this other lady some, she played for the choir I belong to." He shrugged.

"I guess you should have tried her out," Casey said coldly. "Before you gave Connie the heave-ho."

It was early evening now, and becoming cool. Casey imagined the sea, only blocks away, and wished he could smell it.

"Let's go inside," said Donald, and he pushed himself slowly out of the chaise. "We'll have another drink before we figure out where we want to eat."

In the living room, which faced the street, Donald closed the drapes against long shafts of rich golden light. Casey sprawled on the sofa while his father refilled their glasses in the kitchen. When Donald came back he handed Casey his drink and sat in an old, worn chair by the window. It had been covered long ago in a material that resembled tweed. "Margaret was up here the other day," he said. "They're moving. Up to Oregon somewhere. Eugene, I think."

"Closer to me," said Casey, pleased.

"And farther away from me," said Donald. "A whole lot farther away from me. I don't have anybody left now, you know that?" He leaned forward. "You want to tell me the point of having all those kids when you get to seventy-four and there's not a single one of them left around?"

He spelled it out, ticking his ungrateful progeny off on his fingers.

"Donald Junior, architect, with a perfectly good job in San Francisco, two years ago he takes it into his head to move east. To Boston. My God.

"Victor, over in Salinas. He gives up his newspaper job there and is himself off to Omaha, Nebraska." He pronounced it with the distaste some people have for words in any language other than their own. "Of course, Marsha, that's where she comes from. Felt this urge to be back there with her parents." He paused, then added, reluctantly, "I hear they're none too well." He looked at Casey. "Just like I'm going to be none too well, one of these days." He waved off Casey's attempt to protest.

"Then we've got Grant," he went on. "Still in the goddamned merchant marine.

"And Paula." He shook his head sorrowfully. "I don't understand that girl. I do not understand her. First Florence, now it's London. Painting at night, working in some damned pub in the daytimes.

"And then there's you. Up there in Canada.

"And now Margaret. Oregon. My God." He sat back and studied Casey with moody defiance.

"What do you want me to say, Pop?"

Donald shook his head. His face was flushed. "Why anybody would want to move away from California when they don't have to I'll never comprehend."

"I'm sorry, Pop," said Casey gently.

"Damned grandkids. They'll grow up, I'll never see them." To Casey's astonishment, he wiped tears from his cheeks.

"Of course you'll see them. They'll come to visit, like Victor and Annie and the kids came last summer. And you'll go to visit them. Us. All of us."

Donald shook his head again, more vigorously. "Everybody's going to be too busy. Donald Junior, and Grant, and Paula; they haven't been back to see me yet."

"So you go see them. And me."

"I don't like flying. And I can't drive to where Paula is. Or Grant. And anyway I don't like driving, either."

"Pop," said Casey, sitting up. "You ought to get married again."

"Of course I ought to get married again," said Donald angrily. "I don't need you to tell me that, Charles. But it's not so easy, anymore." He looked down at his hands, clenched in his lap, and opened them, spreading his fingers, and placed them again on the arms of the chair. "I'm not saying there aren't any ladies out there wanting to marry a man of my age." He glanced swiftly at Casey. "I'm in pretty good shape, for a man of my age."

Casey nodded. "I can see that, Pop."

"And I'm reasonably well fixed, financially speaking." He hesitated. "I guess you know that Connie got herself a job."

"Yeah. She's selling real estate, right?"

"Selling real estate," said Donald with contempt. "I never thought I'd see the day." He reached for his glass and took a drink. "Anyway, as soon as she landed this job, which was about six months after she took it into her head to move to Florida, she started sending my checks back." He looked at Casey, wide-eyed and indignant.

"I guess she wants to be independent," said Casey with a grin.

"The other two—well, you know. They both remarried years

ago. So I don't have any financial responsibilities. Except for myself. Which leaves me, like I said, reasonably well fixed."

"So what's the problem? With the ladies?"

"Oh, hell, I don't know, Charles," said Donald miserably. "I just can't get interested in any of them. In a permanent sort of way."

"What about in a temporary sort of way?"

"Yes, well . . ."

"Yes, well, what?"

"That doesn't fill the bill, you might say. It makes me even lonelier. It makes me depressed." He looked at Casey, narrowing his eyes. "I guess we're different, you and me."

"I guess," said Casey, and thought immediately of Linda.

He'd rented a car at the hotel that morning, and driven her to the airport. He'd lugged her bags into the terminal for her, and her friends were already there. She greeted the two girls with small shrieks and giggles and hugs; even though he knew them, he maintained at first a formality that was almost stiff, because he saw the bright hard curiosity in their eyes when they looked at him. Linda laid a proprietary arm around his waist and chattered with the other two about the flight time and the gate number. Casey knew that as soon as he left, it would be him they'd be chattering about. He withdrew from the clasp of her arm, smiled pleasantly at the three of them, and announced his departure.

There were a great many people in the terminal, and it occurred to Casey as he was about to leave that to a casual onlooker, he might well be a father, seeing his daughter off on a trip with a couple of friends.

He was suddenly violently angry. He wheeled around and grabbed Linda in a hard, almost brutal embrace; unprepared, her mouth flattened beneath his and he ended up kissing her straight, smooth, perfectly maintained teeth.

He heard little gasps from the other two. When he released Linda he looked at them and saw that they had not approved.

"Have a good flight," he said, and heard the bitterness in his voice, and stalked away.

"Why don't you come up to Vancouver?" he said now to his father. "Spend a few weeks with me."

"You'll be busy at school."

"You can explore the city during the day. Walk around. Take bus tours. I've got a concert in November. Come for that."

Donald looked at him hopefully. "You're not doing the *Messiah*, by any chance?"

"Jesus, Dad. I don't have the horses for it. I've told you and told you."

"You ought to start your own choir. Professional."

"I'm doing the *Magnificat*. How about it; will you come?"

Donald sighed. "I don't know. I don't know anybody up there."

"I'll introduce you to people. Then you'll know somebody."

Donald snorted. "People? What sort of people? Kids? Like the ones that answer your telephone?"

"I know a lot of people," said Casey, trying not to get angry. "All sorts of people. People who teach with me. People who sing in my choir. You'd like them. And," he found himself adding, without having thought about it, "I know a very nice woman, for instance, she owns a bookstore."

There wasn't anything unusual in his voice, he was sure of that. And yet Donald cast a sharp eye upon him. "What kind of a woman?"

"Just a woman," said Casey irritably. He drank up the last of his gin and tonic.

"If she owns it," said Donald, "she can't be a kid."

"Oh, for Christ's sake," said Casey. He stood up. "Let's go and eat."

They went to Monterey for dinner, to a restaurant on Fisherman's Wharf. They had ordered and were drinking more gin and tonic and Casey was gazing out at the bay, feeling wistful and slightly melancholic, when Donald said, "So she isn't a kid, this bookstore lady."

Casey looked at him wearily. "Pop, you said it yourself. We're different. Stop trying to get me settled down. For some of us, once is enough."

"What are you talking about?" said Donald indignantly. "I'd just like to know, I'd be mightily relieved to know, if you've found yourself an interesting woman to get yourself involved with instead of all these kids."

"Pop, for Christ's sake," said Casey in a furious whisper. "Keep your voice down." He picked up his glass and drank, to calm himself. "I do occasionally have relationships with young women. That's true."

"They're your students, right?"

"They are young women, Pop. They don't want to marry me. I don't want to marry them."

"They want sex, right? And that's what you want, too. Sex."

Casey felt himself flushing. "That's right," he said with dignity.

"Can't you find anybody your own age to have sex with?"

"What the hell has age got to do with it?"

"It seems to have quite a lot to do with it, as far as you're concerned. I'd like to know, is it because this is the way you want it, or is kids all you can get?"

He was looking at Casey with bright composure; enjoying himself.

"I mean, I can certainly see the appeal," said Donald earnestly, leaning forward. He folded his arms on the table. "Young flesh, no sags or wrinkles . . ."

"Jesus Christ," said Casey, sitting back in his chair. He looked out again across the water, edged with glittering lights strung along the bay all the way around to Santa Cruz.

". . . shiny hair, shiny eyes; I bet even their sweat smells like perfume."

Casey turned back to Donald in horror. His father was gazing dreamily into space, smiling, his face ruddy, his moustache thick and white.

"Oh, I can certainly see the appeal," said Donald. "And I envy you. No point in denying it. I do. Now tell me about the lady with the bookstore," he said, sitting back, lifting his glass.

"I don't know what to say about her," Casey protested.

"When did you meet her?"

"I met her in January. At a dog class."

"A dog class," Donald repeated, carefully.

"She's got a German shepherd with these black markings around her eyes. And I told you about the guy who went back to the States and saddled me with his poodle. We happened to take our dogs to the same obedience class. That's all."

"But this is August," said Donald. "And you're still seeing her?"

Casey shifted uncomfortably in his chair. "Look, Pop, you're making this out to be more than it is. Really." Yet he had spent every available minute with her, during the two weeks before he left. He looked up and with great relief saw that their dinners were about to be served. "Ah," he said heartily. "Food!"

But when the waiter had left, Donald said, "Tell me some more. About the bookstore lady."

"I don't think I want to talk about her," said Casey.

"Is she married? Do you fool around with married women, as well as kids?"

"No, Pop," said Casey. "She doesn't happen to be married. She's divorced."

"How many times?" said Donald with interest.

"Just once," said Casey. "Kinda boring, huh?"

"Any kids?"

"One. I haven't met her. She doesn't live with Michelle."

"Michelle. That's her name?"

"Michelle. Yes."

They ate in silence for a while. Then Casey said, "She tries to—to keep things separate."

"What things?"

"Sex. From—I don't know. Everything else, I guess."

"Don't you? Isn't that what you're doing with all these kids?"

"I don't know, Pop. Yeah. But it's not the same." He dug into his clam chowder. "I don't like talking about it."

"Charles." Casey looked up at him. "Charles, I am a man who's had three wives. Three wives, son. And that's a hell of a lot more complicated than love affairs. Or whatever you call them these days." He waved his soup spoon. "Don't talk, if you don't want to. But there's nothing you could say that would embarrass me."

"I'm absolutely sure of it, Pop." said Casey. "But let's talk about something else anyway. Can we? Okay?"

Casey got up early the next morning. His father still wasn't up, so he wandered quietly around the house, looking for something to read. Eventually he rummaged for breakfast. The fridge contained a large bottle of white wine, several cans of beer, a jug of apple juice, the remains of a Chinese dinner, and a chunk of butter on a plate. There was also some yogurt, but its expiration date had long since passed. In the shuttered alcoves in the door of the fridge Casey found a chunk of cheddar cheese, moldy behind its plastic wrapping, and most of a pound of butter. In one of the drawers, three withered potatoes. In the other, a small head of lettuce, wilted.

The freezer compartment held three trays of ice cubes, half a loaf of sliced brown bread, and seven TV dinners.

He left the kitchen and went to the piano. He was playing quietly when he heard his father come into the room.

Casey stood up and gestured to the piano. "Play something for me, Pop," he said.

"I don't play much anymore," said Donald, shoving his hands into the pockets of his plaid bathrobe.

There was an awkward silence. Then Casey said, "I'll get breakfast."

He put on some coffee and put two slices of the frozen bread into the toaster. He set the kitchen table with plates, knives, coffee mugs, and glasses. He filled the glasses with apple juice and put out butter, peanut butter, and the bowl of sugar.

He heard Donald shuffling out of the bathroom and poured the coffee.

When his father came into the kitchen, Casey pushed down the bar on the toaster. "You were right," he said. "You don't have much in the way of food around here."

"I eat out a lot," said Donald. He sat down at the table and spooned sugar into his coffee.

"How many pieces of toast do you want?" said Casey.

"I don't usually eat breakfast," said Donald. He drank his apple juice. "One, I guess."

"Pop," said Casey as they crunched their way through the peanut-buttered toast, "I don't like this much."

"You don't like what?"

"The way you're living."

"And what's wrong with the way I'm living?"

"You're not eating right, for one thing. There's dust all over everything, for another. You've got it looks like six months' worth of newspapers piled up in the laundry room. You can't see through the windows. Don't you have anybody come in to clean the place for you?"

"You pay too much attention to externals, Charles." He brushed crumbs from his lap onto the floor. "Some things just aren't that important. That's one of the things wrong with women. Always dusting, scrubbing, some damned thing."

Casey leaned toward him across the table. "What things *are* important, then? To you, I mean?"

"Sure as hell not clean windows and tidiness."

"What, than? What do you do with your days? I want to know. I really do. Do you still sing with that choir?"

"Why this sudden interest in what I do with my life?" said Donald. He smoothed his moustache with both hands.

"It's not sudden. It's just not something you think to ask about in a letter." Casey looked around the room. "Last year—I don't know. I guess I saw all this, but I wasn't worried. Now, I'm worried."

"You've got no call to worry about me." Donald's voice was strong and sure. "I'm doing just fine."

Casey got up and poured them more coffee. "Tell me what you'll do today, once I've left."

"It's none of your damn business," said Donald.

"Okay. You're right. Tell me anyway."

"I don't plan my days. There's no need, when you're as free as I am. I just go where I want, do what I want."

"Like where? Do what?"

"What do you want from me?" said Donald quietly. He set down his coffee mug. "Do you want me to start moaning and bitching? Tell you how empty my life is? How I wake up in the morning and remember that I'm still alive and all I feel is sick and empty? How I get little aches that I imagine into arthritis? A funny feeling I convince myself is cancer of the prostate?" He sat back. "Shit, boy. It's age. That's what it is." He studied Casey for a moment. "And I don't feel like discussing it," he said, "with some half-assed jerk supposed to be related to me who spends his middle age running backwards, going to bed with kids, and thinking he's going to find himself young again." He took a deep breath. "No, Charles. I don't think I want to talk to you about getting old. I don't think I want to talk to you about how I spend my time. I don't think I want to discuss with you whatever plans I may have for my future. Such as it is."

After a while Casey got up and cleared the table. He washed the dishes and dried them and put away the peanut butter and the bread and the butter and the bowl of sugar. His father watched, silent. Casey pulled the plug in the sink and the dishwater began to drain out and Donald got up and left the kitchen.

By the time Casey had wiped off the counter and the table and dried his hands, Donald had carried his suitcase to the front door.

"You'll want to go, now," said Donald. "So you don't miss your plane."

"Yeah, Pop," said Casey. "You're right." He carried his bag to the car and stowed it in the backseat with his jacket.

Donald stayed in the open doorway of his house.

He said good-bye, but he didn't wave as Casey drove away.

From the San Francisco airport Casey called him, but there was no answer.

There wasn't any answer when he called from the Vancouver airport, either.

19

Casey lived on West Tenth Avenue, only a few minutes by car from the university gates. His house had three bedrooms, a living room, a dining room, a basement crammed with junk, and no garage. Almost none of the houses in that part of Vancouver had garages. People parked their cars on the narrow streets. On summer evenings, when the forty-foot oak trees were wrapped in leafy embraces that spanned the pavement, and cars were tucked in bumper to bumper next to both curbs, the streets were narrow tunnels with roofs that quivered and rustled; when it rained, in the summer, the middle of the streets remained dry for quite a while.

It was evening when Casey arrived. He got out of the cab and checked to see that his car, parked almost directly in front of the house, was as he had left it. Then he lugged his bags to the front porch and let himself in. The house felt musty and sullen. He threw open a few windows before going next door to collect his mail from the neighbors, who had each day emptied his mailbox and collected the two Vancouver newspapers and the national edition of *The Globe and Mail* from his doorstep. When they went away in the winter, to their condominium in Hawaii, he would do the same for them.

He dumped the mail and the forbidding stack of newspapers on the dining room table. Then he went to the phone and once more tried to reach Donald, and once more got no reply.

He refused to worry.

He called the kennel to make sure they were expecting him, and left to pick up Corky.

He would call Donald first thing in the morning. If there was still no answer—then, he told himself, it would be all right to start worrying.

At noon the next day Michelle left her bookstore in the capable hands of Barbara Simmons, who worked for her part-time, and walked home with George for lunch.

George heeled dutifully, looking around eagerly but being careful not to step out in front of Michelle, who whenever she did so turned swiftly, ramming her knee into the side of George's head. It was one of the little tricks she'd picked up at the dog class.

Although she was generally extremely pleased with George's behavior she wasn't sure enough of the dog to walk her down the streets unleashed. Which was illegal, anyway.

They strolled through Dundarave, the smaller of West Vancouver's two shopping areas, and along a residential block; between the houses, Michelle glimpsed the sea, two blocks away. At Twenty-third Street they turned right; then left, on Bellevue Avenue; and then they were home.

Michelle unlocked the door and while George rushed through the house to the glass doors leading to the backyard, she picked up the mail from the hall floor.

She let George outside and watched, smiling, as the dog raced several times around the yard, barking wildly, before squatting to pee.

She looked idly through her mail, which consisted of bills from Eaton's, Petro-Canada, B.C. Hydro, and American Express; and a letter, postmarked New York City. Michelle recognized Alexandra's handwriting immediately.

She quickly put it down on the kitchen counter and made herself consider what to have for lunch.

Outside, George had discovered a forgotten piece of rawhide

and was wriggling wildly around on her back with the disinterred treasure in her mouth.

Michelle wondered why she hadn't heard from Casey. Surely he ought to be back by now. Maybe she'd gotten it wrong, the date he'd expected to be home.

George was now furiously digging a hole in the narrow flower garden at the back of the yard.

Of course there was no reason to expect him to call her the minute he got into town. Or at all, for that matter. There hadn't been anything much between them, really.

Her hands were cold, and she wasn't hungry.

George had buried the rawhide and was leaping at the glass doors, barking.

Michelle let her in and clipped the leash to her collar. She grabbed the letter and her purse and took the dog outside. "Come on, George. Who needs to eat. We're going for a walk."

They went back to the corner at Twenty-third Street and turned left, where a concrete path led between a sprawling, low-slung apartment building on the left and a private home on the right. On both sides of the path grew profuse gardens, with small signs asking that admirers please refrain from picking the flowers. There were rose bushes and lupines taller than Michelle, and pink hydrangea bushes much wider than the stretch of her open arms. There were bright gold California poppies, and masses of dark-centered, white-petaled daisies, and in the spring there was orange blossom and forsythia and a little later, wild broom and peonies.

George began straining at the leash. They crossed the railroad tracks. Michelle bent to remove the leash from George's collar. Dogs and cyclists weren't allowed on the seawalk, but there was a path for them between the railroad tracks and the chain-link fence that ran behind the low stone wall bordering the walk.

George raced along the path, barking at nothing, and Michelle followed on the other side of the fence. To her left, beyond the railroad tracks (which were seldom used), a fifteen-foot incline was covered with long grass, white and purple clover, fireweed, blackberries, wild daisies, salmonberries, and the dark green broom that was a rich yellow-gold earlier in the summer.

To her right was another low stone wall, a rocky, barnacle-encrusted beach, and the sea.

The sun was hot on her shoulders but the sea breeze cooled and soothed her.

The walk was wide, made of smooth concrete. A man in his seventies, bronzed and fit, approached her and smiled in greeting. A middle-aged couple wearing shorts and tennis visors passed her, silently. A group of female joggers in sweatpants, short-sleeved T-shirts, and headbands panted by. Nobody but Michelle was dawdling; all strode along purposefully, or ran. It was, she thought, like being in the middle of an exercise track.

Soon she came to a bench and sat down, facing the sea. She watched a seaplane flying toward the Lions Gate bridge, which she wouldn't be able to see unless she went considerably farther along the seawalk to where it curved northward; she knew that the plane would land in Coal Harbor, behind the Bayshore Inn.

She looked at the green mass that was Stanley Park, and across English Bay to Point Grey; she could see some of the buildings of the university there, and thought about Lizzie.

Beyond Point Grey she saw the fuzzy, purplish outline of Vancouver Island.

There were many sailboats in English Bay, like a crowd of white-winged butterflies flitting around the great hulking freighters that waited patiently for their turn to pass under the bridge and enter the harbor to take on loads of bright yellow sulfur, or grain, or potash, or lumber.

She heard George barking and turned to see the dog on her hind legs, her front paws clutching at the chain-link fence. George's long, pink tongue hung from one side of her mouth and her eyes were bright. "Go on," said Michelle. "Run. I'll be a few more minutes."

George dropped from the fence and took off along the path, trotting, her nose to the ground.

Michelle turned back to face the water. A sea gull flapped past at the level of her eyes. The sound of the waves against the great chunks of rock that made up the beach was gentle; there was just a little bit of froth.

Finally she pulled Alexandra's letter from her purse and opened it.

Dear Michelle, she read. *It's been so long since I heard from you that if it weren't for your sweet mother, with whom I continue to exchange gossipy Christmas greetings, I wouldn't even know that this is still your correct address.*

Michelle looked up, shocked. She hadn't been aware that her mother sent Alexandra Christmas cards. She thought this ought to make her angry.

It's obvious that you don't want to hear from me or you would have answered at least one of the letters I wrote when I first came to New York. But it is my opinion that this sullen, deadly silence has gone on quite long enough.

" 'Sullen and deadly?' " said Michelle aloud. " 'Sullen and deadly?' "

I'm coming to Vancouver at the end of the month, the letter went on. *It isn't my first trip home in the last four years, of course. But I knew you didn't want to see me.*

Of course, she must have come home. She had family here. And friends besides Michelle, too. Yet this had never occurred to Michelle. There had been times, then, in the last four years, when Alexandra had been in Vancouver and Michelle hadn't even known it. She looked quickly to her left and right, as though Alexandra might materialize before her right then and there, but nobody appeared except another jogger, and a young couple with their arms around each other.

This time, though, she read, *I really must see you, Michelle. I do have a particular reason, but it's not something I want to talk about in a letter—especially since I imagine you reading this with your eyebrows pulled together and a look of general hostility on your face.*

In this she was certainly wrong. Michelle knew that the only expression she wore was a squint, because of the sun bouncing from the white notepaper.

It's important to me. And that ought to be enough for you. I'll let you know soon exactly when I'll be arriving.

She'd signed it, *Love, Alexandra.*

Michelle folded the letter and put it back in the envelope. She put the envelope in her purse, which she slung over her shoulder. She stood up, turned around, and called to George, who soon caught up with her; they walked to the break in the fence, Michelle on one side, George on the other.

She told herself, calmly, as she attached the leash to George's collar, that there was no reason for her to see Alexandra if she didn't want to.

But as she and the dog went back along the flower-bordered path that led to her street, she was already composing in her head a letter. She stopped to nuzzle an enormous red rose, full-blown and sun-faded, and was amazed to think that this time she was going to write a letter that would actually get mailed.

20

That afternoon Casey was waiting around to hear from his sister Margaret.

He had called Donald first thing in the morning. Still no answer. And he had realized then that he didn't know any of his father's friends, and that he'd only nodded over the fence at Donald's neighbors and didn't even know their names.

He thought wildy about calling the Carmel police, or the fire department.

Finally, he called Margaret in Los Angeles instead. She said she knew a couple of Donald's cronies and his neighbors, too, and that she would phone them.

So Casey waited, since there was nothing else for him to do, and Corky sat in the chair by the living room window watching him pace. Casey figured that if he'd ever been a smoker, which he never had, this was the sort of situation that would probably cause him to take it up again. He saw for the first time that smoking could be useful. He would have to rush out for some cigarettes. He'd have to get a lighter, and an ashtray. Then he'd rush home and start puffing. It would keep him occupied, give him something to do.

Of course he could always drink, he thought. But he decided that it was a bit early in the day for that. If Margaret hadn't called back by seven o'clock, say; or six; maybe five . . .

He thought about calling someone. But his male friends—what was he going to say, for God's sake? It wasn't as though his father was sick, or senile; he just wasn't answering his phone.

He thought of calling Michelle, and pondered this for a minute, looking at the telephone.

No. He shook his head firmly. He wasn't sure that they knew each other well enough for him to be able to call upon her now, in what was something close to panic, quite unreasonable panic, he was certain, yet disconcerting enough to occupy all of his attention.

Besides, it was ridiculous to think about phoning somebody while he was waiting so impatiently for the damn phone to ring. He looked at his watch. She'd had hours and hours to make the damn calls.

He started going through four weeks' accumulation of newspapers but couldn't concentrate on anything. He looked with disbelief at the headlines, which seemed either ludicrously enthusiastic or incomprehensibly gloomy. The only thing that held his attention even briefly was "Doonesbury."

Soon he got up from the table and shoved the whole pile into the blue plastic bag that was collected every two weeks by the paper recycling people.

Corky suddenly jumped from her chair and trotted to the back door. She stood looking up at the door handle, her tail wagging. Eventually she turned around and gave one sharp bark.

"Okay, okay," said Casey, and he let her outside.

Corky stood for a moment on the patio, looking warily around the yard. Then she spotted a robin poking its beak into the grass near the back fence. She streaked toward it. Casey watched the bird, who was watching the dog hurtling in its direction. He thought that to the robin Corky must look like a locomotive gone berserk. The bird waited until the last possible second, then rose into the air and perched on the bottommost branch of the apple tree. Corky skidded to a halt and looked up at the robin, who looked down at Corky. The dog glanced back at Casey, who retreated indoors, grinning. He was glad that Ed had saddled him with a dog, if he had to saddle him with anything. He wouldn't have enjoyed having a cat. Cats actually caught the birds they went after, and sometimes brought them home and laid them before their owners as some bizarre sort of gift.

He began wandering around the house. When the phone rang he was in what he called his workroom—a combination music room and office. He grabbed it on the first ring.

"Well, he isn't dead," said Margaret.

"For Christ's sake," said Casey.

"Obviously, that was a possibility. He could have had a heart attack or something and been lying there dead. Don't tell me that hadn't occurred to you."

"For Christ's sake, Margaret," said Casey, slumping into his desk chair.

"I got Joe Gregson who lives next door on the right to poke around. All the curtains are open and he looked through the windows in every room and Dad isn't there."

"What about the bathroom? It's got that frosted glass, you can't see through it."

"That's true," said Margaret, patiently. "So knowing that we were worried, and prepared to pay for new glass himself if Dad gets mad about it, he took it upon himself to break the window and peer inside and the bathroom was empty, too."

"Great. Now anybody can get in there."

"Casey, will you just shut up and listen?"

"Yeah. Okay. So he isn't there. Does this Dotson guy know where he might be? Did Pop tell him anything?"

"Casey. Shut up."

"Yeah. Okay."

"It's Gregson. Joe Gregson. And no, Dad didn't tell him anything. He says he saw him outside late yesterday afternoon, putting away the lawn furniture. But they just said hello, that's all. I called a couple of his friends and they don't know anything.

"Now, Dad phoned me yesterday, after you'd left, and he sounded—it's kind of hard to describe."

"Never mind how he sounded. What the hell did he say?"

Margaret hesitated. "He rambled, sort of. Went on about

Connie for a while, what the hell did she think she was doing, selling real estate in Floria. Went on about us moving to Oregon. Went on about you. What are you up to, anyway, Casey? He really doesn't like it, whatever it is."

"I sell dope to kids. I hover around elementary schools and deal with them at recess. They pay me in jelly beans."

"Ah," said Margaret. "Well, I can see why he'd be upset."

"Margaret? Go on, will you?"

"Heroin? Cocaine? Or just pot?"

"Jesus Christ, Margaret. Okay. He—I—he doesn't approve of my love life."

"Have you turned gay, or what?"

"Oh, you're funny. Funny. This is ridiculous. I'm coming down there. I'll leave today. Now. I'll bring my dog."

"Is he a bloodhound? I thought he was a poodle. A poodle isn't going to do much good."

"Good-bye, Margaret."

"Hey, Casey, wait. I'm sorry. Really."

"You're laughing. This isn't a laughing matter, Margaret. The man is seventy-four years old, for Christ's sake, and we don't know where the hell he is."

"Sure he's seventy-four years old. He's also healthy, perfectly able to make his own decisions, financially secure, and free to do exactly what he wants. It seems that what he wants to do right now is disappear for a while."

"*What?* How do you know that?"

"Because when Dad called yesterday he said, kind of abruptly, 'I've had it up to here.' I said, 'With what, Dad?' And he said, 'With everything. With life. I've had it shit up to here, forgive the expression, Margaret.' That's what he said. I got worried. Thought he might be—you know, suicidal or something. Except he sounded too angry to be suicidal. I tried to calm him down, I asked him lots of questions, trying to figure out exactly what had him so upset. But he just went on about life, and there's got to be more to it than this, even at his age, and things like that. I swear, if he weren't so old I'd be convinced he was having some kind of mid-life crisis."

"Maybe he is," said Casey gloomily. "Maybe he's going to live to be a hundred and forty-eight."

Margaret thought about it. "That's possible," she said. "*Hmmm.* Anyway, he said not to worry about him, he'd be in touch, and he was writing you a note."

"Writing me a note? What note?"

"I'm getting to it. After Joe Gregson reported in, I got on a plane and went to Monterey and hired a car and it's from Dad's place that I'm calling. I'll make sure the bathroom window gets fixed before I leave. I guess he knew I'd come—I've got a key—because he left your note right here in the middle of the kitchen table."

Casey heard Corky barking at the back door and thought about his neighbors, not the ones who collected the mail and the newspapers for him when he was out of town but the other ones, the pinch-faced, perpetually scowling woman and her small-eyed, overfed husband, a retired couple who complained to him at every opportunity about his dog and who had once called the health department because he'd put his garbage bags out in the alley the night before the 8:00 A.M. collection instead of first thing in the morning. Screw you, he thought savagely, listening to Corky bark.

"Open it," he said to Margaret. "Read it to me." He heard her tear the envelope open; he heard the rustle of paper.

" 'Dear Casey,' he says. Oh, dear. Not 'Charles.' "

"Just read it, Margaret."

" 'Your visit disturbed me,' he says. 'You've got some problems, whether you admit it or not. But I've got some, too. I guess I knew I did. But talking to you, having you ask me all those questions, that made me start thinking about them. And pretty soon I realized that they aren't going to go away by themselves. I have to do something about them. So I'm going away for a while. Going to look at new places, think about things. There's no call for any of you to worry. I may be in touch with you from time to time. I can't say for sure. But you'll hear from me eventually, even if it isn't until I'm finished with this, whatever the hell it is. And meanwhile, I'd be eased in my mind to know that you were doing some thinking, too. I'm fond of you, and I don't want you to screw up your life.' And then he signs it. 'Donald.' "

"What the hell is he up to?" said Casey.

"He's gone traveling, obviously."

"He hates to drive. Is his car there?"

"Yes. And I checked the airlines. Apparently he hasn't flown anywhere. Unless he used another name."

"Another name?" said Casey, incredulous. "Another name?"

"It's unlikely, I know. He's probably taken a train."

"But where? Where the hell has he gone?"

"How should I know, Casey? He doesn't want us to know, remember?"

"Oh, my God."

"The fridge is cleaned out, he's asked the post office to hang on to his mail, he's canceled the paper and the milk delivery."

"For how long?"

" 'Until further notice,' is what they told me."

"Margaret." He was hunched over the phone, elbows on his desk, his right hand clutching his hair. "What are we going to do?"

"Nothing, Casey," she said softly. He could hardly hear her for Corky's increasingly angry barking at the back door. "There's nothing we can do, and nothing we should do. He wants to be on his own for a while. Incommunicado. When he feels like it, he'll get in touch with us."

"But Margaret."

"I know."

"My damn dog's barking."

"I can hear him."

"I've got to let her in."

"If I hear from Dad, I'll call you."

"Yeah. Thanks, Margaret."

He opened the back door and stepped belligerently onto the patio, staring across the fence into his neighbors' yard. But nobody was out there. After a minute he followed Corky back inside.

He decided to call Michelle. Maybe they could get together that evening. Take the dogs to the beach or something.

He'd ask her about her mother. Casually. Maybe dramatic things happened to everybody when they hit seventy or so.

This was not a cheery thought. He did not like the idea of some damned crisis attacking him when he got to be old. He'd always figured you were finished with that kind of thing, when you got old.

Ah, Casey, he thought wearily, picking up the phone. You're so fucking ignorant.

21

They met at Spanish Banks, down the hill from the U.B.C. endowment lands. It was late enough so that there weren't a great many other people there, yet still daylight.

Casey in his agitation got there first and parked as they had agreed in the westernmost parking lot, under a willow tree. He walked Corky on her leash across the concrete and the grass and onto the sand, and for a while they strolled up and down the beach while Casey furtively observed the people nearby. Some of them had dogs, and they were letting them run free, so after a while Casey let Corky loose and sat down on a big log, one of many arranged along the beach like a single horizontal row of rough-hewn pews.

Corky immediately began trotting out to sea, across a wide expanse of hard, smooth sand darkened by the outgoing tide to a color that was almost chocolate. Casey stood up and watched her uneasily. But the sea was very calm, and as soon as it sloshed gently over her paws Corky withdrew. She stood small and black and still, looking west toward the setting sun, and a breeze from the ocean flapped her ears back. She looked like something that might be carved on the prow of a tiny sailboat, Casey thought, sitting down again. A lurching, shrieking child closely followed by its mother approached Corky, who watched it warily but didn't move away. The child put out a violent hand and poked the dog in the side of her head. Corky gave a single truculent bark and hurtled across the sand toward Casey. She sat close beside him, her side pressing against his leg, while the mother bridged the distance that separated her from Casey with exaggerated shrugs and shakings of the head that were meant to denote apology. He smiled and nodded and spread his hands in acceptance, and gave Corky a comforting pat on the flank which she ignored.

He glanced behind him, but Michelle's car had not yet arrived.

The log nearest to his was occupied by a young couple. Casey gradually determined that they were trying to separate, that each was expected somewhere else, and that both of them were already late. They kept falling into close embraces from which the girl would finally extricate herself, laughing, pushing her boyfriend away, telling him that really, they had to go. "Go, then," the young man grinned, running his hands down her back, grabbing hold of her buttocks and pulling her close again. She gave a little moan in her throat and kissed him with a passion that Casey thought unseemly, upon a public beach; he moved uncomfortably, adjusting himself within his shorts, and began to feel vaguely depressed. He was extremely relieved when, reluctantly, their arms around each other, the young couple moved away from the log and slowly up to the parking lot.

Corky stood up, stretched, yawned, and looked at Casey expectantly. "Sorry," he said. He'd forgotten to bring her ball. The dog looked east and west and out to sea again. Then she lay down on the sand in front of him, her head between her paws, staring out across English Bay to West Vancouver. "Where the Christ is she?" muttered Casey, looking at his watch. He turned around and saw Michelle's car pull into the parking lot, next to his own.

Casey stood up, suddenly curious but detached. He didn't know how he would feel, seeing her again.

He watched dispassionately as she swung her legs out of the car, ducked her head and stood up. She closed the door and went to the back of the station wagon, opened it, and George erupted onto the parking lot.

"*Come!*" ordered Michelle, without moving, and George made

an immediate U-turn. She sat beside Michelle, who clipped a leash onto the dog's collar. Then she stood straight and shaded her eyes with her hand and looked around for Casey.

She wore a short denim skirt, a loose, pink sleeveless top, and sandals. She wasn't at all tanned; her face and arms and legs looked positively white, compared to most other people found on the beaches in August. Her hair was different; short, and wavy all over, and the low, slanting rays of the sun seemed to shoot sparks from it. He had forgotten that her hair was that color—reddish brown, like cinnamon.

Then she saw him standing by the log, and lifted her right hand in a wave, and smiled at him.

Oh, Jesus, thought Casey. How could I have forgotten about that smile . . .

They let the dogs run for a while, until the sun had almost set. Corky led and George followed. "It's because she's older," said Casey, almost apologetically, and Michelle laughed. Corky raced in enormous circles along the beach, energized by the presence of a canine companion, and George loped along good-naturedly behind her.

"How was New York?" said Michelle. "And San Francisco?"

"Good, good," said Casey heartily, trying to push from his mind images of honey-skinned Linda, and Donald, scowling.

"Are you glad to be home?"

"I'm always glad to come home," said Casey. He suddenly wondered if there was somebody else in her life. He sneaked a look at her. She was sitting next to him on the log, but not close. Her hands rested in her lap, her feet were crossed at the ankles. She was watching the dogs and smiling, and had not, it seemed to him, been paying much attention to what he was saying. He felt prickings of resentment.

She raised her head and looked across the water. "This really is a beautiful city."

Casey looked blankly right, left, and straight ahead. "Yeah."

"Greener than San Francisco."

Across English Bay the North Shore mountains, tree-furred

and massive, rose dark against the deepening blue of the sky.

"Yeah. I guess," said Casey.

"Much more serene than New York."

To his right was the city's downtown core, a sprawling cluster of towering glass and concrete crammed onto a peninsula bordered on the north by Burrard Inlet, on the south by False Creek, and on the west by English Bay and the acres and acres of forest, rose gardens, zoo, and aquarium that was Stanley Park.

"Yeah," said Casey seriously. "But trees and serenity aren't everything." He looked at her, then, and saw that she was laughing at him. "What the hell," he protested. "You're mocking me, woman."

"Let's gather up the beasts and go somewhere for coffee," she said, only smiling now.

They went to a place on Fourth Avenue called Kalisa's. It was big and hardly ever busy, and served what Casey insisted was the best cappuccino in town.

He noticed, sitting across from her, that her skin wasn't actually white. It had been touched by the sun with a gentle hand which had laid upon her face a golden flush, and scattered freckles across her nose and the tops of her cheeks.

"What are you staring at?" said Michelle, dumping sugar into the milk froth that crowned her cappuccino.

"Nothing," said Casey quickly. "I was wondering. You've got a mother, right? And you said she's a widow, right?"

"Right. Why?"

"I have a problem," said Casey, stirring. He tasted his coffee, added more sugar, stirred again.

"What kind of a problem?"

"With my father. Is your mother married?"

Michelle laughed. "She isn't looking for a husband, if that's what you mean. As a matter of fact, she's just gotten herself engaged."

Casey leaned toward her. "Does she know what she's doing? Do you approve of the guy?"

Michelle studied him, tilting her head. He noticed that some of the hair along her forehead was lighter than the rest. "What's the matter?" she said. "Has your father gotten himself married to somebody . . . inappropriate?" He didn't like the way she said it; as if she were amused by his concern—or, worse, as if she had eagerly created for herself out of absolutely nothing at all an image of his father that was wholly inaccurate.

"No," he said, sitting back. "It's nothing like that."

"Then what?" she said. When he didn't answer, she laid her hand on his. He saw that there were freckles there, too. He wondered where else they might be found, and tried to remember if he'd seen any when they made love, but he couldn't. "Casey," she said. "I do worry about my mother. No, I'm not sure that she knows what she's doing—or at least why she's doing it. But what can I say to her? She's been making her own decisions for a lot longer than I have."

Casey turned his hand palm side up and grasped Michelle's, running his thumb across her knuckles.

"Tell me about your dad," she said.

"He lives in Carmel," said Casey. "All of us kids used to live in California. I was the first to leave. And now, suddenly, nobody's left. Well, my sister Margaret's still in L.A., but she's moving, too. She and I are the only ones who sing. He's a musician. His name is Donald." He squeezed her hand and released it. "My father had three wives and six kids. He divorced all of his wives, and now all of his kids are gone. All of a sudden he doesn't like his life, much. Maybe it's not all of a sudden, I don't know." He shrugged and sat back. "I don't see him all that often. Once a year, or so. Anyhow, he's disappeared."

"Disappeared? What do you mean, he just vanished?"

"He left a letter behind. He's gone off to see the world or some damned thing. Get his shit together. Although he didn't put it quite that way." He slurped up some of his cappuccino. "So?" he said glumly into his cup. "What do you think? Does he sound—does he sound senile to you? Do you think maybe he's got Alzheimer's?" He looked at her apprehensively and saw that she was smiling.

"He sounds like an adventurer, your old man."

"An adventurer?" said Casey indignantly. "Michelle, the man's seventy-four years old."

"Why did he get divorced three times?"

"Something about relationships having a natural life, or some damned thing. Personally, I think he just got restless, and couldn't bring himself to screw around, so the damned fool got divorced instead."

"An adventurer and a gentleman," said Michelle wryly.

"He made an awful mistake the last time," said Casey with a grin. "Got himself divorced, then couldn't find anybody to take her place."

"*Hmmm,*" said Michelle.

"So you don't think he's sick? Or crazy?"

"Do you have any idea where he might have gone?"

Casey shook his head.

"But he knows where to reach you, and your brothers and sisters, if he needs you?"

"Yeah. Sure."

"Is he healthy?"

"In his body, you mean?" said Casey grimly. "Yeah, as far as I know."

"Can he afford to travel?"

"Oh, yeah," said Casey impatiently. "But look, you're missing the point. He's just up and disappeared, for Christ's sake."

"He hasn't disappeared, exactly." said Michelle. "He left you word that he was going."

"In a goddamned letter, he told me."

"I can see why, too. Look how you're reacting. He probably didn't have the energy to go through it with you face-to-face."

"I don't know where the hell he is!" said Casey loudly.

"And why should you? Do you tell him where you are all the time? Why can't he just go off, if he wants to? See the world, get his shit together? What difference does it make if he's seventy-four years old? Don't seventy-four-year-old people have the same rights as the rest of us?"

He stared at her. "What are you so mad about?" Her face was extremely red. She looked positively hostile. He was amazed.

"I like the sound of him," she hollered.

"Keep your voice down," Casey hissed, although there was no need. The few other patrons of the café were buried in books or conversation or, in one corner, a chess game. Only the proprietor was looking uneasy. Casey gave him a weak grin, and he turned away.

"You've got a damned nerve," said Casey in a low voice, "saying it's just fine for my father to do a fool thing like this, and getting all jumpy about your own mother, who only wants to get married. Christ," he said in disgust.

Michelle burst out laughing.

"I think we'd better go," said Casey sullenly, and went up to the counter to pay the bill.

They went outside into the warmth of the summer night, and at the sight of them Corky began barking from Casey's car and George started howling from Michelle's.

"*No!*" hollered Casey, but Corky paid no attention. With her beady brown eyes fixed on him, she continued to bark shrilly.

Michelle reached a hand through the partly open window of the station wagon and stroked George's head. George stopped howling and began to pant. With a smug smile, Michelle leaned against her car and folded her arms.

"Do you want to come to my place?" said Casey, surprising himself; he'd thought he was still irritated with her. "It's not far from here. We can let the dogs cool off in the backyard. It's fenced."

"Have you got any gin and tonic?"

He nodded vigorously. "I have indeed."

"I'll follow you," said Michelle, getting into the wagon.

He put the dogs in the backyard and mixed the drinks, while Michelle prowled around his living room. When he brought in the gin and tonics she was standing, facing him, with her feet apart and her hands behind her.

She was almost frightened. What if they didn't do it? What if they did?

He put the drinks down carefully and wrapped his arms around her, hugging her tightly. "I've missed you," he said. "I like your hair like this. All short and sparkly."

"I've missed you, too."

"Let's go to bed," he said. "But let's take it real slow. Okay?"

"Okay," she said, pressing her hands flat against his back.

"Just seconds at a time. Thinking about every one of them. Okay?"

"Okay," said Michelle. "Okay."

"Yeah, I missed you, all right. I didn't know how much until I saw you. You got out of your car and smiled at me. Then I knew it." He hugged her still closer. "I missed you."

"Good," said Michelle.

"Did you miss me?"

"I don't know," she said. "But I hoped I'd see you again."

"Let's see each other a lot." He kissed her hair. "Come on upstairs," he said, turning her head, his mouth searching for hers, "and lie down on my bed with me, and we'll see what happens, from second to second."

22

The next morning Lizzie called Michelle at the bookstore.

"How about we have lunch sometime soon?" she said. "Maybe tomorrow?"

"I've got a better idea," said Michelle. "There's a book signing going on here today. If you aren't working, why don't you come over at the end of the day and meet the author, and then I'll take you for dinner at Peppi's." She knew that Peppi's was one of Lizzie's favorite places. It was an Italian restaurant on Dundarave beach, right down next to the water at the bottom of Twenty-fifth Street in West Vancouver.

"Yeah, well," said Lizzie. "Who's the author?"

"Alma Glendenning. You probably haven't heard of her."

"*Alma?*" said Lizzie. "What kind of stuff does she write?"

Michelle laughed. "Romance novels."

"Yuck."

"Yuck, hell. They sell like the proverbial hotcakes. So? What about it?"

"I'll skip the romantic novelist, if you don't mind," said Lizzie. "But I'll take you up on the dinner. Mom—"

"Yes? What is it, Liz? Hurry up, this place is a madhouse today."

"Are you still seeing the music teacher?"

"Yes," said Michelle cautiously, after a minute. "I think so. Yes. I am. Why this sudden interest in my love life?"

"I don't know," said Lizzie. "It's the first time you've really had a boyfriend, isn't it? Since Dad, I mean?"

"He's not exactly a boyfriend," said Michelle. "And I really do have to run, Lizzie."

"Yeah, okay, but Mom—Alma won't have to come with us, will she?"

"Good heavens, of course not. She's got three interviews after she leaves here."

"So it'll be just you and me?"

Michelle, behind the counter in the bookstore, felt a burning in her eyes. She had to turn around and stare at the floor so that nobody in the shop would know how close she had suddenly come to tears. "Just you and me, sweetie," she said to Lizzie. "We'll have a terrific time."

Late that afternoon the door to the bookshop stood open, to let some air in, and from the sidewalk outside could be heard the excited chatterings of the fans gathered to purchase autographed copies of Alma Glendenning's latest book, *A Woman Scorned.*

A clutch of women gathered around the author, who was seated at a table in the middle of the store. On another table set up a few feet away there was a large coffee urn, Styrofoam cups, miniature tubs of cream, and envelopes of sugar. There were also cakes and cookies, napkins, and small paper plates.

It was about five o'clock when Michelle, feeling flushed and disheveled but well pleased, spotted Lizzie helping herself to coffee and a slice of carrot cake, and she immediately made her way through the crowd to Lizzie's side.

"I won't drag you over to meet her, don't worry," she said with a smile. "Twenty-five copies so far," she murmured in her daughter's ear.

"Mother," said Lizzie, staring. "What have you done to your hair?"

Automatically, Michelle's hand went to her head. "I got it cut, and had a perm. What do you think?" she said.

Lizzie looked at her critically. "I think they did a good job. It looks sort of finger-waved. I like it. You look younger. Did you get it streaked, too?"

Michelle felt herself bristle. "It wasn't my intention," she said coolly, "to look younger. And no, of course I didn't get it streaked."

Lizzie was nodding. "It looks like you did." She took a sip of her coffee. "It looks like you got highlights put in, right there, in the front."

"That, my dear, is grey. Natural grey. Silver threads among the red." She glanced over to see Alma Glendenning cast a pleading look her way. "Just another twenty minutes," she said to Lizzie. "I promise. Now I'd better get back to my author."

The women gathered around Alma Glendenning were Jane Fonda worshippers all, thought Michelle as she joined them; tanned and fit. They wore casual but expensive dresses, their hair was tinted and coiffed, and they used a great deal of makeup. Michelle wondered if they were disappointed in their favorite author, in the flesh; she was middle-aged and shapeless, with grey hair, straight and short, and she wore something that looked like a parachute suit. Upon her face instead of makeup was a fixed smile, and she was nodding a lot, and not talking much. But then she wasn't being asked many questions anymore, Michelle noticed. The women were busy telling her about their own lives, or things they had heard or read, suggesting among shrieks of laughter plots for future Glendenning romances.

Michelle, surreptitiously collecting empty coffee cups and crumpled napkins, thought it must be getting difficult for the poor author to breathe; her fans had applied generous amounts of perfume before bustling out to meet her, and the combined scents were strong enough to permeate the entire shop. Michelle wondered why the scents of flowers didn't clash in the same kind of olfactory battle, filling the air with a strident sweetness that made you have to breathe through your mouth.

She glanced over at Lizzie and saw that she was amusing herself among the biographies.

Eventually the women began leaving, in groups of two or three, until only a dozen or so remained, encircling Alma Glendenning's chair and chatting companionably among themselves.

Michelle waited until the part-time assistant, Barbara Simmons, had rung up a final sale. Then she saw the customer to the door, walked over to the author, and placed a firm hand on her shoulder. "Ladies," she said with a smile, "I'm afraid we're going to have to let Miss Glendenning go, now. She's due at the television studio in half an hour."

At that moment Casey Williams walked into the bookstore.

Michelle's heart gave a tremendous leap.

He stopped, read the author's name on the large card propped up against the diminished pile of books in front of her, and took a couple of steps backward. Then he looked up and saw Michelle. His face crinkled with joy. His green eyes sparkled. He thrust his hands into the pockets of his baggy-kneed corduroy pants, shrugged apologetically, not wishing to interrupt, and ambled over to the side of the store.

Michelle looked around for Lizzie, just in time to see her disappear behind the rack of cookbooks.

As quickly as possible Michelle ushered the last, diehard fans out of the shop, locked the door, and flipped over the sign so that from the street it read CLOSED.

Casey came toward her, his hands outstretched. She took them, and felt herself lean toward him, and then felt his kiss upon her cheek.

"Oh, God, Michelle," said Alma Glendenning, in her high, melodic voice. "I hate these things. I absolutely hate them."

"You'd hate them a lot more," said Michelle briskly, "if nobody showed up for them." She introduced the author to Casey, then called out to Lizzie.

"I've got to get to my hotel," said Alma. "I'm exhausted."

"TV first, then your hotel," Michelle reminded her. "I'll call you a cab."

"It's on its way, Michelle," said Barbara Simpson.

"Thanks, Barbara. Do you want to use the washroom, Alma,

before the cab gets here?" She led the way, and when she returned she saw that Casey had been joined by Lizzie. "You've met," she said, with satisfaction.

"Not exactly," said Lizzie. Her voice sounded clipped and cold.

"Casey Williams," said Michelle, smiling at him, "I'd like you to meet my daughter, Lizzie."

"Elizabeth," said Lizzie, with a furious glance at Michelle. "Elizabeth Paparo," she said to Casey.

"She uses her father's name," Michelle explained, feeling awkward.

"It happens to be my name, too," said Lizzie.

"Here's the cab," Barbara called out just as Alma emerged from the washroom, and Michelle hurried to escort her to the car.

When she rejoined Casey and her daughter, Lizzie was saying, "We're having dinner together, Mother and I. Would you like to join us?"

"No," said Casey, quickly. He was already backing toward the door. "No, thank you." He turned to Michelle. "I should have called first," he said. "I'm sorry."

"You can at least have a drink with us," she protested.

"No, no," said Casey. "Believe me, I can't. I have to go." He smiled, but without much conviction. "I'll talk to you tomorrow."

Barbara let him out.

Michelle looked around the shop. "What a mess," she said. "I'm really terribly tired, all of a sudden. Barbara, I can't thank you enough for volunteering to clean up. For God's sake, take tomorrow off."

"Don't worry," said Barbara, a small, neat woman of about thirty-five, with enormous serenity and a quick grin. "I will."

Michelle put an arm around Lizzie's shoulders and gave her a hug. "Let's go pick up George and take her home. Then we'll go to Peppi's."

"Don't you want to know what I think of him?" said Lizzie, following her mother through the store and out the back door.

"Not much, is what I think you think of him," said Michelle

grimly, as she led the way across the alley to the building that housed the veterinary clinic and the dog groomer. "You were rude, Lizzie. Making all that fuss about your name."

"I wasn't rude. He's quite attractive, really."

Michelle stopped and looked at her. "He is, isn't he?" She ran her fingers through her hair and laughed. "He's very nice, too. Did you think he was nice?"

"I'll tell you absolutely *everything* I think about him, Mother, I promise," said Lizzie slowly: she looked, thought Michelle worriedly, rather pale. "But let's wait until we get to the restaurant, okay?"

Michelle nodded. "Okay," she said with a smile.

23

"I'm going to treat you like an adult," Casey said the next day. He knew that his intense discomfort was obvious.

"I should certainly hope so," said Lizzie, rummaging in her bag for her cigarettes and lighter.

Casey saw that she handled the accoutrements of smoking with some awkwardness, and realized that she must be feeling a certain amount of tension herself.

She had approached him in the bookstore the previous day, while Michelle was busy with her author. Stuck out her hand and said, "Hello. I think we've met."

Even while he looked at her admiringly, taking in the slimness of her waist, the richness of her dark hair, the flash in her eyes, he was shaking his head regretfully. He took her hand. "Have we?" he had said with a smile. "Are you sure?" Oh, Jesus Christ on a cross. He shivered, now, remembering the look on her face.

It wasn't until all that chit-chat about her goddamn name happened that it had finally dawned on him. He knew that she had seen his face when remembrance swept sickeningly across it.

Later, when Michelle took the writer out to her cab, Casey had said, "I don't—I can't think of anything to say."

Lizzie smiled at him then. Very coldly. "I'm not surprised," she'd said.

"I think we have to talk," he said grimly.

"Oh, really?" she said, and laughed, and then Michelle had come back.

He'd looked her up in the student directory and phoned her that very night.

"I was pretty sure I was going to hear from you," she said calmly.

He'd suggested they meet the next day for coffee. But she had a summer job, at a clothing store or something, and the only time she had free was dinnertime.

So here they were. In the White Spot on Broadway.

Casey had to admire her style. She'd made sure she got there before he did. White Spot restaurants didn't accept reservations and they were always busy; you had to leave your name with the waitress and then hang around making conversation until there was a table free.

By the time he arrived, she had already been seated.

A middle-aged waitress bustled up and deposited glasses of ice water in front of them. With a flourish she whipped out her order pad and a pen. "And what can I get for you folks today?" she said, beaming. The tag on the lapel of her uniform announced that her name was Bernice. Casey didn't think he'd ever before met anyone called Bernice.

Lizzie ordered a hamburger platter with fries and a chocolate milkshake.

"Just coffee for me," said Casey. The waitress whisked up the menus and hurried off.

"I remember you very clearly now," he said, looking at Lizzie. "You're Josh's friend."

He had seen them at a party, arguing. Josh was a music student, and the party had followed a recital attended by all the faculty, most of whom had decided that their presence at the party was also obligatory, if only for a few moments.

Josh had been talking about dropping out of school and joining a rock band. Casey, among others, had tried to dissuade him. So he was pleased when he overheard some of the conversation between Josh and his girlfriend, because it was obvious that she was even more impatient with Josh than were his professors.

She became so angry with her boyfriend, in fact, that she ended up shouting at him and running out of the house without her coat.

It was a cold day in early winter, and Casey was about to leave anyway.

When he emerged, she was standing on the sidewalk, looking up and down the street, and he offered her a ride, after introducing himself. He delivered her straight to her doorstep. Nothing happened at all.

Josh, as it turned out, wouldn't listen to anybody. He left school and disappeared with the rock band.

Then Lizzie—who was called Elizabeth at U.B.C.—began showing up in the cafeteria near the music building from time to time.

And she and Casey had conversations.

And one thing had led to another.

"Josh's friend," said Lizzie at the White Spot. She gave a sputter meant to be a laugh. "Great." She took a deep drag on her cigarette. "I guess you disapprove of smoking," she said, "you being a voice teacher and a choir leader and all."

"Did you know that he's back?" said Casey. "Josh, I mean?"

"I don't care whether he's back or not."

"He was out for two years. Played with that band of his in every tavern and club in every little town in B.C. Then he came back. He's doing well." During all this he watched her steadily.

"I really don't care," said Lizzie, tapping cigarette ash into the ashtray.

"You cared then. I remember. That's why we met."

"Well I don't care now."

"Here we are, sir," said the waitress, arriving with a cup of coffee for Casey. "Would you like your milkshake now, dear, or with your meal?" she said to Lizzie.

"With my meal, please," said Lizzie. "No, wait. Yes, I'll have it now, please. It's kind of warm in here."

"Did I treat you badly?" said Casey, when the waitress had left.

Lizzie's eyes shot to his face. He saw the blood pounding in her throat, her cheeks, and knew he'd said the wrong thing.

"You don't remember anything about it, do you?"

He didn't try to deny it.

"You're a real son-of-a-bitch, aren't you?" she said, her voice shaking. "A real jerk. A complete idiot."

Casey rubbed absently at his temple. "Yeah. I probably am. But I'm going to try to explain why."

"Forget it," said Lizzie, violently stubbing out her cigarette. "We're not here to talk about me. We're here to talk about you and my mother."

"And here you go, dear," said Bernice, delivering the milkshake, into which was stuck a large straw and a long-handled spoon. "Your burger'll be up in a couple of minutes. You want your coffee warmed up there, sir?" she said to Casey.

"No, no thanks," he said, picking up his cup. "It's fine." He took a sip and returned the cup to its saucer.

"You have some hell of a reputation," said Lizzie bitterly. "And don't try to pretend it isn't true, either. You'll fuck anything female that's of age, attractive, reasonably well-adjusted, and not looking for a commitment," she said. "Everybody knows it."

"Did you know it?" said Casey, with sudden anger. He leaned forward, aiming his ice-green eyes at her. "When you made it a point to start having lunch in the cafeteria frequented by staff and students of the music department?"

"I had a boyfriend in the music department."

"Not by then, you didn't. By then he'd dropped out."

"I had other friends in the music department. People he'd introduced me to."

"Then why, every time I saw you, were you eating lunch alone?"

"You bastard," said Lizzie, and he saw that she was almost speechless and perilously close to tears.

Casey sat back, rested his head in the corner where the booth met the wall, and closed his eyes.

Meanwhile, Bernice set Lizzie's hamburger platter in front of her. "Enjoy," she said, smiling encouragingly.

"Lizzie," said Casey. "I'm sorry."

"Elizabeth," said Lizzie. "I told you, I'm called Elizabeth." She looked at him bitterly. "Elizabeth is what you called me then, you know. When—when—"

"When we were involved," he said. "When we had our thing. It was long time ago, Elizabeth."

"Is that what you're doing with my mother?" she said bitterly. "Having a 'thing'? You know, you'd better watch yourself, you bastard. I don't think my mother *has* 'things.' "

He sighed and rested his forearms on the table. "I'd like to tell you—I loved my wife very much."

Lizzie snorted, and sucked up some of her milkshake.

"I haven't loved anybody else since her," Casey went on, with some effort.

"You've sure been looking hard," said Lizzie. He gave her a sharp glance and then almost smiled, for a minute.

"No, I haven't," he said. "That's just it. I've been enjoying myself. It's not the same."

"Better, probably," said Lizzie, with a world-weary tone that seemed to please her.

This time he really did smile. "Maybe," he said. "Who knows?"

"So," said Lizzie, businesslike. "My mother. Now you're enjoying yourself with her."

"Yes. But it's different."

"She's older."

"Yeah."

"Not so many complications, maybe," said Lizzie. She looked at him critically. "You really are getting on, you know." she said. "All those lines in your face. All that grey hair. You've even got a little paunch."

Casey decided to ignore that. "I wouldn't say there aren't as many complications," he said. "No, I certainly wouldn't say that."

Lizzie pushed French fries around on her plate. "She's got secrets, you know," she said softly. She sounded suddenly sly; almost malevolent. "She probably hasn't told you about them. She probably never will." She darted him a glance. "I know what they are.

You wouldn't like them. Believe me, you wouldn't."

"Have you told her your secrets, Elizabeth?" he said softly.

Lizzie looked at him coldly. She picked up her hamburger and started to eat.

"I'd like to be the one who does that," said Casey. "If it isn't too late."

"Hoo, hoo," said Lizzie, with her mouth full. She chewed and swallowed. "I'd sure love to be there for that." She drank some more of the milkshake. "She'll dump you so fast it'll give you a concussion."

He was nodding, slowly. "You're probably right."

"You'll probably decide she isn't worth the trouble," said Lizzie, spearing three French fries with her fork. She stuffed them into her mouth. Casey waited, watching her. "After all, you could pick up another adolescent"—she snapped her fingers—"just like that." She took a deliberately long, slow look at him. "I don't know, though. You're getting a bit long in the tooth for cradle-snatching, or whatever they call it. Is that it? Is my mother kind of a last resort, or something?"

Casey shook his head again.

Lizzie shoved her plate aside. Her fork fell off, bounced on the tabletop and dropped to the carpeted floor. "I haven't told her. Not yet. But I will. I just haven't found the right time, that's all." She burrowed into her bag for a Kleenex and blotted savagely at her eyes. "You damn—you damn degenerate." She shoved her cigarettes and lighter into her bag. "Let me tell you this. If you happen to get up your goddamn nerve before I do, which I doubt, then you'd better tell her everything, do you hear me? Not just about me. You'd better tell her about every damn one of us." She shoved herself from the table and rushed out of the restaurant.

The waitress came by with a coffeepot. "Fill your cup?" she said cheerily. Then she looked at Lizzie's half-eaten hamburger, the glass almost full of milkshake, and glanced at the door just in time to witness Lizzie's hurried departure. "Is your daughter not feeling well, sir?" said Bernice, worried.

Casey felt a stab in his chest, and laughed.

24

D*ear Allie,* wrote Michelle that evening. She looked up wearily from the dining room table through the big window into her backyard. The light was fading. She'd been at the damned letter for what seemed hours. On the floor were dozens of crumpled sheets of notepaper. Maybe I ought to be using the typewriter, she thought.

But what the hell difference would that make? She'd still have to come up all by herself with just the right words.

She sighed and went into the kitchen to mix herself a gin and tonic. George followed her, and she realized that it was long past the time that the dog usually ate. So she fixed George's dinner and put the dish down for her. She took her drink into the dining room and got a coaster so as not to mark the finish of the table. She sat down, picked up her pen, put it down and went over to the stereo to put on the tape deck Mozart's Piano Concerto No. 21, from which *Elvira Madigan* had borrowed the middle section.

Again she picked up the pen.

Oh, Allie, she wrote. *I don't know what to say to you.*

What the hell, thought Michelle. I'll just write as though it's another one of the letters that never gets mailed, and then I'll edit it and copy out safe parts.

Of course I want to see you. It even hurts me to know that you've been back here before, and never called me. But then why should you have called me, when I'd never answered your letters?

She drank and shut her eyes for a moment, listening to Mozart. The first movement was irrepressibly joyful, that's why she'd put it on—to lighten up her for this letter-writing task. The music rippled through the air like elegant sweeps and flicks of a jeweled lariat.

Actually, she went on, *I did write to you. I've been writing letters to you regularly the whole time you've been away. I just never mailed them, that's all. Tore them up and chucked them, as soon as they were finished. You wouldn't have wanted to read the first few—they were angry and bitter. But then I calmed down and got sensible and in my mind, anyway, you were my friend again, my good friend, and so I told you pretty well everything that was going on in my life.*

She stopped for a moment to let George outside, and she decided to leave the glass door open a bit, the scent of the evening was so sweet and strong; it went well, she thought, with Mozart.

While you're here, she wrote, *we can have long conversations like we used to and bring us both up to date.*

I'm very happy that you're coming, Allie. And that you want to see me. (You're probably going to tell me you're getting married. Or maybe you're already married. My God, maybe you've even got a child or two.) She had to stop writing to ponder this for a while. She didn't like the idea that Alexandra might have gotten married and become a mother without letting Michelle know. Surely, she told herself, Allie would have told Michelle's mother, in one of her Christmas cards. Besides, Alexandra was hardly likely to alter her attitude toward children at this late date.

Anyway. When you're here I want you to see Lizzie. With whom I have a tenuous but what I hope is a steadily improving relationship. She loved you, too, you know. Her pen remained suspended over the paper. She remembered Allie's furious hollering at Lizzie: "Your father fucked around, your father was a fucker-around . . . "

She couldn't think of anything more to say about Lizzie.

The man I've been telling you about during the summer (though you didn't know I was telling you about him) has come back from his month-long sojourn in New York and San Francisco. Again she paused.

How to say it? What was there to say, exactly? She didn't want to give Alexandra the wrong idea. *We're going to a movie tomorrow night,* she wrote, carefully, and felt her lips begin to smile, and her crotch begin to throb gently. And here was *Elvira Madigan,* fields full of bright poppies and the sound of the wind in summer-heavy trees, and a sky so blue it could stop your breathing.

And also, she wrote, *it seems that my mother's getting married. It might even happen while you're here. I do hope so—and so will she. Let me know immediately exactly when you'll be arriving, and how long you can stay . . . and whether you can be persuaded to occupy my guest room.*

I'm not entirely sure that she wants to get married. Michelle reread the sentence, lifted her pen to cross it out, and then changed her mind. She'd said as much to Casey, who hadn't even met her mother. She could certainly tell Alexandra. *There's just something about the way she discusses it. Actually she never brings it up herself, but I do. And she seems uneasy, or uncertain, or something.*

Hell, wrote Michelle, *she's probably just nervous.*

She got up to turn on the light that hung low over the table.

My business is doing okay, she went on. *I love it, and although it's a struggle, and always a worry, so far it's managing to support me and that's all I ask.*

She drank some more of her gin and tonic. Outside, night had come; she could see her reflection in the window.

Please write me quickly, she wrote to Alexandra. *I'll meet your plane. Bring you flowers. Give you a hug.*

She left the letter on the table and sat down in her favorite easy chair to listen to the end of the concerto. She'd do the editing later, she thought.

But already she knew that she would put it into an envelope unchanged, and send it off special delivery first thing in the morning.

25

The next morning Michelle mailed off her special delivery letter to Alexandra, and Casey received one from Donald.

He poured himself some coffee and sat down at the kitchen table to read it, resolved despite a ferocious headache to remain calm no matter what news it contained.

It was postmarked Reno. Oh, Jesus, Casey moaned to himself as he ripped open the envelope. He's taken all his money with him. He's discovered that he's a gambler. He's lost every cent he had.

Dear Charles, the letter began, and Casey was at least grateful for that. *I've come here to look up an old friend, name of Harry Miner. You probably don't remember Harry. He and his wife Isabel were our neighbors when we lived in Monterey, before the War, and during it, too.*

Who the hell was Harry Miner? thought Casey. He imagined him as somebody who was now important in the gambling industry, if you could call gambling an industry; somebody purely delighted to see a long-lost buddy with his pockets stuffed with cash.

Isabel's dead now, God rest her soul. Cancer, it was. Five years ago. Truth is, I was kind of relieved to hear it, though I'm ashamed to say so. She turned against me, some, when the first divorce happened, in '46. Stopped speaking to me, as a matter of fact. Then they up and moved here to Reno. But Harry and I, we stayed in touch.

Casey shook his head. His father had stayed in touch with practically everyone he'd ever met and felt some liking for. Casey clearly remembered that Sunday was sacrosanct in the household of his childhood not because it was Sunday, but because it was Donald's day to spend at his desk in the den, laboriously pecking out letters on his antiquated Smith-Corona.

Harry did well out here, I guess. Got into real estate, (Like Connie. Ha ha.) Has himself a real big house out by Lake Tahoe. He invited me to stay there—Christ knows the place is big enough. Not sure why I turned him down. But I did. He's retired now, Harry is. Very active in community affairs.

Casey poured himself more coffee and took three more aspirins—that made nine since he'd gotten up, but who was counting—before turning the page.

By the time this gets to you I'll be gone from here. Not much around this town to engage a fellow's interest. And I found I couldn't really talk to Harry, after all.

He's going home, thought Casey excitedly, and read quickly on.

But if you want to get in touch with me for some reason—maybe send me a letter, tell me how you are—this is where I'm going next. Casey, incredulous, saw that his father had provided an address in Wyoming. *I'm leaving this afternoon,* said Donald's letter, *on the Greyhound bus.* Casey tried without success to imagine his father on a Greyhound bus. *Going to visit a lady, maybe you remember hearing me talk about her, her name is Mirabelle Potskin. Used to be Mirabelle Owens.*

Casey looked up, staring blankly at the cupboard over his kitchen counter, his head still pounding. Mirabelle? Mirabelle Potskin?

Mirabelle's the one who nursed me in Guam, his father went on. *Probably saved my life. Anyway, we started writing to each other, and just kept on. Irene knew all about her, of course. She even wrote Mirabelle herself, just to say thank you. She had a lot of class, your mother did.*

Enough for fourteen years of marriage and not a second more, thought Casey bitterly.

This town in Wyoming, it's pretty small, I think, Donald wrote. *They've got a ranch near there, Mirabelle and Walter—it's Walter Potskin she married. Sent me photos when it happened, in '52 or '53. He plays the trombone. She says he's looking forward to meeting me. Huh.*

What the hell is he going to do on a ranch in Wyoming? thought Casey. He struggled to see his elderly father forking out horse stalls, or whatever people did on a ranch.

That's where I'll be when you get this letter, his father went on. *So if you want to drop me a line, send it here. I probably won't be here very long—I just want to see Mirabelle again, talk to her in the flesh.*

Why? thought Casey, incredulous. Why the hell did he want to talk to a woman he hadn't seen in forty years?

It's been such a long time, said the letter, *I don't expect much . . .*

Ah, Charles. I don't know what the hell I'm doing. I've got this list of people, spread out across the whole damn country. Friends, acquaintances, people I started corresponding with through the papers. I got myself a map of the U.S.A. and made little circles around the places where I know people. It made me feel real good to see how many of them there are, how many places I can go and be welcome, at least for a little while. I did it after you left, that Sunday. And then I made a few phone calls, just to see if it was possible. And then I packed my grip, got a taxi to the bus station, and started out.

I'm only at my first stop and I don't know what the hell I'm doing.

Harry doesn't sing anymore. And he doesn't seem to miss Isabel much. She's been gone five years. Connie and I have only been divorced for four. Maybe another year, that's all it'll take and then I'll be ready to get myself active in goddamn community affairs.

There's a big distance between some of these places. I might even have to get on a plane, once or twice. You know how I hate flying. If the damn plane gets anything wrong with it, it's a hell of a long way down. And now there's lunatics putting bombs on them, too.

I think about you quite a bit. It would please me if you could find the time to write me, c/o Wyoming (see above).

Love, Donald

P.S. Maybe you could phone Margaret and let her know where I am, and that I'm okay. Thanks.

Casey slumped in his chair, holding the letter loosely in his hands. His father, his seventy-four-year-old father, was trundling across America in a Greyhound bus. Did he buy sandwiches and apples and bottles of mineral water to consume as the landscape passed behind his window? Did he strike up conversations with his fellow travelers? Of course he did, thought Casey. By the time he got home he'd have had to buy another address book.

He tossed the letter on the table. He had to call Margaret right away.

But before that, he wanted to talk to Michelle.

It wasn't until he was dialing her number that he remembered Lizzie. Elizabeth. He hung up quickly, feeling frantic.

What the hell was he going to do?

After his meeting with her he'd come home and gotten blind drunk. He remembered wanting deep in the night to drive over to Michelle's house, tell her everything, then take her roughly to bed to make a point. He didn't know, now, what point that could possibly have been.

He groaned and rubbed wearily at his face.

When his doorbell rang he was tempted to ignore it. But Corky had raced into the front hall and was yapping with such penetrating shrillness that Casey thought his head might split in two. She'd stop as soon as whoever was outside went away, but his head couldn't wait that long. He went to the hall, scooped Corky up and held her under his arm, and opened the door.

"Hi!" said Linda Thornton. She looked like she'd stepped out of a commercial for yogurt, or a health spa.

Casey was immediately aware that he had not shaved that morning, he was still wearing the T-shirt in which he'd slept, the shorts into which he'd stumbled were rumpled and soiled, and he was barefoot. His toes involuntarily curled themselves into the carpet, as if trying to hide.

"Hi," he said, with such dignity as he could find. When he reached down to set Corky on the floor his headache fed savagely upon the blood that rushed to it; he straightened with a groan.

"Have you strained your back?" said Linda solicitously.

"I've got a hangover," said Casey.

"Coffee," said Linda, walking past him into the kitchen. "That's what you need. Coffee and aspirin."

"I've had two cups of coffee," said Casey, trudging after her. "And about sixteen aspirins."

"Then," said Linda, smiling, "I've got another suggestion." She put her handbag on the table.

"Listen, Linda," said Casey. "I've been meaning to get in touch with you."

"I thought you might have been trying," she said, kicking off her sandals. "I've been out a lot. I've got to get one of those answering machines."

Casey watched with a mouth suddenly dry as she began slowly to pull down her zipper. He attempted to distract himself from the flesh being revealed to him by trying to decide what the thing she was wearing might be called. It was like a pair of very short shorts and a low-cut top with thin shoulder straps, the two sewn together into one—garment. "What's that thing called?" he said conversationally, backing away from her.

She went on smiling at him, pulling the zipper down. Then she slipped the straps down over her shoulders and stepped entirely out of it, whatever it was.

"Oh, Jesus," said Casey, turning away.

She took his hand and gently tugged at it. "Come on. Let's go into your bedroom."

"Linda, listen. Put that thing back on. There are windows in this house." He pulled his hand away and sat down at the table, averting his eyes from her naked body. "This headache—you wouldn't believe it. I really tied one on. I think it would be better if you left."

"Come on, Casey," she said impatiently. She sighed, then walked behind him and began rubbing his neck and shoulders. "Come on," she said. "It'll make you feel better. You know it will."

"To be quite honest with you, Linda," he said, gripping his

hands together in his lap, "I just don't want to." He glanced at her over his shoulder. "Sorry."

"I don't believe this," she said, exasperated. She stalked away and put her clothes on.

"I don't think it's a good idea," said Casey, "for you to come here uninvited."

She looked at him disbelievingly. "You've never said anything before."

"I know. But I should have. It isn't a good idea."

She stood silently in the middle of his kitchen. "Is it anybody I know?" she said coldly.

Casey hesitated. "If there were anybody else," he said, "no, it wouldn't be anybody you know."

"So who is it?"

He stood up. "Mostly, Linda, I've got a bitch of a headache and also a kind of a family problem. I'm sorry. Thank you for coming. I wish I were better company this morning." He moved past her toward the front door, Corky padding at his heels, and held the door open.

She swept out onto the steps, her head high, and turned to face him. "Am I going to see you again?" she said.

She was really very beautiful, he thought, looking at her longingly. "I don't know." he said.

"It isn't entirely up to you, you know," said Linda.

"I know," said Casey seriously.

"I'll see you again, all right," she said. "If I don't hear from you pretty soon, you can be damn sure I'll be in touch with you." She looked him up and down. "Not that you're such a prize, you understand."

"I do," said Casey humbly.

"But you fuck good," said Linda. " And I have a strong aversion to being dumped."

Oh, my God, thought Casey, closing the door behind her.

He went into the bathroom and gulped down two more aspirins.

Then he called Michelle.

"I've had a letter from my father," he said.

"That's wonderful," she said. "See? He hasn't disappeared after all. Where is he, anyway?"

"Reno," said Casey. "Next stop Wyoming. Can I show it to you tonight? The letter?"

"Of course. After the movie let's come back to my place for coffee and something to eat. You can show it to me then. Okay?"

"Okay," said Casey, relieved.

He hung up and called Margaret and read her the letter. She took down the Wyoming address and said she'd write Donald immediately.

Casey decided he'd better do the same.

He wrote a long letter, much longer than he'd expected to write.

He told Donald all about Michelle.

And about Lizzie.

I know she won't see me anymore, once she knows, he told his father. *I can't decide which would be worse—to wait and let Lizzie tell her, which might at least give me more time with her; or to tell her myself, right now, which is probably what I ought to do but it's sure not what I want to do.*

How about calling me up, he wrote, *if they've got telephones on Wyoming ranches, and giving me some advice?*

He knew, of course, what advice he could expect from his father, once Donald finished yelling at him. He hadn't asked for it because he wanted it. He just thought it might do Donald some good to be distracted from his fruitless musings upon life by the unsavory problems of his wayward son.

He took the letter to the post office and sent it off special delivery.

While he was out he had dim sum and copious quantities of Chinese tea. This seemed to have gotten rid of his headache, so when he got home he cleaned the house and mowed the back lawn.

Then he shaved, had a shower, and spent considerable time deciding what to wear that evening. If honor were to prevail (which he doubted), it might well be the last time he ever saw Michelle.

He thought that if honor insisted upon prevailing, he'd at least persuade it to hold off until they'd been to bed.

It was this, he realized, poking through his closet, that had caused him to send Linda away. He didn't want to make love to both of them in the same day. Maybe he wasn't even capable of it. And if he was to have only one of them, apparently he would prefer to have Michelle.

He sank onto his bed to think about this.

26

The following Saturday, Michelle met her mother at Pacific Center and they went shopping for Mrs. Jeffries's wedding dress. First they had an Orange Julius, sitting on one of the benches in the middle of the underground shopping mall, and discussed where they would be most likely to find something that was just right.

"I would have suggested Holt-Renfrew . . ." said Mrs. Jeffries. She stopped, and followed with her eyes a swaggering young man wearing black leather whose head was shaved on either side, leaving only a strip from forehead to nape which was a couple of inches wide, about eight inches high, stiffly gelled, and dyed a brilliant orange. "You know, I like it," she murmured to Michelle. "All these outlandish heads you see downtown. They look like a bunch of exotic birds."

"They huddle in flocks, too, like birds," said Michelle, trying unsuccessfully to imagine Lizzie with a haircut like that.

"I would have suggested Holt-Renfrew," her mother said again, "but while I was waiting for you I had a look in the windows. They seem to have changed their minds about who they want to shop there. I couldn't see a single thing fit for a woman my age."

"How about The Bay, then?" said Michelle. "We could try the Mirror Room."

And so they did, and Mrs. Jeffries was pleased to discover that there happened to be a dress sale going on. She found, almost immediately, not one, not two, but three dresses that she considered appropriate. They all fit her, and she ended up buying two of them.

They went then to the cafeteria next to the skywalk that led across Seymour Street to The Bay's parking garage.

They each got a pot of coffee, and Michelle had a salad and her mother got a slice of Black Forest cake. They sat at a small round table which was separated from the lingerie department by a low, white, fence-like barrier. Mrs. Jeffries stowed her parcels carefully behind her chair, against the wall.

"My goodness, that's a relief," sighed Mrs. Jeffries, pouring her first cup of coffee. "It was right on the top of my list of things-to-do, and I was absolutely certain that it would be the hardest thing of all to accomplish." She looked at Michelle and said passionately, "I loathe shopping. For clothes, that is. I absolutely loathe it."

"I know, Ma. But you were lucky today. Both of those dresses look lovely on you." And it was true, thought Michelle. The grey one brought out the silver in her mother's hair; the rose-colored one made her cheeks look pinker, and her hazel eyes brighter.

"I'll have to get a hat, I suppose," said Mrs. Jeffries, looking uneasy. "Oh, dear. I haven't bought a hat in years."

Michelle reached across the table and patted her mother's hand. "I know just the place. I'll take you there whenever you like. You've still got three weeks. That's lots of time."

"Maybe I won't wear a hat. What do you think, Michelle?"

"I don't think it matters, Ma. It's your wedding. I think you ought to wear exactly what you want to wear."

"Good. I won't buy a hat." She picked up her fork and started on the chocolate cake.

"I remember that photograph of you and Dad on your wedding day," said Michelle. "You're wearing a kind of a tailored dress, and a hat with a little veil. But you were married outside, weren't you?"

"In Mom and Dad's garden. It was a beautiful day. George wore a white suit," said her mother. "He looked terribly handsome." She pushed her plate to one side. "I don't seem to have much of an appetite these days," she said, poking nervously at her hair, which was fastened into a loose bun; some strands had come free, and she tucked them behind her ears. "I don't have much concentration, either. There are many, many things on my list. So far I've only done one of them."

"But you said yourself, Ma, that it was the hardest one of all."

"My God," said Mrs. Jeffries flatly, her eyes caught by the nearby displays of lingerie. "I guess I'm going to have to buy myself a new nightie." She turned to her daughter in dismay, and Michelle saw that her eyes were shining with unshed tears.

"Ma." Michelle took Mrs. Jeffries's hand. "You don't have to do this, you know, if you don't want to."

Her mother blinked vigorously, squeezed Michelle's hand and let it go. "Oh, pay no attention to me. It's only to be expected. A bit of nerves, that's all. Go on, eat your salad. I'm sure it must have happened when I married your father, too." She poured herself more coffee. "And I'm sure you must have gotten the nerves when you married Max, too. I'm sure it happens to every last one of us. The men, too, probably."

"I remember," said Michelle, "that I peered through the crack in the door and looked down the aisle and when I saw him standing there by the altar all of a sudden I got into a cold sweat. I told Dad I thought I'd changed my mind."

"I know," said Mrs. Jeffries. "He told me. Poor George. He didn't know what on earth to say to you."

"He just looked at me in horror," said Michelle, laughing. "And then Alexandra said, 'Well, I don't care whether you do it or not, just make up your mind one way or the other,' and I remember thinking that I'd made the decision to marry him when I was calm and rational, and so I ought to trust that decision, and not try to change it now, when I was anything *but* calm and rational. Then Allie said, 'Okay, I'm heading through the door now and up the aisle, and I want you two to be right behind me or I'll feel like a complete fool.' So off she went, and I took Dad's arm and we followed her." She sprinkled salt on her salad and took a bite.

"Your father liked Max."

"So did I," said Michelle, through a mouthful of spinach. "I still do. I'm not even sorry anymore that I married him."

"I'm glad Alexandra's going to be here," said Mrs. Jeffries. "I've always been very fond of Alexandra."

"Have you invited a lot of people?"

"As many as the house will comfortably hold. That's what I told Van. He's doing it. The invitations, the food; everything, really."

"Ma." Michelle put down her fork. "Would you mind if I brought a friend?"

"Michelle. For heaven's sake, you're as red as a beet. What kind of a friend? A man friend?"

"Yes."

"Of course I wouldn't mind. Who is he? What does he do?"

Michelle laughed self-consciously, and told her mother about Casey Williams.

"For heaven's sake," said Mrs. Jeffries, beaming. "How long has this been going on?"

"Ma, I'm just going out with him, that's all."

"Oh, I think there must be more to it than that. You wouldn't ask to bring somebody you were 'just going out with' to your mother's wedding. Now would you?"

Michelle looked at her, amazed. "No. I guess I wouldn't." She looked away from her mother into the racks of nightgowns and peignoirs and silk pajamas.

"What's the matter, Michelle?"

"Nothing, Ma. I just don't want to get serious about him. That's all."

"Why not?"

"I don't know." A small child peeked from behind a rack of black and lacy nightgowns; she disappeared as soon as she saw Michelle looking at her. "I don't think it has anything to do with him personally. I think I don't want to get serious about anybody."

Mrs. Jeffries looked at her with weary contempt. "Don't be ridiculous, Michelle," she said.

Michelle turned to her quickly, hurt.

"I'm sorry," said her mother. She made an exasperated gesture. "It's just so naïve of you to think you have a choice."

"Of course I have a choice," said Michelle indignantly.

The small child reappeared from behind a collection of thigh-length T-shirts meant to be slept in, each emblazoned with something foolish like "MAYBE—and that's my final offer." She leaned on the white fence that surrounded the café and peered at the plate on which most of Mrs. Jeffries's Black Forest cake still lay. Mrs. Jeffries glanced at her irritably. The small girl continued to look at the cake. "Go away, child," Mrs. Jeffries snapped, and the girl turned and ran, wailing for her mother.

"Ma," said Michelle. "I can't believe you did that." She began to laugh.

Her mother rubbed her forehead, "I have the most awful headache," she said.

Michelle went to fetch a glass of water from the young woman tending the cafeteria. When she got back to the table Mrs. Jeffries had found the small bottle of aspirin she always kept in her handbag.

"Thank you, Michelle," she said, and swallowed two aspirins and the entire glass of water. "I will be extremely glad," she said, setting the glass down, "when this is all over."

"Where are you going to live?"

"I don't know. He has a nice house. But so do I. His is bigger. But I like mine better." She shook her head. "Oh I don't know. What does it matter?"

"Ma, are you really, absolutely, totally certain that you want to go through with this? You don't sound particularly happy about it. It isn't too late to change your mind, you know."

"I always wanted to have a dog." said her mother dreamily, her chin in her hand.

"Ma," said Michelle, but her mother ignored her.

"I didn't think I should, though," said Mrs. Jeffries. "I'd expected to be traveling a lot, and that wouldn't be fair to a dog. But as it turned out I didn't travel very much at all, and I could have had one." She sat back with a sigh. Then she looked irritably at

Michelle and said, "I'm very fond of your dog, but I certainly wish you hadn't named her George. I really do, Michelle. I can't possibly call her that. Which makes it exceedingly awkward for me. The dog probably thinks I'm mad, never calling her by her name."

"Why don't you and Van get a dog, then," said Michelle, exasperated, "and call him 'Michelle'? That ought to make you feel better."

"Don't be ridiculous," said Mrs. Jeffries, pushing at her hair. "You really are being quite ridiculous today."

"I think Dad would be honored," said Michelle, "to know that I'd named my dog after him."

"I doubt it," said her mother coldly, "very much indeed."

A woman wearing a summer suit had sat down at the table next to theirs; a steaming cup of coffee sat in front of her and she was frowning at some papers she had apparently taken from the briefcase that was propped against a table leg.

Michelle bent over her salad. She ate it all, and drained her coffee cup, and looked up to see her mother smiling at her. "It's just nerves, Michelle," she said, "I'm truly sorry to have been so bad-tempered. Especially when you've done me the favor of coming shopping with me."

"It's nothing, Ma. I just wish you'd let me do more. There must be tons of things to do, to get ready for the wedding."

"Oh, yes," said her mother vaguely, stuffing the bottle of aspirins back into her bag. "But Van's taking care of most of it. He insisted. My list is just a list of personal things I have to do. You can imagine how long his is."

"He really does seem to be a very nice man, Ma," said Michelle softly.

"Oh, he is," said her mother. "He certainly is. A very nice man indeed."

"Why didn't Granny and Grandpa like Dad?" said Michelle suddenly.

Mrs. Jeffries smiled and shook her head. "Oh, my. Well, I guess there are certain advantages, after all, to getting married at my advanced age. At least I don't have that to worry about, this time." She glanced at Michelle. "Of course they never said they didn't like him."

"But it was obvious."

"Yes, I know. Even though they were always very polite to him, he knew how they felt. And it hurt him. He tried very hard to make them like him. He never stopped trying."

Michelle looked at her mother curiously. "Ma. Did you like Max?"

Mrs. Jeffries gave her a slow smile. "You mean, you couldn't tell?"

"I always thought you did."

"Well, then."

"But did you?" said Michelle insistently.

Her mother sighed. "Never," she said. "I couldn't stand the man. Ever. From the first moment I laid eyes upon him. I looked at him and I said to myself, 'There's a womanizer if ever I saw one,' and I was afraid he was going to break your heart. And that's the God's truth."

Michelle stared at her, and began to laugh.

"But at least," said her mother softly, "he gave you Lizzie."

"Yes," said Michelle. "Lizzie."

27

"I've been divorced for quite a while now, you know," said Michelle, a week later.

"*Hmmm,*" said Casey, rubbing his hand slowly up and down her back.

"But you're the first man I've slept with. Since Max."

His hand stopped moving, settled around her waist.

"I thought you ought to know," she said.

They were sitting on a bench at Dundarave beach: dogs were prohibited, fires were prohibited—but children were not. There were dozens of them whooping it up in the playground, digging to find sand on the rocky beach, shrieking in the cold waters of the Pacific, racing up and down the long pier that thrust into English Bay. Their mothers tanned themselves upon blankets and towels which lay in scattered clusters upon the grass that stretched between playground and beach.

"Why?" said Casey.

She put her hand on his warm bare thigh and squeezed. "Don't worry," she said seriously. "I'm not making any assumptions. I just wanted you to know, for some reason." She looked at him and laughed. "There's apprehension in your eyes. Tons of it. Relax."

"Not apprehension," he said, shaking his head. He squinted at her, and pushed the fingers of one hand into the waves that fell across her forehead. "Well, maybe it is apprehension. But it's not the kind you mean." He tightened his grip around her waist, giving her a hug, and his other hand pressed against the side of her head; she felt his lips on her hair.

"What kind, then?" said Michelle into the curve of his neck. She kissed him there, and felt his pulse beating beneath her mouth. She touched his skin with the tip of her tongue, tasting heat and sweat, and felt him shiver. You ought to be ashamed, she told herself. A middle-aged woman like you. On a public beach.

"Not the kind you mean," he said again.

She pushed gently away from him and combed her hair with her fingers. In the water she saw a rubber kayak piloted by two boys wearing life jackets. There were wind-surfers, too, and swimmers, and somebody in a canoe. Across the bay sailboats in a swarm departed from the jetties at Jericho beach.

"I have a friend coming," said Michelle. "From New York."

"Male or female?" He put his arm around her again, and she settled comfortably against him, her head on his shoulder.

"Female."

"That's good."

"Her name is Alexandra."

"Alexandra," said Casey. "Makes me think of Tutankhamen, and the Sphinx."

"Of course."

"What's she like?"

Michelle hesitated. "I don't know," she said. "I haven't seen her for a while."

He half turned, to look down at her, but she knew he couldn't see much of her face.

"We were best friends when we were kids," said Michelle. "We climbed other people's cherry trees after dark and stuffed ourselves until our mouths turned purple."

On the left, on the other side of the pier, was Peppi's restaurant, windowboxes overflowing with geraniums.

"It was Alexandra that I went to stay with. When I left Max."

She felt so good, sitting next to him, so near to him. He smelled so good, and felt so good; and there was still, she knew, so much to be discovered about him.

"Then she moved away," she said. "We kind of lost touch."

"Are you nervous about seeing her again?"

A small amount of panic shot into her chest.

"It's hard," said Casey, "to meet somebody you haven't seen for a while. If you used to care about them. Maybe they've changed. Maybe you'll find out that you've changed. Maybe you won't care about them anymore. Maybe you will." She felt him shrug. "Either way . . ."

"Do you ever see your mother when you go to California?" said Michelle. "You never mention her. Or your stepmother."

"No, not anymore." He pulled Michelle closer to him. "My mother made that bedspread. The one that's on the sofa in the cabin."

"I know. You told me."

"I was seven when she and my father were divorced. Margaret was six and Donald Junior was twelve. We didn't understand what the hell was going on.

"The second time it happened I was grown up and married.

"I loved them both. My Mom and Barbara. But I kind of grew away from them. We send cards and presents, that's about all." He laughed. "They still send cards and presents to my dad, for God's sake. Both of them." He shook his head. "It's damned hard to figure people, isn't it?"

To the right of the public beach private beaches began, lawns and gardens sweeping down to driftwood, stone-covered sand and the sea. The land curved inward, here; far away Michelle could see Lighthouse Park, and the blinking light on Atkinson Point, which marked the northern boundary of English Bay.

"I've got some things I've got to tell you," Casey said softly, close to her ear. His warm breath penetrated right to her brain, her nipples, her genitals. She shivered, and snuggled closer to him.

They had been spending a lot of time together, since he got back. They'd gone back to his cabin and cooked dinner on the wood-burning stove and read aloud to each other by the light of the kerosene lamps. They had washed each other in the cold sweet water from the spring-fed, hand-operated pump in the kitchen sink.

They'd taken the dogs to the beach, and had dinner at the Salmon House, high above the Upper Levels Highway, and lunch at the Tea House in Stanley Park; they'd walked through the rose gardens in the park and at U.B.C.; they'd taken the ferry from Horseshoe Bay to Bowen Island, and had a picnic; they'd gone to Captain's Cove and Mosquito Creek to look at sailboats, and Casey had almost decided to buy one, right there and then, but she had persuaded him that first maybe he ought to learn to sail.

Now, when they walked together, they held hands. When they stopped to look at something, his arm went automatically around her.

They had made love often, and each time it got a little better, each time Michelle let herself become a little more free. She had decided that Max must have destroyed a certain kind of trust she had once possessed, and that Casey was slowly helping her to regain it.

They talked about making love on hot sand; under running water; on sweet-smelling grass. But they hadn't yet done these things.

They had known each other less than three months.

Well, thought Michelle, it was longer than that, if you counted the dog class.

"Did you hear me?" said Casey.

"I heard you," she said. "What are these things you've got to tell me?"

A large beach ball hurtled past their heads.

"There are too many kids around here," said Casey. "Far too many." He stood and held out a hand to help her to her feet. "Let's go back to your place."

They sat side by side on lawn chairs in her backyard while George lay in the shade, panting.

For a long time they didn't talk. Michelle put her head back and closed her eyes and listened to birds, and traffic, and muffled shouts and laughter from a volleyball game that was going on in the backyard of the house that lay behind her high wooden fence. She tried not to think of anything at all, just to listen to things, and feel the sun on her face and her bare arms and legs; but everything that her senses brought her was filtered through an intense physical awareness of Casey's presence.

When he took her hand she opened her eyes and smiled at him, and felt a ripeness in her, an exhilaration; she wanted him to get up from his chair and kneel on the grass next to her and put his lips on her thigh; her thighs parted slightly, in expectation of this. She loved it, the moments just before they began to have sex.

He looked over at her, not moving from his chair, and while holding her hand he said, "Michelle. Listen. I think I love you."

She didn't want any tears in her eyes. It bewildered her; where could these unwanted tears be springing from? She blinked them away.

"This isn't entirely a good thing," said Casey. He didn't look at all happy. Shouldn't a person be happy, if he thought he was in love?

"No, well," said Michelle. There was an inordinate amount of confusion in her. Perhaps it was joy. Was it joy? She couldn't be sure. But Casey certainly wasn't experiencing any joy. "Maybe it isn't entirely true," she said, feeling her way.

"Maybe what isn't true?"

"Well, I just mean, maybe you only think you love me. Maybe you love my body, or something." She laughed out loud. "No, I guess that can't be it. But there are other things it could be besides love. You could be infatuated with me for some reason." She knew she was babbling, and took a firmer grip on his hand, in case he decided to take it away.

"Fuck that," said Casey angrily, and Michelle laughed again.

It's hysteria, she wanted to tell him, but she thought it would sound too pompous.

"What's so goddamn funny?" he said. "I'm making a serious declaration of permanence here, and all I get from you is hysteria."

Ah, she thought with relief, good, he knows I'm hysterical.

Now he did try to wrench his hand away. She grabbed it with

both of hers, and in order to keep hold of it she had to get out of her chair.

So she ended up on her knees beside him, instead of the other way around, and this struck her as funny, too.

"Jesus Christ," said Casey in disgust, looking away.

"Casey. I'm sorry. Really I am.

"I wanted to have a serious conversation."

"You took me by surprise," said Michelle, calming down. "I didn't expect it. That's all."

"It has to be a *serious* conversation. And it's not going to be easy."

"What isn't?"

"The conversation, for Christ's sake. This conversation we have to have."

"Okay," said Michelle. "Okay. I can be serious. I quite agree. This is very serious business. Do you want me to stay on my knees, here? Should we have this conversation outside? Or should we go into my house?"

He looked at her hopelessly and shook his head.

Michelle let go of his hand and sat back on the grass. George came over and flopped down beside her. The dog wriggled around until she could put her head in Michelle's lap. Then she sighed and closed her eyes, and Michelle stroked her head and rubbed behind her ears.

"I'm sorry," said Michelle. "I've sobered up, now."

Casey sighed, and didn't say anything.

"Maybe you should think about it some more," said Michelle. "It could be a thing you just blurted out in a moment of affection, you know. It's quite possible that you don't actually mean it."

"Have you slept with your ex-husband since your divorce?" said Casey suddenly.

She felt herself blush, and kept her head lowered, concentrating on the dog.

"I know you could say it's none of my business," he said. "But I do love you. I don't have to think anymore about whether I do or not. I've been thinking about nothing else for days, and I'm certain of it. I love you." He glanced at her. "I'm not totally happy with the idea," he added, "but what can I do. I love you."

"Well, thanks a hell of a lot," said Michelle.

"You don't have to tell me if you don't want to," he went on. "But I would like to know. And of course I'm not asking how it was. Just if it ever happened."

"Yes," said Michelle quickly. "Yes, it did. I have. But not for a long time, now."

She looked up to see him nodding. Her face was still burning.

"I see," said Casey bravely. "That's good. Really."

Michelle pushed George aside and got to her feet. "I don't feel like having a conversation right now," she said.

He climbed out of his chair. "Michelle. We really do have to talk. There are a lot of things I have to tell you."

"I'm not at all sure that I want to hear them," said Michelle, striding toward the French doors. She flung them open and walked straight through the house to the front hall, where she waited for Casey. "I'm quite irritated at the moment," she said when he got there.

"I can see that."

"I'm not used to having people tell me they love me and then add that this is quite against their will and their better instincts."

"Goddamn it," said Casey, exasperated, "that's not what I said."

"Maybe." She opened the door. "You may call me sometime in the future, if you like, and make an attempt to explain yourself more clearly." She closed the door before he'd had a chance to step through it. "I forgot. Would you like to come to my mother's wedding with me? It's in two weeks. September fifth."

"I would be very pleased to come with you," he said politely.

She opened the door again. He grabbed her and kissed her hard. Then he kept his arms around her for a minute, and she thought he was going to say something, but he didn't. He just hugged her tightly, and then he left.

28

She knew Alexandra at once, of course. Four years wasn't all that long.

Allie came through the frosted glass doors from Customs carrying a single bag. She was wearing a cream-colored suit, long-jacketed, with a mid-calf swinging skirt, and a patterned blouse with a loose-looped tie. A handbag was slung over her shoulder.

Michelle saw her first, but only a couple of seconds passed before Alexandra's eye caught hers and a smile spread across her face, erasing weariness.

There was a crowd, for which Michelle was grateful. They met easily and gracefully; Michelle handed over an armful of roses, and Alexandra hugged her in thanks. Theirs was just one of so many reunions going on there, in a variety of languages, that it turned out to be a comfortable thing, anonymous and soothing.

Michelle insisted on carrying the bag. She hurried Alexandra outside and was relieved to find no ticket on her windshield; she had double-parked, figuring that it was worth ten bucks, if she got caught, not to have to tramp in from the too-distant parking lot, and then back, with Allie.

She stowed the luggage in the trunk, and she and Alexandra got into the car.

"I hope you don't mind," said Michelle, "but I told my mother that we'd go to her place for tea before I take you to your parents' house. We're practically there already. It's just a couple of miles from the airport."

Alexandra shook her head, smiling. "I don't mind at all. I'd love to see your mother." She shifted in her seat in order to face Michelle. "You said in your letter that you weren't sure she really wanted to get married. But since then I've gotten an invitation to the wedding. Does that mean all's well?"

"I'm not sure," said Michelle, carefully. "Tell me what you think, after we've seen her."

As they drove to Richmond Michelle got Alexandra talking about her job, and Alexandra asked Michelle about the bookstore.

And then, "Tell me more about this new man in your life," said Alexandra.

"It's gotten a bit complicated," said Michelle, turning onto the Steveston highway. "I haven't seen him for a few days."

"Is there a problem?"

Michelle drove for a while without speaking. "He says he loves me. He says he wants to have a serious talk. About permanence."

Alexandra chortled. "Well?"

"Well, I've been busy. Inventory. You know. That kind of thing."

"Bullshit," said Alexandra.

"What do you mean, 'bullshit'?" said Michelle heatedly. "I've got to think of the store first. It's my livelihood, for God's sake."

"Do you love him?"

"I don't know," said Michelle. Then, "Probably."

"Good," said Alexandra, with satisfaction.

"I'm not ready to have a serious talk, though."

Alexandra laughed. "You're just scared to get married again, that's all. It's perfectly natural."

"Marriage," said Michelle uneasily. "I don't know if that's what he's got in his mind. 'Permanent' doesn't necessarily mean 'married,' does it? Not anymore."

Alexandra leaned back against the headrest and closed her eyes. "Ah, well," she said. "Loving's the only thing that counts, anyway." A little later she said, "How's Lizzie?"

"Fine," said Michelle quickly. "She's just fine."

Soon she pulled up in front of her mother's house.

When they got out of the car Allie surprised her by putting her hand on Michelle's arm and looking straight into her eyes. "I'm so glad to see you," she said.

Michelle said, "Me, too," flushing, feeling awkward, and they followed the sidewalk under the dark-leaved ornamental cherry trees to Mrs. Jeffries's front gate.

They went along a flagstone path flanked by rhododendron bushes up to the front door, and Michelle rang the bell. When her mother opened the door she looked past Michelle at Alexandra and held out her arms. Allie stepped inside and Mrs. Jeffries hugged her and began to weep.

"Good heavens, Ma," said Michelle, and realized that her own eyes were wet.

For a few moments they all stood around crying and laughing. And then Mrs. Jeffries took them into the living room, where roses from her back garden bloomed as usual in several vases.

They had tea, and sandwiches of thinly sliced ham, and brownies. Michelle ate ravenously—she'd been too nervous to have any lunch, and it was now mid-afternoon—but Alexandra, although she drank several cups of tea, managed only one small sandwich and no brownies at all. "I ate on the plane," she said apologetically to Mrs. Jeffries. "Twice, I think." She sat back and got cigarettes and a lighter from her purse. "Do you mind?" she asked Michelle's mother, who said no.

Alexandra's hair was jet black—she must touch it up, thought Michelle, but it didn't matter, it suited her. She looked older, in her face. But then so did Michelle. And it had been a long trip and Allie was tired. She hadn't put on an ounce, Michelle noticed; she was as svelte as ever, maybe even svelter.

"Only a week of freedom left," said Alexandra to Mrs. Jeffries with a grin.

"Eight days, actually," said Michelle's mother.

"How do you feel? Any jitters?"

Mrs. Jeffries moved uneasily in her chair. "Some. Yes. But that's only to be expected."

"He's a very nice man, Alexandra," said Michelle.

"I'm so glad you'll be there," said Mrs. Jeffries.

"I wouldn't miss it for the world. Maybe I'll catch your bouquet," said Allie, stubbing out her cigarette.

"You look a little pale, Alexandra. Tired. And you're much too thin," said Mrs. Jeffries.

"Haven't had my holiday yet. Just wait, by the time I go back I'll have such a tan, and I'll have eaten so much of my mother's cooking"—she looked down at herself— "this suit won't fit me anymore." She reached for another cigarette.

Mrs. Jeffries refilled their teacups. "He has a great deal of china," she said. "I guess it was his wife's, actually."

"I never thought of it before," said Alexandra, casually, "but each of you must have a whole houseful of possessions. How on earth are you going to decide what to keep?"

"I think they should buy a house twice the size of the ones they've got now," said Michelle, "and keep everything." She looked fondly around her mother's living room. "If I were you, Ma, I wouldn't want to part with a single thing."

"Well, I don't, Michelle. But he says he doesn't mind, he'll sell everything and live with my furniture, if that's what I want." Her hands were stroking the arms of the stuffed chair in which she sat. It was covered in a fabric that displayed pink roses upon a background the color of sand.

"What is it, Mrs. J.?" said Alexandra gently. "What's making you unhappy?"

Tears spilled with shocking suddenness from Mrs. Jeffries's eyes. Michelle got up quickly, but Alexandra was there first, crouched next to Mrs. Jeffries's chair; so Michelle hurried into the kitchen to get a box of Kleenex. When she returned, her mother was sobbing into her hands and Allie was patting her back.

"Ma, Ma," said Michelle in dismay. "Don't cry. You do not have to get married, for heaven's sake. I've told you and told you."

"Oh, I want to. I want to," said Mrs. Jeffries. Michelle thrust some tissues at her and she took them and wept some more. Michelle and Allie exchanged bewildered glances.

Gradually Mrs. Jeffries stopped crying. She reached out blindly and Michelle put more tissues in her hands. She wiped her face and took a skittery breath. "I'm all right now. Oh, dear, I must look a sight." She raised her hands to her hair and unpinned her braid, and then pinned it up again.

"Now what on earth was that all about?" said Alexandra, sitting down again.

"I don't understand it at all," said Mrs. Jeffries. "I've been over it in my mind again and again and each time it comes out the same: I do want to marry Van." She said this with such conviction that Michelle had to believe her. "Yet I seem to be astonishingly reluctant to do any of the things necessary to cause this to happen. I don't even like it that the days are passing, time is passing, and pretty soon it will be Saturday." Her eyes brimmed again, and she reached for the Kleenex. "It's just an old woman having an attack of nerves. That's all it is."

"Have you talked to Mr. Hudson about it?" said Alexandra.

Mrs. Jeffries shook her head. "Oh, no. I could never do that. The poor man." She sobbed, and clutched the tissues to her face.

"Ma, for heaven's sake," said Michelle. "Have you talked to your doctor, then? Or a friend?"

Again, a violent shaking of the head.

Michelle looked helplessly at Alexandra, who shrugged.

"Well, Ma," Michelle said firmly, "you can't possibly get married in this state."

Her mother straightened, dabbed once more at her face, and lifted her head. "You're absolutely right, Michelle. And yet I am certainly going to get married. So what is your advice?"

"Mrs. J.," said Alexandra quickly. "I know you don't want to talk to Mr. Hudson about this. It would hurt him to know that you're having doubts. Is that right?"

Mrs. Jeffries nodded.

"Okay. But just hypothetically, now; if you were upset, like this, but for some other reason, having nothing at all to do with getting married, would you have wanted to see him? Would you have called him?"

"Of course I would have," said Mrs. Jeffries, and began again to cry. "I love him, for heaven's sake."

"Well, then," said Alexandra with satisfaction. "I don't think you've got a thing to worry about." She reached over and patted Michelle's knee. "She's going to be just fine."

29

"Goddamnit, Michelle," said Casey the following Wednesday. "I'm sorry I ever brought it up." He stalked around his workroom, holding the phone in one hand and the receiver in the other, kicking the long cord out of his way. "No, I take that back." He sat in the swivel chair behind his desk. "I meant it. I still mean it. And it isn't going to go away, just because you refuse to talk about it."

"I'm not refusing to talk about it," said Michelle. "I've just been terribly busy, you know that. And now Allie's in town, and my mother's wedding's only three days away—"

"But last week, Michelle. Last week your friend wasn't in town. You wouldn't see me then, either. What the hell's going on? Do you want to call it quits, break it off? Is that it?"

"No. Oh, Casey . . . "

"Don't cry, for God's sake. Are you crying? What the hell are you crying about?"

"I don't know."

"Look. You completely misunderstood me."

He listened until he heard her breathing return to normal.

"How?" she said.

"It isn't that I don't want to love you. I love loving you. I want to love you permanently." His grip on the receiver was much too tight. He tried to relax. "But before we can talk about that, before

I can even ask you whether you feel the same way that I do, I have to tell you some things. And that's what I don't want to do."

He swore he could hear her thinking, wheels and cogs—or microchips—busily lumbering away, putting two and two together and maybe coming up with four.

No, he told himself. Not possible. Not unless her daughter's spilled the beans. In which case she wouldn't be talking to him at all.

"What kind of things?" said Michelle calmly.

"I can't tell you on the phone."

She thought some more. "I can't see you until Saturday," she said.

"I don't believe you."

"All right, then, I *won't* see you until Saturday," she said. "I need more time."

"For what, for Christ's sake? This is urgent, can't you understand that? It's urgent, Michelle. Why do you have to have more time? We haven't *got* any more time."

"I need time to figure out if whatever I feel for you is enough to make me listen to whatever it is you've got to tell me. And this is your own fault, Casey. You've filled me full of dread. Maybe you didn't mean to, maybe I shouldn't be full of dread, but I damned well am. You've got to have this urgent talk. It can't happen on the damned telephone. I keep thinking, he's got a fatal disease, or his wife isn't really dead—don't interrupt me, I don't want to know! I'm not ready yet."

Casey dropped his head into his hand. "But you'll be ready on Saturday."

"I'll try," she said. "No. I will. I'll drink a lot of champagne at my mother's wedding, and then I'll listen to you. I have to go now."

Casey got himself a beer and talked to Corky for a while, until she turned her head away and shot him uneasy glances from her beady eyes.

Then he got out the letter from Donald which had arrived that morning, and reread it.

I don't feel like phoning, his father had written. *Probably I'd just start hollering at you, and then you'd start hollering back at me, and we'd both hang up on each other.*

How you ever got yourself into such a mess God only knows. Have your goddamned brains pickled themselves, or what? I knew you were going to get your comeuppance. But Lord Jesus, even I couldn't have thought of a better one.

You know what you're going to have to do. I feel weary sitting here with my pen in my hand, going to all the trouble of saying it and knowing damn well you know it without hearing it from me.

So I'm not going to tell you.

Figure it out for yourself.

That's what we've all got to do, sonny boy.

Farm life ain't for me, I've decided, which won't surprise you or Margaret or anybody else.

Tomorrow I'm off again, to the next spot on my map.

That was it. He hadn't even told Casey what the next spot on the map was.

Casey wondered if Margaret knew. Margaret hadn't gotten any letters at all, so far. But Donald obviously felt it necessary to let somebody know where he was. If he was now too disgusted with Casey to communicate with him again, surely he'd start writing to Margaret.

He'd gotten up to phone her when his doorbell rang, sending Corky into a paroxysm of barking.

"Hi," said Linda with a smile.

"What are you doing here?" said Casey coldly.

"Aren't you going to ask me in?"

"I told you, Linda. I don't want you coming here anymore. I meant it."

Her smile faded. "I haven't heard from you."

"I know. I'm sorry. I should have called."

"So ask me in, and we'll talk about why you didn't."

"There's nothing to talk about. I'm not going to see you anymore. That's it."

"You know," she said, studying him thoughtfully, "I don't believe that."

"It's true."

"Then there's got to be somebody else."

"That's true, too. I'm sorry. I should have told you."

She stepped closer to him. With the index finger of her right hand she poked him several times in the chest. He heard Corky behind him begin to growl.

"I could make trouble for you, Casey."

"What would be the point of that?"

"I'm very mad at you, Casey." she said slowly. "That would be the point of it."

"I'm sorry that you're angry. I know I haven't handled it very well."

"It's humiliating, you know?" She tilted her head and looked at him thoughtfully.

"I'm sorry."

She smiled at him. "Not half as sorry as you're going to be."

My Jesus, he thought wearily.

She was much closer to him than felt comfortable, but he didn't step back, so that when she whirled around to leave and her long hair flew out, strands of it whipped across his mouth.

He closed the door and leaned against it. "Christ," he whispered to himself. "Christ."

He thought about Saturday.

About talking to Michelle.

After her mother's wedding.

Where Lizzie would be.

"Christ," he muttered, staring down at Corky. "Is it worth it? Is it really worth it?"

30

The first person Michelle saw when she stepped into her mother's living room, with Casey right behind her, was Max.

It hadn't occurred to her that he might have been invited. She felt a surge of indignation, remembering her mother's confession that she didn't even like Max. Then she realized that he had probably been invited because of Lizzie.

But she still thought her mother ought to have warned her.

It was a small house, so although there weren't more than twenty people gathered there, it was crowded. Fortunately the day was sunny and warm, and some of the crowd had been able to spill out onto the patio.

Many of the guests were strangers to Michelle; they must be Van Hudson's friends, she thought—or rather, friends of both her mother and Van Hudson whom Michelle had not met. She looked around but could see neither Mrs. Jeffries nor the prospective groom. She wondered if they were both going to stay out of sight until three o'clock, when the ceremony was to be performed by the Unitarian minister who'd agreed to come to the house.

She couldn't see Lizzie, either.

Or Alexandra, who was supposed to be coming with her parents.

Casey grabbed two glasses of wine from a tray carried by a young woman in a waitress's uniform.

From across the room Max spotted Michelle and began making his way toward her.

"I think," said Michelle, "that you're about to have the pleasure of meeting my ex-husband."

"Terrific," said Casey. "Just what I need."

When he reached them Max wrapped his arms around Michelle and hugged her tightly. She experienced this embrace with great curiosity, only slightly distracted by Casey's feigned indifference. It was a familiar embrace, and comfortable.

Max held her at arm's length and looked at her tenderly. His eyes hinted at secrets she couldn't remember; he had become a conspiracy of one.

Smiling, she patted his cheek. "Max," she said, "I'd like you to meet a friend of mine. Casey Williams, this is Max Paparo."

Max absorbed this and all that was implicit in it smoothly, easily. He and Casey exchanged remote how-do-you-do's while Michelle watched and was pleased to detect nothing triumphant in her. She listened as the two men attempted to exchange small talk. Then Lizzie appeared from the kitchen, and Max excused himself politely and escaped to talk to his daughter.

"Well?" said Michelle, "What do you think?"

"He's nice enough, I guess," said Casey, watching Max and Lizzie. He drained his wineglass and looked around for another one.

"Here, have mine," said Michelle. "I'm not thirsty."

And then several things happened.

It felt later to Michelle that they had all happened at once, as a single apocalyptic event, but of course this wasn't true. It was just that the cumulative effect was rather like having been run over by a truck.

Alexandra arrived, pale and slender in a red dress, her black hair like a gleaming cap. Michelle piloted Casey over to her friend and introduced him to Alexandra and her parents. Alexandra turned from Casey to Michelle and gave her a slow wink and Michelle knew that she approved.

And he certainly was attractive, she thought, smiling at Casey's profile. She loved his curly hair, his green eyes, his sun-browned body; and she loved the distracted expression which so often appeared on his face, as though he were working constantly on a problem which when he solved it would change his life, set him free.

Alexandra's parents drifted off to get themselves glasses of wine.

Michelle saw that Lizzie was by herself now, studying the contents of a bookcase against the wall behind the sofa. She took Casey and Alexandra by the arms and headed for her daughter.

"Oh, Christ," said Casey, when he saw where they were going.

"Are you sure this is a good idea?" said Alexandra.

"Lizzie," said Michelle. "Look who's here."

She really didn't know why she was doing it. Just to get it over with, maybe. Or maybe, uncertain as to how Lizzie would react to Alexandra, she'd decided to make sure that the first words they exchanged were exchanged in public, where Lizzie couldn't embarrass herself. Or anyone else.

But it turned out that Lizzie had been at her grandmother's house for some time, helping her dress, helping the caterers when they arrived—and helping herself to several glasses of wine.

The face she turned to Michelle was flushed, flinty-eyed, and mutinous.

"Oh, Christ," said Casey again.

"Hello, Lizzie," said Alexandra quietly.

"Elizabeth," said Casey, and they all looked at him. "She likes to be called Elizabeth," he explained, reddening.

Lizzie stared at him. "You don't know about her, I bet, do you?" she said. Her voice was slurred.

"I beg your pardon?" said Casey.

"I bet my mother hasn't told you about Alexandra," she said, trying to articulate more clearly, drawing out Alexandra's name contemptuously.

"Lizzie," said Michelle. "My God, child. You're drunk." She felt as if she were teetering on a roof edge, aware that it was far too late to call for help.

"I bet she's told *you* all about *him,* though," said Lizzie to Alexandra. "All she *knows,* that is. Has he told you the good stuff yet, Mom? Or is it going to be up to me?"

Casey took hold of her arm and tried to say something.

"Don't touch me." She shook him off, and staggered a little. "Don't you dare lay your hands on me ever again."

"Lizzie," said Michelle. She put a hand on Lizzie's shoulder, steadying her. "What's the matter? What do you want to say?"

Lizzie looked around wildly. "Dad!" she cried, and there was such pain in that word that Michelle wanted to weep.

Instead, she, too, looked around for Max, and saw him, engrossed in conversation. From across the room she concentrated intently on the person her ex-husband was talking with—a person she had never seen before, an old man whose neck was so skinny that his shirt collar stood out from it—as if by watching this stranger she could cause the whole room to watch him, and whatever was happening around Lizzie would stop happening.

Then she heard Alexandra say, "You haven't changed a bit, have you, kid?"

Michelle whirled to face her. "Allie! Don't!"

"You were a selfish brat when you were seventeen," said Alexandra. "And you're a selfish brat now." She turned and walked away.

"You don't know so much!" Lizzie shouted after her. "You don't know anything!" She took a deep breath. "Bitch!" she shrieked.

Michelle looked at her and felt a great coldness in her chest. Well, she thought. Well. That's it.

She raised her hand and slapped Lizzie's face.

"Jesus Christ," said Casey, appalled.

Lizzie burst into tears. Michelle watched her cry, feeling not much of anything.

She heard Max say, "What the hell?" He hurried over to Lizzie and embraced her protectively. "What's going on?" he said to Michelle. Lizzie buried her face in her father's suit jacket.

Michelle didn't reply. She noticed that she was shaking.

Every conversation in the room had come to a dead stop.

Casey put his arm around Michelle. "Come on," he said. "What was that all about?" he muttered, pushing her toward the kitchen. On the way he cadged another glass of wine. "Here. Drink this."

In the kitchen the caterers were busy putting food on trays, so he turned her around and aimed her back into the living room.

"Let's go outside," said Michelle unsteadily, and then the front door opened and the Unitarian minister came in.

He spread his smile around at the crowd, which rushed forward almost as one to greet him with cries of relief. The room cleared, except for pockets of the elderly or the maimed: the skinny-necked man, who had collapsed into a sofa next to a woman whose left leg was in a brace; Lizzie, still huddled against Max, who was glaring across at Michelle; Alexandra, standing next to the fireplace and puffing furiously on a cigarette while her parents watched her, worried and uneasy, from several feet away; and Michelle and Casey, clutching each other uncertainly, wondering if they could possibly slip past the group clustered around the minister and sneak out the front door.

Then Van Hudson stepped inside, and the guests became even more excited. They ushered the two of them into the living room, the minister and the groom. Lizzie gave her eyes a fast, final wipe and stepped away from Max. Alexandra reluctantly put out her cigarette.

And Mrs. Jeffries appeared upon the stairs, descending slowly, hanging onto the banister as she came.

Michelle detached herself from Casey and went to meet her. "Mom," she said, her voice trembling. "You look lovely." But she was pale and grim, and Michelle wondered with a sinking heart how much she'd been able to hear from upstairs.

Mrs. Jeffries looked behind her, at Casey, and managed a smile, and Michelle introduced them.

"Grandma!" wailed Lizzie, and hurtled across the room to throw herself into her grandmother's arms.

Mrs. Jeffries, startled, hugged her and then pushed her away to peer into her face. "Elizabeth. Are you drunk?" she said incredulously. She looked quickly at Michelle.

"You're right, yes, she's had too much to drink, I'm afraid," said Michelle crisply. "Now I think we'd better get on with things, don't you? The minister's arrived, and so has your groom." She stepped back and gestured into the living room, where Van Hudson waited, beaming, flanked by beaming friends.

Mrs. Jeffries's hands were still on Lizzie's shoulders. Now she moved slightly, so that Lizzie stood between her and Van Hudson like a shield. Michelle could see her thinking, busily.

Oh, my God, thought Michelle.

"I don't think I'm up to it," said Mrs. Jeffries, eventually.

Lizzie stopped crying and looked at her in disbelief.

"Not today," said Mrs. Jeffries.

"Oh, Ma," said Michelle. "Please."

Her mother drew herself up; Michelle was reminded of the Queen Mother. "Please give him my regrets," she said to Michelle. "Or whatever you do, in a situation like this." She began climbing the stairs.

"Mother!" said Michelle. "For God's sake," she hissed after her. "You can't do this. You had your chance. It's too late. It's not fair!"

"Elizabeth's had too much to drink," said Mrs. Jeffries, climbing. "And the house is too full of people. Too full of—of stuff. I just can't do it," she said, almost cheerfully, as she disappeared. "I'm not up to it," she said loudly from the top of the stairs.

Everybody in the house heard her.

"Your mom throws one hell of a party," said Casey.

They were back at Michelle's house. Michelle was lying on her sofa, a hand thrown over her eyes. Casey was pacing.

"I guess you were right," he said. "She must have had some doubts about it, all right." He sat down, his hands clasped between his knees. "I got another letter from my father."

She lifted her hand. "What did it say?"

"He's left Wyoming. Didn't tell me where he's going next."

"You're worried about him again, aren't you."

"Yeah."

"You'll hear from him, Casey."

"Yeah. Maybe." He took a deep breath and looked at her.

"Oh, God. You're going to do it. Have that serious conversation."

"Yeah."

"I thought maybe, after this afternoon—maybe it could wait a day."

"I know. I'm sorry. I'm not completely insensitive, you know. If it could wait . . . But it can't. Some of it has to do with Lizzie."

"Lizzie?" She sat up. "I don't want to hear this."

Casey stood and looked out the window. Michelle knew he couldn't see much out there, not through the sheer curtains. She figured he just didn't want to look at her.

"When Aline died," he said, "I kind of fell apart for a while. I think I even thought about killing myself. I can't remember for sure. Anyway, it was pretty bad. Couldn't teach, couldn't sing, couldn't do anything. Then I had an affair."

"I told you I don't want to hear this."

"With a student. It made me feel a lot better. And so after it was over I had another one. And that's been going on now for just about four years."

"Shut up."

"Most of them didn't last very long. Some of them only lasted for one night, or one afternoon. And one of them was Lizzie."

He must have written this out, thought Michelle. And memorized it.

He didn't turn around.

I guess he's waiting for me to say something, she thought.

She sat there for a long time but she couldn't think of a single thing to say.

She had felt a terrible pain, so savage and intense that her heart had stopped beating, the blood had stopped flowing in her veins. And now she felt nothing.

I guess I'm in shock, she thought.

Finally, "Excuse me," said Michelle. He turned, then, and watched as she got up and went into the bathroom.

She looked at herself in the mirror. Oh, boy, she said to her reflection. Is this ever going to hurt.

She looked more closely, and seemed to see herself love-bruised, love-swollen.

You can take this, she told herself, nodding confidently.

She took hold of the door handle and turned it and pushed the door open and went out into the hall. She clasped her hands together when she got back to the living room, because they were cold.

"You had to know," Casey said to her from the window. "Because I do love you."

"Yes," said Michelle. "It must have been difficult for you to tell me," she said politely.

"I had to tell you. If I hadn't, then Lizzie would have."

"Ah, yes," said Michelle. "Of course." She shivered and rubbed her arms. "I think you'd better go now."

"I want it to be permanent between you and me."

"Yes," said Michelle thoughtfully. "So you said."

"I don't want to leave you like this."

Michelle looked into his face for the first time since he'd begun to talk. "You haven't any choice," she said.

"May I call you?" he said when he got to the door.

"Oh. Well."

"I'll call you," he said, and left.

31

About four o'clock the next day somebody rang her doorbell. She waited for the ringing to stop and it did, but it soon started up again and George was barking and then there was a banging on her door and from the sound of it she knew the person outside was not going to go away.

She would have to get out of bed and go downstairs . . .

When Casey'd left after his serious talk Michelle had fed the dog and let her out and then she'd gone to bed, because she couldn't think of anything else to do.

As she lay there she was channeled through shock into pain, from pain into anger, and then back to shock, a dizzying, maddening torture against which she was helpless. Michelle hated being helpless.

She had turned over in bed again and again, finally got up to put a Mozart tape on the small player she kept in the bedroom, threw the pillows onto the floor, arranged herself in the position most conducive to sleep, but nothing worked. The shock and anger and pain kept returning in waves that drenched her soul yet left her body dry. At one point she did feel physically sweaty and shaky and sick but she wasn't sweaty; when she held her hand out in the light of the bedside lamp it didn't tremble and when she made her way unsteadily into the bathroom and knelt in supplication before the toilet her retchings produced nothing, especially not relief.

She couldn't understand where her brain was. She had a good brain, she knew it, what the hell had happened to it, where had it gone, what had taken over from it? Just being able to think these thoughts, she told herself, was proof enough that her brain hadn't been atomized, merely traumatized, and would soon shake itself back into shape and embark upon some kind of positive action.

It didn't do so during the night, though.

She decided that was okay, and finally gave up altogether the idea of sleeping and went downstairs to pour herself a huge brandy.

She had sat in bed, in the dark, drinking it. This was better, she thought. Much better to sit here, quietly sipping, than to toss and turn. She put her head back and closed her eyes, calmer . . . and then the pain took over; there was no anger, no shock—only pain.

It leapt in there with such obviously evil intent she knew it couldn't be a product of any of her own cells or nerve ends. It had to be an outside thing, a devil of some kind, one of hell's minor fiends. It projected scenes upon the insides of her eyelids and even when her eyes flew open in panic it made her watch them anyway—Casey and Lizzie, Lizzie and Casey, and she heard herself cry out, turned on the light, set her brandy glass on the bedside table and wept and wept until George got up uneasily from her place on the carpet at the foot of the bed, whined, jumped up on the bed, and began frantically licking at Michelle's hands, which were clapped over her mouth and nose.

Eventually Michelle had to stop crying in order to soothe George. She let the dog stay on the bed, and George was soon curled up there, asleep again. Michelle cleaned off her face with tissues from a box she kept under her night table, turned off the light, and resumed sipping her brandy.

In this way, the night passed.

She might have dozed off, when the brandy was gone. She wasn't sure.

When morning came she had to get up to let George go outside.

She made herself some coffee, called George back into the house, and returned to bed.

At least, she thought, it's a Sunday. Nothing is required of me. She decided to let the pain have her for the day. Maybe it would exhaust itself. She knew a day wouldn't be enough to get rid of it entirely. But maybe when it came back it would be weaker, of shorter duration, if for an entire night and an entire day it had been allowed to have its way with her.

The thought of this day ending with another night filled her with terror. But surely her body was smart enough not to deprive itself of sleep for two nights in a row.

And even if it wasn't that smart, she told herself, two nights without sleep wasn't going to do her any damage. Tomorrow she'd have to go back to work, and that would distract her. She would be forced to concentrate on familiar, important things. If necessary she'd go to her doctor and get a prescription for sleeping pills. She'd start getting herself back together, start really thinking, deciding what to do.

And so she spent the day in bed, suffering, watching things she didn't want to see, remembering things she didn't want to remember . . .

. . . and then suddenly the doorbell rang and she was obliged to climb out of her bed and shove her feet into slippers and make her way down the stairs to deal with George's barking and somebody banging on her door and as she made herself do these things the pain was transformed into fury.

She really was shaking, now. With rage. She knew who was banging on the door and as she marched down the steps she tried to think of a weapon with which to strike him, something that would draw blood, bruises wouldn't be nearly enough. "Shut up, George!" she roared, looking wildly around her, but of course there was nothing on the stairs and in the hallway, nothing, but as she threw open the door she remembered the poker in the living room.

She ran to the fireplace and picked up the poker. She heard the door close and whirled around, holding the poker in both hands, like a baseball bat.

"Hi," said Allie. George was sniffing delicately at the knee of her blue jeans.

Michelle lowered the poker.

"You haven't been answering your phone," said Allie. She put her purse down on a chair and patted George, who had moved in front of her, still sniffing concentratedly.

Michelle looked at her with great intensity, almost believing that Alexandra was Casey in disguise. She was holding her breath.

"Have you got any coffee?" said Allie, and walked into the kitchen.

She came back with two mugs and held one out to Michelle, who looked at it uncomprehendingly. Allie put it down on the coffee table and then sat down, at one end of the sofa. George, who had followed her to and from the kitchen, sat on the floor next to her and rested her head in Alexandra's lap. Allie stroked the dog, and drank some coffee.

"What are you doing here?" said Michelle. She noticed that she was breathing again.

"You haven't been answering your phone. I got worried."

Slowly, Michelle put away the poker. She gathered her green terry cloth robe around her and tied the belt. She was very tired, and her throat hurt. She slumped onto the other end of the sofa. "I didn't have a very good night. I didn't get much sleep."

"Drink your coffee."

"I had some when I got up."

"Have some more."

Michelle picked up the mug and drank. "It's awful."

"When did you make it?"

Michelle thought. "I don't know. The birds were singing. I left the back door open while George was out there and I remember hearing the birds."

"That was probably a long time go. It's after four, now. In a little while I'll make some fresh stuff."

Michelle lay back and closed her eyes, but they wouldn't stay closed. She saw the ceiling, and noticed some spiderwebs in one of the corners where it met a wall. She was always seeing spiderwebs, but hardly ever a spider. Maybe George eats them, she thought.

"Your mom's okay, you know," said Alexandra.

Michelle felt a violent constriction somewhere inside her. "Oh, my God," she said, "I forgot all about her."

"You want to know what happened?"

Michelle turned to look at her. "I forgot all about her. Alexandra. How could I?"

George lay down with a sigh upon Allie's feet.

"Obviously," said Alexandra, "because something more important has happened to you."

Tears started working away at the ache in Michelle's throat, planning to dissolve it; she swallowed several times, preferring the ache to another bout of weeping.

"Anyway," said Allie, "let me tell you. It was really rather sweet."

As soon as her mother had disappeared up the stairs, Casey had grabbed Michelle and run for the door. She had let him, although she knew it wasn't the daughterly thing to do.

It wasn't motherly, either, for her to desert Lizzie, drunk and disorderly, obviously in need of a firm and loving hand. But she'd figured Max had a perfectly good firm and loving hand, not to mention a great deal more influence on Lizzie than Michelle had had for a long time now.

But she hadn't given much thought to who might come to the aid of the reluctant bride. Maybe she'd intended to go back later. Yes, she decided; that must have been what she'd intended to do. Yet she knew that wasn't enough to exonerate her for having fled in what was clearly, for her mother, a moment of considerable crisis.

"Everybody just stood there for a minute," said Alexandra. "It was fascinating. Must be what happens when a volcano erupts, or a bomb drops. At first you can't figure out what's going on.

"Then the groom took over. Was he a soldier or something, before he retired?"

"An engineer, I think," said Michelle dully. "Some sort of an engineer. Not the kind that operates trains. Another kind."

"Anyway. He thanked the minister and briskly dispatched him. Then he said to the rest of us thanks for coming, he was sorry we hadn't gotten to see the main event but he hoped we'd enjoyed the wine.

"People were shuffling around by now, murmuring things rather furtively to one another. Including my parents." She laughed, and Michelle was momentarily indignant. "They didn't know what to say to the groom, any of them, that was clear," Allie went on. "They just did not know what to say to poor old Van. Here, sweetie," she said to George, "just let me get my feet loose, okay?" She gave the dog a pat, picked up her coffee, and put her feet on the coffee table. "But it didn't seem to bother him. He looked a wee bit shaken, as you might expect, but he's got a lot of dignity, old Van. Stood at the front door and shook hands with everybody as they left. Didn't make any apologies. I thought his behavior was—" She tilted her head thoughtfully. "Meticulous. Meticulously correct."

She squirmed slightly on the sofa, getting more comfortable, and crossed her legs at the ankles. "I hung back, told my parents to wait for me in the car. Wanted to see it all, so I could give you a full report.

"Lizzie started blubbering again, hanging onto Max, who looked decidely uncomfortable and not a bit happy. She was saying things to him but I knew if I got close enough to hear, she'd probably start shrieking at me again. He wasn't really listening to her, I think. He just wanted to get her out of there. But when he began pushing her toward the door she resisted, and started calling out for your mother. At this point, Van stepped in again.

" 'Don't you worry about your grandmother,' he said. 'She's going to be just fine. The best thing anybody can do now is just go on home. I'll look after Eleanor.'

"Lizzie started to argue with him, and Max suddenly looked kind of uncertain, too, but old Van was very firm. 'Eleanor and I understand each other,' he said. 'She's going to be just fine.' And so Max and Lizzie left."

"But you were still there?" said Michelle.

"I was leaning against the wall in a corner by the windows. Not hiding, exactly. Just not in plain view."

"What happened then?" said Michelle, aware that she was sitting up straight now, the mug of coffee clutched in both hands. She felt like she had felt years ago when, as a child, during a visit from her grandmother, she would sit on a stool in the kitchen drying the dishes while her grandmother, her father's mother, washed them. When they did the dishes together her grandmother always told her stories that she made up as she went along. Sometimes she had to stop to think what ought to happen next and then Michelle would say, "What happened then? Hurry, Grandma—what happened then?"

"What happened then?" she said again to Allie, her voice a croak.

"I just stayed where I was, half obscured by the curtain." She winked at Michelle. "Van went into the kitchen, to talk to the caterers, I guess; they'd vanished, simply vanished, as soon as the significance of your mother's retreat sank in.

"Then he came back and stood at the foot of the stairs. He looked down at the floor for a minute, hanging on the post at the end of the banister with both hands. I guess he was thinking."

She's almost as good at this as Grandma was, Michelle thought admiringly, caught up in the tension of the tale, freed temporarily from guilt.

"I guess the caterers were leaving," said Alexandra. "Is there an outside door from the kitchen?"

Michelle nodded.

Alexandra was looking through the doorway to the dining room, through the glass doors there, into the backyard. "He waited until everything was quiet in the kitchen," she said. "Then he lifted his head and called out, 'Eleanor.' There wasn't a question in his voice. There wasn't any anger, either. He just called her name, once. And I guess she must have come to the top of the stairs. I couldn't see her, of course. But he smiled a big smile, and held out his hand, and said, 'It doesn't matter a tinker's damn, Eleanor. Come on. You look so pretty. Let's go out and get some dinner.' That's exactly what he said. In this big, soft, slow voice." She turned wonderingly to Michelle and a grin spread across her face.

"And did she go? What did she say?"

"I didn't hear her say anything. But as I was slipping discreetly out the front door to make my cautious way around to the back, where my parents were waiting for me, I saw just her hand stretched out toward him, and some of the skirt of her dress—that's a lovely color for her, Michelle; rose. She was coming down the stairs, all right.

"And that's the end of my report." She looked questioningly at Michelle. "Now I want to hear yours."

Michelle shook her head and stared at her hands, lying loose and helpless in her lap.

"First maybe we'd better have some fresh coffee." Alexandra collected the mugs and disappeared into the kitchen.

Michelle went into the bathroom. She washed her face and combed her hair. She wondered how long Alexandra was going to stay in Vancouver, and why it hadn't occurred to her to ask before now. She was surprised to realize, inspecting her pale, hollow-eyed, indisputably worn and unattractive face, that she wanted to talk. To Allie.

She returned to the living room and sat down again on the sofa.

"Do you want cream or sugar?" Alexandra called from the kitchen.

"No. Black." She smelled the coffee and was reminded that she hadn't eaten anything since breakfast the previous day.

"Okay," said Allie, putting down the mugs. She fetched her bag, got out cigarettes and lighter, and curled up at the opposite end of the sofa. "Shoot."

Michelle spoke rapidly, getting it all out in one big breath, huddled over her steaming coffee. "Casey has a thing about students, he's slept with a lot of them since his wife died, he's slept with Lizzie." Jesus God, there were a lot of tears still in there, wanting very badly to get out. She took a big loud slurp of coffee; it was so hot it burned, and some of the tears took advantage of this. She put down the mug and dabbed viciously at her eyes.

"Oh, boy," said Allie softly.

"The son-of-a-bitch," said Michelle. "I'm going to kill him. I am."

"When?"

"He'll show up here eventually, the bastard. I'll do it then. With the poker, I think. Unless I can think of anything better in the meantime. I want a lot of blood," she said grimly to Alexandra.

"No, Michelle. I mean, when did it happen? With Lizzie?"

"I don't know. What the hell difference does it make?"

"Since he met you?"

Michelle looked at her with outrage. "Since he met me? Of course not! Good God, Alexandra."

"Was it a big thing, do you know? Was he serious about her? Was she serious about him?"

"Oh, God, I don't know. It wasn't serious with him. I think. I think he said—it only happened once. I can't remember for sure."

"What about Lizzie?"

Michelle hesitated. "We haven't talked about it. She didn't tell me about it."

"How long has she known you've been going out with him?"

"Since it started. Since—I don't know. June."

"Michelle." Alexandra moved closer to her and took her hand. "You mean, the kid's had this on her mind all summer, and never said a word to you?"

Michelle took a shuddering breath, and nodded. "I'm going to have to talk to her. I'm going to have to see her, and talk to her."

"Oh, God. Poor Lizzie. I wish I hadn't spoken to her like that." She squeezed Michelle's hand and let it go, so she could light a cigarette. "How do you feel about him?"

"I told you, I'm going to kill the son-of-a-bitch."

Allie smoked for a while, and rubbed her foot gently, absently, in the space between George's ears. Michelle noticed that she was wearing sneakers. And a big sweatshirt, even though the sun was shining and it was hot in the house, probably even hotter outside. It pleased some small, uninjured part of her to see Allie in jeans and sneakers and sweatshirt. It reminded her of good times, long-ago times. She felt old, and terminally melancholy.

"Tell me something, Michelle," said Alexandra. "He confessed this to you, right?"

"Right," said Michelle. " 'I love you,' he says, 'and we have to have a serious talk.' He was so grim, I thought he was dying or some damn thing."

Allie gave a high-pitched, inappropriate laugh, and Michelle glared at her bitterly.

"How would you have felt about it," said Alexandra, after a minute, "if Lizzie hadn't been one of his conquests?"

"But she was," said Michelle. She banged her fist on her knee. "The bastard's slept with my daughter! My *daughter*!"

"Yes, " said Alexandra patiently, "and no."

"What do you mean, 'no'? He told me, Alexandra. It's true."

"Nobody sleeps with somebody's daughter, or somebody's son. They sleep with a person. Lizzie's a person. Apparently one of many, in his case."

"So?" Michelle fished another tissue from the pocket of her robe. "Shit," she said, when it turned out to be used and soggy.

Alexandra got a package of them from her purse and handed it to Michelle.

"Thanks."

"Do you see what I mean? He must have been absolutely horrified, when he found out."

Michelle snorted.

"I mean, the poor man. He finds a way to deal with his widowed state—did he love his wife?"

"He says he did," said Michelle. "I personally don't now believe a word he's ever said to me."

"Well, let's say he did. He loves her, she dies, he's still youngish, sexy—you can't deny that he's sexy, Michelle."

Michelle grunted.

"He's devastated. His life is over. Then all of a sudden—hey!" She threw up her arms, assuming an expression of wonder. "It's not over after all. 'People want to sleep with me,' he says to himself. 'Hey, Casey, let's give it a try,' he says. And so he does. And it works. His life's not over after all." She laid a hand upon Michelle's arm. "Can you blame him for that? Would you blame him for it, if Lizzie weren't involved?"

"But she is," said Michelle stubbornly.

Alexandra sighed. She put out her cigarette. She stood up and shoved her hands into the pockets of her jeans. "I want to tell you a story, Michelle. Okay?"

"Go ahead," said Michelle, sullen.

"It's a story about me," said Allie, leaning close to her. "You aren't the only one with problems. I want your complete and undivided attention for a moment. Do you think you can pry yourself loose from self-pity long enough to grant me that?"

Michelle looked up. Self pity? This was full-fledged tragedy, for God's sake; not self-pity.

"Yes," she said.

"Good." Alexandra stood straight and addressed her as though making a speech. "I have gotten myself into a mess. It's a real cliché-type mess. I've been having an affair for two years now with a man who's married. That's want I wanted. No strings, freedom, all that shit. And now, guess what, I'm not free at all, can't handle it, not as strong and independent as I thought I was . . ." She sat down again and lit another cigarette. "A real mess, Michelle."

"What are you going to do?"

"I don't know. That's why I came home. To try to figure it out. Thought it would be easier, away from New York." She looked at Michelle and lifted her eyebrows. "And what do I find? My best friend's mother backing out at the very last second from marrying a perfectly nice man, my best friend involved with yet another fucker-around, my best friend's daughter all in an ugly turmoil because she was one of the fuckees and what to do, she must have thought, who to tell. . . . And she ends up telling nobody, keeping it all stuffed inside, then getting pissed to the gills on her grandmother's wedding day." She smiled, with an effort. "I think we ought to have a drink, now. Where do you keep it?"

"Sit," said Michelle. "I'll get it." She fetched brandy and glasses. "I haven't eaten anything," she said, as she poured. "I ought to eat something."

"We could order in Chinese." Michelle looked at her sharply. Alexandra gave her a slow wink, and started to laugh.

"We could invite Lizzie over," said Michelle thoughtfully, and Alexandra laughed harder, doubling over.

Michelle sat down next to her and gave her a hug. "Come on," she said decisively. "Drink up. I want to hear all about this son-of-a-bitch you've got yourself mixed up with. We'll compare notes."

32

The chairman of the music department was a man named Gordon Pointer. Casey had always gotten along well with him. He was absentminded and hearty, seldom wore a tie, and always looked as though he'd forgotten to comb his hair. This was because he was continually running his hands through it, perhaps believing that stimulation of the scalp encouraged stimulation of the memory.

He came to Casey's office the second Friday in September, which was the end of the first week of registration. Corky gave a token growl from beneath the desk.

"Got to see you, Casey."

"Come on in, then, Gordon," said Casey, removing his feet from his desk. He'd been staring out the window, thinking about sailboats and sunshine and serenity. He could buy himself a sailboat, the sun had shone before and would do so again, but he was convinced that serenity was forever out of his reach.

"I'd rather you came down the hall, if you don't mind," said Gordon. He tried an apologetic grin.

Casey got up and followed Gordon to his office. He shuffled along after the head of his department, his legs heavy, his arms dangling, and felt vaguely like an orangutan. Corky, as usual, was at his heels.

Gordon waited for Casey to enter his office and looked down

with dismay at the dog. "Suppose he absolutely has to be here, does he?"

"I appreciate your tolerance, Gordon. We both do." He sat down. Corky circled the room, sniffed suspiciously, before lying at his feet.

Gordon seated himself behind his desk, lined up some pens and pencils that he found lying there, ran his hands through his hair. It was thick and grey. His face was tanned. Probably from weeks on a sailboat, thought Casey gloomily, eyeing him.

"How are your rehearsals going?" said the department head. "For the *Magnificat?*"

"I have to tell you, Gordon," said Casey, relieved and heart-lightened, "that they are the joy of my life. Those rehearsals, which are going very well, by the way, are the focus of my existence. And thank God I have one."

"Well," said Gordon uneasily. "That's fine. That's really very fine. We're all looking forward very much to the performance.

"There's one other thing, Casey, unfortunately, that I am forced to discuss with you."

Casey cast upon his face what he hoped was an expression of polite expectation.

"Some trouble, here," said the department head.

"What kind of trouble, Gordon?"

"Student trouble."

Casey looked thoughtful. He couldn't imagine what kind of trouble the students might be stirring up. Classes had only begun three day ago.

"No official complaint. Not yet."

The skin on the back of Casey's neck began to prickle. He scratched it.

"But open talk." Gordon shook his head. "Bad business, Casey. Bad business."

Foreboding. That's what it was. Filling up his chest, like he'd dived into deep water without having taken a big enough breath. "I think you'd better be a little more specific, Gordon."

"This girl. Thornton." He picked up a file folder and held it about fifteen inches from his face, narrowing his eyes. Among the things the chairman habitually misplaced was his glasses. "Good student?" He peered at Casey over the top of the file.

"If that's her file, you can see for yourself."

"You've given her A's, it says here."

"I think other people have given her A's, too, Gordon."

Gordon studied the file. "Right," he said, and Casey thought he looked relieved. "Yes. All her courses. A's." He looked again. "Except English."

"Well, that's not our department, is it."

Gordon laughed heartily.

"Gordon. What's the problem?"

He looked at Casey unhappily. "She's been talking. Loud and long, you might say. In the cafeteria. Among other places, probably. Making implications."

"What kind of implications?"

Gordon sighed. His nervousness dropped away. "She says you seduced her. Then when she wanted to end it, you threatened to—to mark her a lot harder, this year. That's what she's saying, Casey. I don't believe it, of course. But it could land you in a great deal of trouble."

Casey rubbed the back of his neck. He felt sick, and unutterably weak. "It's not true, Gordon."

"I know you pretty well, Casey. And I'm sure it isn't. But you have been sleeping with her. Haven't you."

"Yes. That part's true. I did sleep with her for a while." He looked out the window and saw that it had begun to rain. It wasn't cold outside, though. Maybe he and Corky would go for a walk.

All he wanted to do was get out of the music building.

Gordon leaned back, and his chair squeaked loudly. "She's been threatening to make an official complaint," he said. "If she does, there isn't much I can do for you."

Casey smiled at him. "I know."

"I should have talked to you a long time ago," said Gordon, heavily. "You're a very special member of the faculty. I was—very upset when your—your activities were first brought to my attention." He leaned forward to rest his arms on the desk, and the chair squeaked again. "I think I can understand what you were going through. I think I know what would happen to me if Carol died. For some reason we always think that we're going to go first. If it happens the other way around, we just aren't prepared." He rearranged some papers on his desk.

Casey shifted position so that he was facing slightly away from Gordon, and looked again out the window.

"I was relieved when you started to recover," said Gordon. "Mightily relieved. And then I started hearing the gossip.

"At first I didn't believe it.

"Then I did.

"I told myself that nobody was getting hurt. But I knew that somebody *could* get hurt. Maybe a student. Maybe you. But I hoped you'd come to your senses before that happened."

"What do you want me to do?" said Casey.

"I should have talked to you."

"It wouldn't have done any good. Other people talked to me. That didn't do any good. What do you want me to do?"

"I don't know. Maybe it would be best to do nothing." He hesitated. "I'm sure I don't have to tell you this, but if you intend that this kind of thing should go on, there's no future for you here."

Casey was shaking his head. "I don't intend that it should go on."

"Good. Well," said Gordon, standing up, "I guess that's all." Awkwardly, he held out his hand. Casey shook it. "We'll see," Gordon muttered distractedly. "We'll see."

Casey went back down the hall, Corky's nails clicking on the tile behind him. He let the dog into his office and told her to stay. Then he closed the door and went down the stairs, out of the music building, and through the rain across to the cafeteria.

He saw her almost at once, among a group of other students, several of whom he recognized. Two were the girls who'd flown back with her from San Francisco.

He walked up to her, approaching from behind. He was extremely calm. Light on his feet again. All senses operating at full capacity. He saw eyes widening, elbows nudging. Before he got there, she had half turned around.

"Linda," he said. "I'd like to see you please. At once. In my office."

"Why, Professor Williams . . ." he heard her say, coquettishly, as he turned and walked away.

What the hell will I do if she doesn't come? he thought. And why should she? What am I going to do, drag her out of there by her hair?

But she'd caught up with him by the time he reached the door to the music building. "You sounded terribly serious, Casey," she said as they went inside.

He entered the music building, walked up the stairs and into his office, and she followed him.

"Hi, Corky," said Linda, and made a big fuss over the dog.

Casey closed the door and waited.

Eventually she stood up and faced him. "Well? Here I am. What do you want?" She was smiling.

"I want you to stop making a fool of yourself." He was still calm, but his heart was racing.

Her smile disappeared. "It's you I'm making a fool of."

"No. You're telling the whole world that I don't want to go to bed with you anymore."

She opened her mouth, but no words came out.

"I'm fed up to the teeth with you, Linda. Which is a shame. I used to like you a lot."

"You used to like to fuck me, you mean." Her voice was trembling, and her hands were fists.

"That, too," said Casey. "Now, I just don't want to see your face. I'm going to get you transferred out of my courses."

"I could ruin you," she said, and it was clear that she'd been feasting on this thought for quite a while.

"Maybe," said Casey. "Maybe you could." He stepped closer to her, and she backed away. "It's time to be a grown-up, Linda. Stop waffling. Stop shooting off your mouth. Get off the pot." He was breathing heavily, and stopped for a minute to get himself under control. She edged closer to the door. "Either have the dignity to keep your mouth shut, Linda. Or go all the way. Report me. Make an official complaint." He went to the door and opened it. "I just don't give a shit, kid. Believe it," he said, and pushed her gently through the door, closing it behind him.

He heard her footsteps, light and rapid, and listened until the stairway door slammed shut.

Then he slumped in his chair and stared out at the rain.

After a while he reached for the phone and dialed the number for the bookstore.

Michelle answered.

"Michelle," he said.

Casey looked down at the small black dog lying beneath his desk. "She hung up on me again, Corky." He replaced the receiver and stood up to put on his jacket. "Come on. Let's go for a walk."

He stopped at the door, feeling dizzy. There was a sick coldness in him; he tasted it at the back of his throat, and it was accompanied by panic so acute that for a moment he couldn't breathe. He rested his head against the door, wondering if he was sick.

33

"May I come in?" said Michelle on Sunday evening, when Lizzie opened the door.

Lizzie didn't say anything.

"It's my fourth try," said Michelle. "I came by twice last week. And then again yesterday. You weren't home."

"You should have phoned first," said Lizzie.

"I wasn't entirely sure you'd see me."

"I don't particularly want to, actually."

They stood there looking at each other.

"Well, now that I'm here," Michelle said eventually, "may I come in, or not? It's raining, in case you hadn't noticed."

Lizzie pulled the door open and stepped back.

"Thank you," said Michelle. She lowered her umbrella and shook it before going inside.

She had been to Lizzie's apartment only twice before. By invitation. Each time she had marveled at how neat it was, compared to the way Lizzie had kept her room, when she lived at home.

Now she looked around, taking deep slow breaths she hoped were unobtrusive, and as she registered what she was seeing, she almost smiled. There were piles of clothes in one corner of the living room, an overturned stack of tapes on top of the bookcase; the desk was a litter of books, paper, pens. The ashtray on the coffee table was full of cigarette butts. Michelle had no desire to look into the kitchen, the bathroom, or the bedroom.

"I've been thinking about getting a cat," said Lizzie, stretching out her hand for Michelle's raincoat.

"Oh!" said Michelle, turning swiftly, tears suddenly in her eyes. "Like Ashes?"

Lizzie shook her head. "There was only one Ashes." She hung up Michelle's coat in the hall closet. "Do you want some coffee or something?"

"Coffee would be nice. Thank you."

Michelle sat on the sofa and waited. She looked around and saw a white standing lamp with a white pleated shade. Prints on the walls. A large bulletin board next to the desk, with a calendar on it, and lots of notes Lizzie had written to herself. On the table, the telephone and a large red candle.

Eventually Lizzie returned with a tray bearing coffee in white cups, and cream and sugar in white containers, a plate with Brie and cheddar cheeses, a cheese knife and some crackers, and two folded paper napkins.

"Thank you," said Michelle, accepting a cup.

Lizzie sat in a basket chair on the other side of the coffee table.

"This is very nice," said Michelle. She looked for a while at the food in front of her. Then she set down her coffee, cut a piece of cheddar, and put it on a cracker.

"I'll be graduating in the spring," said Lizzie. She crossed one leg over the other. "It's hard to believe."

"Yes, it is," said Michelle. She put the cracker down upon a napkin.

"I don't know what I'm going to do then," said Lizzie. "I might look for a job and I might go on to graduate school, if I can get some kind of scholarship or something."

"Max would go on paying for school," said Michelle. "You know he can afford it."

"I've decided," said Lizzie, "that I don't want to take anything more from Dad. It's time I started being more independent."

"Oh, Lizzie," said Michelle. She put her hands on her chest.

"It's—we want to give. Each generation—we all think that we discover something special, something important."

Lizzie made a small, impatient movement with her shoulders.

"And we want to pass it on." said Michelle, trying to push past Lizzie's indifference.

"But we don't have to take it from you," said Lizzie. "You can't make us take it from you."

Michelle shook her head wearily. "No. You don't have to take it. So we give you other things instead. Like money. Or whatever you'll accept." She lifted her hands and pressed them against her temples. "I guess we all say no, when little bits of wisdom are offered to us. Maybe because by the time that happens, we can only see the hypocrisy of it." She stood up, frustrated and angry. "But it's such a waste, Lizzie. We all end up having to go around in the same stupid circles, learning the same damned things, and by then life's all gone. And there's never any damned progress."

Finally Michelle sat down again.

"Why are you here, anyway, Mom?" said Lizzie. She was wearing furry slippers, old jeans, a shirt Michelle recognized as once having belonged to Max, and no makeup. "I've already apologized to Grandma for ruining her wedding. I've apologized to Dad for embarrassing him. I've even called Alexandra and apologized to her, for God's sake. Do you want me to apologize to you, too? Is that it? Okay. I apologize for getting drunk and calling your friend names. Okay?"

Michelle picked up the cheese-laden cracker and kept her eyes on it as she said, "Casey told me that you and he once slept together. You knew months ago that he and I were seeing each other. It must have been extremely difficult for you." She looked up at Lizzie. "I don't know how you did it. Kept it to yourself."

"He finally got up the nerve to tell you, did he?" Lizzie put her feet flat on the floor and slumped back into her chair. Her eyes were blazing. "I wasn't even in love with him, you know," she said. "It was nothing." She tossed her head impatiently. "Nothing."

"But—" Michelle struggled for the right words.

Lizzie leaned forward with a suddenness that startled Michelle.

She put her hands on her thighs and said to her mother, articulating slowly and clearly, "Did he say, 'I want to make love with you'? Did he say that, the first time you went to bed with him?"

Michelle's face burned.

Lizzie picked up a cracker and thrust it into her mouth. "That's his line," she said, chewing. "That's what he says to everyone." She shrugged. "I was just curious. Maybe he'd say something different to somebody his own age. I just wondered."

Michelle stood up. "Lizzie."

"What?"

She sat down again. "I don't know."

Lizzie cut a piece of cheese, put it on another cracker.

"He wasn't sleeping with people's daughters, you know," said Michelle.

Lizzie glanced at her, then nodded. "Oh, I see what you mean," she said casually. "Well, no, of course not. He didn't think of us as people's daughters. He didn't think of you as somebody's daughter either. I understand what you're saying." She picked up her coffee cup. "But just think how you'd feel if you found out he'd gone to bed with Grandma."

Michelle tried to imagine this.

Lizzie popped the cheese-laden cracker into her mouth. "You see what I mean," she said. She took a sip of coffee.

"Why didn't you tell me, Lizzie?"

Lizzie put the coffee cup back on its saucer and brushed crumbs from her thigh.

"Well? Why didn't you? Were you getting a big laugh out of it, your mother falling for a jerk who slept with his students? Including her own daughter?"

Lizzie looked up quickly.

Michelle knew that her face was red again, but she didn't care. "Didn't you think I ought to know? Didn't you want me to know? What the hell was going on with you?"

"I go to see this psychologist."

Michelle stared at her.

"I started going in my first year. Then I stopped because I

didn't need to do it anymore. But I went back when I found out about—about you and him."

Michelle nodded, slowly, looking at the floor. "I'm glad you had somebody to talk to about it."

"What are you going to do, Mom?"

"I don't know." She got up and moved restlessly around the room, pushing her fingers through her hair.

It occurred to her that it was the things that had been kept from her that were the things that had actually shaped her life. First there is the unknowing, she thought. In the unknowing she had lived a married life that was a lie; in the unknowing she had had affectionate congress with a man to whom she had gradually revealed all she knew of herself, while he, as it turned out, kept secret most of what he knew about himself.

And then finally there comes the knowing, she thought; you are given truths you didn't know existed, and have to flounder stupidly around in an excruciating bewilderment which robs life of all sense, all meaning.

"And then," she said aloud to Lizzie, "I suppose it just happens all over again, not knowing things and then knowing them whether you want to or not, it's another one of those fucking vicious circles, and would you care to tell me what the point is of that?"

Lizzie was watching her apprehensively.

"I think," said Michelle, considering, "that people have to be careful not to feel sorry for themselves."

"Well," said Lizzie, hesitantly.

"Anger is okay," said Michelle with conviction. "For a while, anyway. But not self-pity."

"Yeah," said Lizzie. "You're probably right."

"Fuck it," said Michelle. She sat down on the sofa.

"Yeah," said Lizzie.

"Why didn't you tell me?" said Michelle.

Lizzie pulled her feet up under her. "Well, let's see. Why didn't you tell me about Ashes? Can you remember back that far?"

Michelle slowly shook her head. She could feel tears filling her eyes. "Ashes. Ah, Lizzie. You know why."

"Because you thought it would be cleaner, or something."

"Easier," said Michelle. "Easier for you. That's what I thought." She laughed, and the tears splashed onto her cheeks. "Oh well, wrong again."

"I wanted to say good-bye to him, you know? I wanted to be the one to hold him while he died."

"I know. But you were so young."

"So you didn't even tell me how sick he was, until it was all over."

"Right. I didn't. That's right." Michelle dug in her handbag for a Kleenex.

"But at least you did a bad thing for the right reasons," said Lizzie.

Michelle looked at her warily.

Lizzie took a deep breath. "Now if I'd told you about—about what's-his-name," she said, "I would have been doing a bad thing for the wrong reasons, I'm afraid."

"Oh, Lizzie." Michelle reached out and put a hand on Lizzie's knee. "Are you ever going to stop wanting to hurt me?"

"I don't know, Mom," said Lizzie seriously. "I sure hope so."

"Well," said Michelle. She tossed the crumpled Kleenex onto the coffee table and let her hands fall into her lap. She was exhausted, and her head ached. "I guess that's a start," she said.

34

On Wednesday evening Casey went out of his house and just started walking, leaving Corky behind because he didn't know where he was going, maybe he'd find a bar, maybe he'd get drunk. He had no intention of going into a bar but he wanted to be free to do it if he changed his mind.

He went along Tenth Avenue to Alma, and up to Broadway, and then he just walked and walked, and the September sun went down and his legs got tired and still he walked. Finally he sat down on a bench at a bus stop to rest. A short, pudgy man with a blond beard was there reading the afternoon newspaper. A remote, disconsolate looking woman holding a plaid umbrella open above her head watched the traffic go by. Casey wondered about the umbrella. The last three days had been hot and golden, haze on the horizon but no clouds in the sky.

When a bus came along and the other two people in the shelter got up Casey did, too, and he ended up following them onto the bus. He had to ask the driver what the fare was. The driver pulled away from the stop while Casey was still rummaging in his pockets, looking for the exact change. He wondered as he dropped it into the box what would have happened if he hadn't had it: would the bus have screeched to a halt in the middle of the block so the driver could toss him out on his ear?

He went all the way to the back of the bus and sat next to a window. He hadn't been on a bus for years. He hadn't even ridden the new rapid transit system, which operated between downtown Vancouver and New Westminster, sixteen miles away, and was said to offer magnificent views when it wasn't too crowded.

This bus, he noticed, wasn't at all crowded. There was the man with the blond beard, engaged in conversation with the driver. And the woman with the plaid umbrella, which was now closed, staring out the window. A few book-laden kids, probably U.B.C. students.

He wondered where the bus was taking him. Wherever he ended up, he decided, it was better than being at home.

Except when he was rehearsing, he was paralyzed by lethargy these days. Waiting for something. For Linda Thornton to lose him his job. For Lizzie's father, Michelle's ex-husband, to appear on his doorstep brandishing an ax. Sometimes, when his mood lightened a little, he even waited more hopefully—for Michelle to call, saying that she'd thought it over and what the hell, let's go for it.

The bus was turning left onto Granville. He was being taken downtown, then. He thought about going to a movie, once he got there, but didn't like the idea of sitting in a darkened theater with a lot of other people, listening to them breathe and eat popcorn and suck at Coca-Cola straws, trying in vain to lose himself in whatever story was being told him up there on the big screen in living color.

The only place he was able to lose himself was in the *Magnificat*. The soloists were doing pretty well; the orchestra, too. But Jesus, he had to get the choruses up to tempo. Why the hell did the choir never seem to be ready to come in on "Omnes generationes"? Why does it always surprise them? thought Casey, exasperated.

He reminded himself that he had lots of time. Almost eight weeks until performance.

Maybe he'd sell the house, he thought, apropos of nothing. Find a townhouse somewhere, with a little yard just big enough for Corky.

The problem was, soundproofing in those places was usually not very good. He wouldn't be able to bang away on the piano, sing at full volume, turn his tapes and records up as high as he sometimes liked to hear them.

They were crossing the Granville Street bridge, now. He wasn't sure where he wanted to get off the bus. His legs were rested and he felt like walking again. He pulled the cord as soon as the bridge was behind them.

He was the only person who got off at this stop. When the bus had driven away he headed north along the Granville mall, where only buses and emergency vehicles were permitted. He swung along feeling slightly more cheerful, firmly ejecting from his mind all thoughts of Linda, teaching, Michelle, his future, Lizzie, music, his father, even the *Magnificat* . . . Which didn't leave him anything, really, to think about; he was content just to walk, and look around him.

All sorts of people set up little stalls along the mall where you could buy cheap jewelry, souvenirs, various kinds of food. Other people played instruments and sang, usually badly but sometimes surprisingly well, and you were supposed to drop coins into a prominently displayed violin or guitar case, or a small cardboard carton. Casey did so, reminding himself as he parted with change and, occasionally, dollar or even two-dollar bills, that he had to make sure he had busfare available when it came time for him to go home.

It never even occurred to him to take a taxi home. He wondered about this, later.

There were long lineups in front of most of the movie theaters, and all along the mall Casey smelled popcorn. By the time he'd reached Georgia Street, beyond which there were no more theaters, he was almost sick from the smell of it. He went into a small café at the corner of Georgia and Seymour and had some coffee, and it was then that he became aware that he was wearing jeans and an old sweatshirt and torn sneakers; he also recalled that he hadn't combed his hair before leaving the house, and he rubbed his hand surreptitiously over his cheeks and jaw and realized that he should have shaved, too.

He felt anonymous, almost invisible, when he emerged from

the coffee shop. He stood indecisively on the corner for a moment before crossing with the light at Georgia and heading down Seymour, past The Bay.

He walked all the way to Hastings Street, then stopped. It was almost ten o'clock now, and getting pretty cold. He decided he'd better be going home. He didn't know where the hell to find a bus that would take him there. But he figured that Hastings was probably a good bet, and he could always stop and ask somebody.

He turned west on Hastings and walked a few more blocks, passing several bus shelters, not wanting for some reason to engage in any communication with anybody, until finally he realized that he was shivering and his legs were aching again. He went into the next shelter he saw, and sat down with a grateful sigh.

The only other person sitting there was a young woman with long, thick, taffy-colored hair pulled back from her face with red combs. She was wearing yellow slacks and a yellow blouse and a suede jacket, and there was an enormous black bag on the seat beside her. Casey noticed that even though she didn't look up from the book she was reading when he sat down, she did put a protective hand on the bag. He was curious as to what it held; its sides were bulging.

The traffic on Hastings Street was heavy, and there were a lot of pedestrians, too, some of them hooting and hollering and carrying on. Casey looked through the glass walls of the bus shelter and saw a couple of young men approaching. They were about half a block away, and they were obviously the ones making all the noise. They were staggering slightly, flinging their arms around one another's shoulders, then breaking away and laughing uproariously.

A bus pulled up, the young woman beside Casey glanced at it, looked back down at her book, and the bus drove away.

"Christ," muttered Casey.

The girl gave him a sideways glance.

"Excuse me," he said.

She leaned slightly away from him, even though at least four feet of bench separated them.

"I'm trying to get to Tenth and Alma," he said. "I don't even know if I'm at the right stop."

"You are," said the woman.

"How will I know which bus to get on?"

She must have seen nothing harmful in him, because she gave him a little smile and said, "It's the Number Ten."

"Thank you," said Casey.

"You're welcome," she said, and went back to her book.

Somebody banged on the bus shelter. Casey whirled around and saw two faces pressed against the glass, features out of whack, like something you'd see in a hall of mirrors. He knew he'd looked startled, because the two young men reared back and roared with laughter.

"Ignore them," said the young woman, not looking up from her book.

Casey took her advice and looked straight ahead, through the open front of the bus shelter.

They went around and came inside, leaning against the walls. Casey smelled booze. He didn't like the look of them, either. One was tall and skinny with long unwashed black hair. Either he was congenitally restless or he had to go to the bathroom; he kept shifting his weight from one workboot-clad foot to the other. "What've we got here?" he said, and giggled.

His friend was shorter, stockier, wearing jeans and a denim jacket and scuffed cowboy boots and pointed toes. He laughed when his friend spoke, and said to the girl, "Whatcha readin'?"

The girl neither looked up nor answered him. She turned the page with what Casey considered admirable self-possession, and read on.

The skinny one reached past Casey and snatched the book from her hand. "He said what're you readin', so what're you readin'?"

"Hey," said Casey.

The girl picked up her bag and put it on her lap. She didn't look at anybody.

"*Shee*-it," said the skinny one in disgust. He tossed the book to his friend.

"It's a philosophy text," said the young woman calmly.

"It's a what?" said the stocky guy.

"A schoolbook."

"A schoolbook," said the skinny one. "She goes to school."

They laughed uproariously.

Casey moved closer to the girl.

"Hey hey," said the guy wearing the cowboy boots. He stuck out an imperious hand. "Watch it, fella." He squeezed in between Casey and the girl. "You're trying to put a move on her. I saw that." He put his arm around the young woman and pulled her resisting head down onto his shoulder. "Don't worry, sweet thing. I'll protect you."

The skinny one threw back his head and gave such a strident shriek of blood-chilling glee that Casey thought for sure a patrol car would magically appear.

Or at least, he thought desperately, a bus.

But no bus arrived.

"Get your hands off me, fuckface," said the young woman, struggling.

Casey stood up. He had a vivid flash of memory, of himself at age five, solemnly and with thumping heart escorting across a vacant lot a five-year-old girl who had told him that sometimes big boys on their lunch hour from school saw her walking home from kindergarten and chased her and threw rocks at her. He remembered that the grass in the vacant lot was almost as tall as they were. He walked first, with the girl close behind him, and he felt like Tarzan creeping stealthily through the jungle, followed by a trusting Jane. They hadn't met any big boys, but the little girl was as grateful as if they had, and Casey had immolated them.

"Leave her alone," he said to the stocky guy, positioning himself so as to be able to keep on eye on both of them. "Fuckface," he added, for good measure.

He couldn't remember if the little girl had ever asked him to walk through the vacant lot with her again. In fact he couldn't even remember ever seeing her again—although he must have, they'd gone to kindergarten together.

"Christ, listen to him," said the skinny one, amazed. He pushed himself away from the wall. "You got a piece? A blade?" Again he laughed, and Casey couldn't suppress a shudder.

"Just get the hell out of here, okay?" said the girl.

"Naw," said the man sitting next to her. "He's gonna take us on bare-handed. Right, fella?" He gave the girl's neck a squeeze, and stood up.

Once a female friend had called Casey in a panic. The man she lived with had fallen off the wagon and was wrecking their house. When Casey had told Aline, his wife had urged him to call the police, but he'd been reluctant to involve the law in the private lives of friends. So he'd gone over there. Tried to reason with the guy—who was usually a very reasonable sort of person. But not that night. He was drunk, wasted, pissed out of his mind. He was also big and very strong and he was methodically destroying the inside of the house. Finally Casey had in desperation hit him. The man wasn't trying to defend himself, he was just looking for things to break; he certainly wasn't expecting to be hit. Casey had never forgotten it. The sensation of smashing his fist into a face, feeling his knuckles against teeth, splitting lips open; seeing the guy lying harmless and bleeding on the floor.

There had been pleasure in it.

"So whatcha gonna do, old man?" said the stocky one. He was standing too close, breathing right into Casey's face. "Whatcha gonna do, huh?" He poked Casey hard in the chest, which caused him to stagger backward a couple of steps. "Huh?" he said, giving him another poke.

Casey fleetingly contemplated slipping out of the bus shelter and running like hell.

"Leave him alone!" shouted the young woman. "Help! Help!" she yelled.

That'll do it, thought Casey with satisfaction. He brought up his fist and struck out, thinking to at least land one blow before the cops arrived.

Then he was lying on the floor of the bus shelter, with excruciating pain in his face and something warm and wet dripping enthusiastically from his nose. The girl had leapt to her feet. She was still yelling for help, and she was standing on his hand. Thank God she's not wearing those spike heels, he thought, trying weakly to communicate with her, and then he caught a quick glimpse of a scuffed and pointed cowboy boot and felt a terrific blow to his chest. "*Oof*," said Casey, curling up into a fetal position, his hand still pinioned to the grimy concrete floor by what he now identified as a yellow sneaker with Velcro fasteners. He closed his eyes and waited to be struck again, and thought about how humiliating this was, and wondered if Michelle might take pity on him and fix his wounds and decide she loved him after all if he were to go straight to her house, when this was all over.

"Oh, my God, are you all right?" She was kneeling beside him, so the juvenile delinquents must have fled. His hand hurt less; he tried to move it and discovered that he could. Good. She wasn't kneeling on his hand, then.

He saw that she was crying. "Don't cry," he said. The tears were ruining her makeup; she badly needed to wipe the mascara from her cheeks.

She was fumbling in the big black bag. Ah, good, he thought, as she fished out a banged-up box of Kleenex. He was surprised when she squatted down beside him, grabbed a handful of tissues from the box, and pressed them against his nose.

There were a lot of people clustered around the bus shelter by now. Casey wondered where the hell they'd been when he needed them.

"You'd better try to get up," said the girl.

He got onto his hands and knees, then grabbed the bench and pulled himself up until he could sit down.

"Shit," he said, breathing shallowly. The girl was still pressing the tissues to his nose.

"Put your head back," she said.

Then the police arrived.

"It's about damn time," said Casey, muffled by the tissues.

There were two of them, a man and a woman. They took descriptions and muttered into their radio and took a look at Casey's nose and pressed gently at his chest until he told them to lay off.

Then they drove the two of them home.

The girl got dropped off first. She laid a kiss upon Casey's forehead as she got out of the patrol car. "Thanks," she said with a smile. She still had mascara all over her cheeks.

"You're welcome," said Casey politely, his head tilted back. He was now holding a thick bandage against his nose.

When the police car pulled up in front of his house he could hear Corky barking.

"Remember, sir," said the female cop. "Call your doctor. Get that nose checked out. I don't think it's broken, but you never know. And the chest, too. Could be you've got a couple of cracked ribs."

"Great," said Casey, struggling out of the car. He hurt all over, as though he's been run over by a stampeding herd of something or other. Which wasn't far from the truth, he decided. "Thanks for the ride," he said, and the cops waved, and drove off.

He turned and shuffled slowly across the sidewalk and through the gate. He made sure it was latched behind him. He'd make sure all the doors and windows were locked tonight, too, which was something he was often careless about.

Corky was still barking, and he would have called out to reassure her except that he didn't have the strength—and besides, somebody seemed to be sitting on his porch.

He hadn't left any lights on, not even the porch light, so he couldn't see clearly but he was goddamn sure somebody was sitting on his porch; there was a kind of whitish glow there that looked human.

"Who the hell are you?" he said, and his voice sounded almost as high-pitched as that of the skinny guy in the bus shelter. "Who's that sitting on my damn porch?"

The figure stood up and came down the steps. "That's a pretty yappy dog you've got there," said Donald.

35

"I saw you got dropped off by a police car," said Donald as Casey fumbled at the door with his keys. "You out on bail, or what?"

"Very funny." He got the door open and reached inside to turn the porch light on. Corky was jumping up and down. At least she'd stopped barking. He tried to pick up Donald's big, battered leather suitcase but it hurt too much. "Bring your bag and come on in," he said, and led the way to the guest room, turning on lights as he went, with Corky skittering along ahead of him.

In the living room he said, "Want some coffee?"

Donald surveyed him from head to foot. "There's blood all over that sweatshirt. Do you mind telling me what's happened to you?"

"Somebody beat me up," said Casey. He cautiously took the bandage away from his nose and was relieved to see that the bleeding had stopped.

"Let me guess," said Donald. "The bookstore lady? Her daughter? Her daughter's boyfriend? Her ex-husband?"

"Her daughter doesn't have a boyfriend. As far as I know. A total stranger beat me up. A punk. Two of them. I was in this bus shelter—" He shook his head wearily. "Pop, let's just forget it. It's too complicated. Okay? Now, you want coffee or not?"

"I'd like a drink, if it's not too much trouble."

"That sounds like a hell of an idea," said Casey, and he fixed them Scotch over ice.

Then he went into the bathroom to clean up his face. He poked gently at his nose, peering into the mirror, and decided it didn't look too bad. It was already swelling, but he was pretty sure it wasn't broken. He looked distastefully at his gory sweatshirt and attempted cautiously to take it off, but decided that it hurt too much.

"You're walking kind of hunched over, Charles," said Donald when Casey returned to the living room. "You got some other injury, besides the nose?"

"Got kicked in the ribs." He sat down slowly and drew a careful breath. "Nothing serious," he said with more confidence that he felt.

"Quite a place," said Donald. "This Vancouver."

Casey smiled at him, and felt a sharp pain in his face that turned it into a grimace. "I'm glad to see you, Pop."

"But I guess you wonder what the hell I'm doing here."

"I don't care. I'm glad to see you."

"Do you mind if I just stretch out a bit here?" When Casey shook his head, he took off his shoes and put his feet up on the sofa. "Not much room to stretch out, in a Greyhound bus."

"Did you come straight up here from Wyoming?"

Donald took a hefty swallow of his drink. "First I called Connie in Florida. Had some fool notion of going out there, maybe trying to patch things up." He put down the glass and rubbed his eyes. "She's got herself attached to some fella," he said painfully. "Well, of course, I knew that was bound to happen. Left it too late. My own fault." He picked up his drink again.

"I'm sorry, Pop."

"Yeah, well, so am I. So then I got to thinking, this is a lot of horseshit, this traveling around the countryside. It was only an excuse to maybe get out there and see Connie. And as soon as I got that figured out, well then I thought, better head north and check up on Charles, see how his rehearsals are going, before I get myself home where I belong."

"I'm happy that you did."

Corky, having observed Donald for several minutes now, advanced upon the couch.

"He's a real estate fella," said Donald. "The guy she's attached to. Hell of a lot of real estate folks in the world, so it seems."

Corky jumped up onto the couch and began sniffing Donald's feet.

"Barks like hell, this dog," said Donald. "It's a wonder one of your neighbors didn't call the cops. I thought they had, when that police car drove up. I was trying to figure out what I was going to say, to explain my presence on your front steps." He held out a hand and Corky stepped between his legs and let him stroke her. "Friendly enough, though. Once you're inside."

"Why don't you stay here for a while, Pop," said Casey suddenly.

"Why the hell do you think I rode that bus all the way up from Wyoming?"

"I mean for a long time. Long enough to get to know the city, see how you like it. Maybe you'd want to move up here. You never know." It surprised him, to be saying this. But he found his father's presence in his house comforting. He had not known that the house felt empty, sometimes, with just him and Corky in it; he had not known this until he was being driven home in a police car, his ribs aching, blood on his clothes, a bandage clutched to his face.

Donald stroked the dog. "How about another drink?" he said. "I'd get it for myself, what with you in that injured state, except I'm seventy-four years old and wore right out."

"So, what do you think?" said Casey, when he returned with fresh drinks.

"Oh, my, Charles, I don't want to talk about my future. Not tonight." He sat up a little, and pushed one of the throw cushions on the sofa behind his back. "Besides, your life's a little too complicated for a person my age to get involved in. There's all this sex stuff, and then this love stuff, and now here you are getting beat up by total strangers."

"That could have happened to anybody," said Casey, gingerly touching his nose.

"It's sure as hell never happened to me. Look at this dog, will you. Curled up like that, right between my feet. I think the damn dog likes me, Charles. You got any marriageable women up here? Women about my age, I mean?"

"Could be," said Casey. "Wouldn't be surprised."

"What about the bookstore lady?"

"She's too young for you, for Christ's sake."

"No, no, Charles. I mean, how are things going, there? With you and her, I mean?"

"She won't talk to me."

"Ah."

"I called her every day, until yesterday. She just hung up on me, as soon as she heard my voice."

"Did you try sending her flowers?"

"Somehow, Pop," said Casey, "I don't think that would work, under the circumstances." He reached for his glass and a sharp, vicious pain in his chest took his breath away.

"No. No, you're probably right."

"Listen, Pop . . ."

"You better go to where she lives. Not where she works. She might have you thrown out. You go to where she lives, and wait outside in your car until you see her come home, and then just charge up to her door and keep banging on it until she lets you in."

"Pop. Have you got your driver's license with you?"

Donald shook his head. "You've got to go alone. She sees two men sitting out in front of her house in a car, she's going to call the cops."

"Pop. I think I ought to get to the hospital."

Donald stumbled to his feet. "What? What?"

Corky leapt from the sofa and began barking.

"Pop, for God's sake. It's nothing. Calm down. It's just my ribs. I think I better get somebody to look at them."

Donald helped him get out of the chair. "Where's your car, son?"

"It's right in front of the house. We aren't far from the hospital. I'll direct you. Okay?"

"Okay. Right, now. We're on our way. Hang in there, son. Damned good thing we only had a drink and a half. Does the dog come with us?"

36

Michelle went to the seawalk that evening. While George raced back and forth behind the chain-link fence Michelle sat on the bench and watched the sunset. The air was almost still; she felt only a single breeze that touched her face softly, curiously, as if it were trying to read her skin like Braille.

Alexandra had left for New York that morning. Michelle had expected her to stay much longer—she hadn't even been here three weeks—but Allie had laughed and said no, she had to get home, there were things to be done before she went back to work on Monday. It had given Michelle a jolt to hear her speak of New York as "home." Yet of course that's what it had become.

She wondered if Allie would take her advice and tell her married lover—Harry something, his name was—to get lost. She didn't think it very likely.

The sun disappeared and the day chilled into evening and finally Michelle called George and walked slowly through the fragrant, shuffling shadows of the path-side gardens leading away from the seawalk, and much too quickly she was home.

Inside, she pulled the curtains closed and turned on all the lights. She flipped through the *TV Guide*, looked at the books stacked next to her bedside table, put on a tape in the living room, and almost immediately turned it off.

She made some tea and sat on the sofa drinking it and trying not to think about anything.

When the phone rang she almost didn't answer it, because she didn't feel at all strong or even angry; she just felt vulnerable. But he hadn't called yesterday, nor so far today. Maybe he'd given up.

"It's Allie. I just wanted to tell you—I've decided not to give up smoking."

"What?"

Alexandra laughed. "It's terribly late here. But I know it isn't late where you are. I'm still on your time, sort of. Can't go to sleep yet, you know? I hope you don't mind my calling."

"Of course I don't mind. I'm sitting here in the living room with a mug full of tea and George snoring away on the carpet and there's nothing to do but feel lonely. I'm very glad you called."

"Good."

"I wish you lived closer."

"And I wish you'd mailed all those letters you said you wrote me."

"I will, from now on. What did you mean, you've decided not to give up smoking? I didn't know you'd even been thinking about it." She pushed off her shoes and tucked her feet under her. "Allie? You still there?"

"Michelle, I meant to tell you something."

"What?"

"I have to have an operation."

Michelle very slowly put her feet back on the floor and sat up. "Alexandra. What's wrong? What kind of an operation?"

"I've got ovarian cancer. That's why I've decided not to quit smoking." She laughed. "Oh, it's such a relief to tell somebody."

"Oh, Allie. Why didn't you tell me when you were here?"

"I don't know," said Alexandra wearily. "I don't know. Anyway, I'm telling you now. I'm going into the hospital Monday. They're going to take out the whole shmear, ovaries, uterus, the works."

"And then?"

"And then I don't know. It depends."

"Does he know about this? Harry?"

"No."

"Alexandra. I'm coming out there."

They argued about it for a while. But Michelle knew that's why Alexandra had phoned, even though she wasn't about to admit it. It was finally agreed that Michelle would get Barbara Simmons to look after the bookstore, and that she'd book a flight to New York on Saturday.

When they'd hung up she just sat there for a while, and then she began to weep.

37

On Thursday the weather was again warm and cloudless. May and September, thought Casey, changing his clothes at the end of the day, were the best months of the year in Vancouver. He was grateful for the weather. It meant he could put on a light, collarless shirt and casually roll up the sleeves and leave the buttons undone just far enough to reveal the taping that had so briskly and painfully been applied to his chest.

He left a vague note for Donald, who was out walking Corky and becoming acquainted with the neighborhood. Then he hobbled out to his car and drove to West Vancouver.

He tried to rehearse during the halfhour drive what he would say when she opened the door. He drove slowly and carefully, to avoid jarring himself, along Broadway, over the Burrard Street bridge, west on Georgia, through Stanley Park, across the Lions Gate bridge and west again on Marine Drive. He rejected several opening sentences because they were too apologetic, and by the time he got there he was irritated. Where's your pride, man? he kept asking himself. He sat in the car for a few minutes feeling resentful and sullen.

He was in pain, too. His ribs hurt like hell, and so did his nose. He'd been in pain all day, despite the pills they'd given him at the hospital. It had been a lousy day. He couldn't even draw a normal breath, much less sing.

And he hadn't liked the way some of his students looked at him, either. "I was in a minor accident" is what he'd said to those who'd inquired, and he knew he hadn't imagined the slightly amused, knowing smirks on some of those adolescent faces.

Not all of them, he admitted. But some.

He didn't want her to glance out her window and see him sitting there looking morose and irresolute, so finally he got out of the car and made his way haltingly up the steps that led to her front door, clutching the wrought-iron banister.

He knocked, and George started barking, and then he heard quick footsteps and his heart was beating hard, pounding witlessly against his cracked ribs.

She opened the door.

"Michelle," said Casey weakly. "You wouldn't talk to me on the phone. So I came over." He couldn't think of anything more to say. The pain in his ribs was considerable, and seemed to have affected his ability to make decisions.

"Casey." She burst out sobbing and threw her arms around him.

Oh, Jesus, thought Casey, tears of pain in his eyes. He found himself embracing her, hugging her as tightly as she was holding him. This intensified his discomfort to an almost intolerable degree. Yet he continued to hang on to her, breathing in her fragrance, burying his damaged nose in her hair. I must love her, he thought, incoherently. I guess I love her, all right.

"Casey," she said, and pulled away from him. "It's Allie. She's sick. I have to go to New York."

Casey let out a garbled sound of protest.

"I do. I have to go." She took him by the arm and pulled him inside. He yelped. "I'm leaving on Saturday," said Michelle, hauling him into the living room. "I've got my reservations and everything."

He fell into a chair and emitted something that sounded like "*Whoof.*"

Finally, she actually looked at him. He wiped sweat from his forehead with the back of his hand. He felt her really seeing him, for the first time, and gave her a small, brave smile.

"Casey. What happened?"

He'd never seen her eyes look so big. There were still tears on her face, but she'd forgotten about them. "Oh," he said, waving a hand. "It's nothing."

She got down on her knees next to his chair and touched his nose so lightly he could barely feel it, but it made him wince anyway and she quickly took her hand away. Then she spotted the tape on his chest. She gave a little gasp and slowly, carefully unbuttoned his shirt. He looked down at himself compassionately.

"Were you in a car accident?" she said, almost whispering.

"Not exactly," said Casey. "I was trying to do a good deed. I'll tell you about it sometime," he said, with an effort. "But I'm okay. Nothing broken. I'm going to be fine." He moved cautiously in the chair, trying to get more comfortable. "It just hurts a little right now. That's all."

She leaned over him, her hands on the arms of the chair, and kissed him all over his face, except for his nose, and as he closed his eyes and lifted his face into her kisses something inside him spilled over and he thought of nothing and he said "Michelle" over and over, until her mouth silenced him.

"We can't do anything," she said, her breath in his ear seductively warm. "It would hurt you."

"Yeah," said Casey. "Well. I don't know. I wouldn't say that. I wouldn't say we can't do anything."

Michelle smiled at him, a slow smile of pure delight. "Let me do it, then," she said. "You just lie there and let me make love to you."

"Oh. Well," said Casey, and he watched her pull her sweatshirt over her head. "Oh, Jesus," he said. "You're going to take off your clothes. Oh, Michelle," he said a minute later. "You're beautiful. Do you know that? You're beautiful."

He lay on her living room floor, wounded and sweating, and she touched him. His eyes were closed and her touch was so light she knew he almost couldn't feel it, but his flesh rippled in the wake of it. She undid the buttons of his shirt and the belt and zipper of his trousers and peeled back his clothing so as to have more of his skin to touch, and when he lifted his hands in search of her she pressed them away. She touched him first with her fingertips and then with the tip of her tongue, watching him shudder, hearing sounds come from his throat. She leaned over him and brushed her nipples against his bandaged chest and his hands cupped her breasts, one at a time, and she let him take them to his lips for suckling. Michelle felt the sun from the window warm on her back and buttocks like warm hands pressing her close to him, pressing her nipples into his warm, wet mouth. She pulled away and moved down to slip off his shoes and tug gently at his trousers and his undershorts. "Just lie still," she told him when he attempted to sit up, to help her, and he did, he lay still and let her take off his clothes, except for his unbuttoned shirt. Then she studied him, as he lay naked in the sunlight, and she touched him, and kissed him, and stroked him with her tongue, marveling at the sounds he was making, loving the sweat on him, patiently pushing his hands away, and finally she raised herself above him, impaled herself delicately upon him and then he clutched her, pulling her with urgency farther and farther inside him, and she smiled as he bucked beneath her and loved him as he cried out and then realized, amazed, that the cry she heard had slid from her own throat.

"We shouldn't have done all that," said Michelle, later. "It was far too athletic. It's probably damaged you some more." They were in Michelle's bed. She had tucked both pillows behind him and gotten them mugs of Mellow-Mint tea, which she thought would in some way be therapeutic for an injured person.

Casey chortled.

"It's true," she said. "Look at you, you can't breathe properly."

"Only because I'm still not recovered from all that passion." He pulled her head onto his shoulder and hugged her, cautiously, to his side. "We are getting to know each other so damn beautifully," he said.

"In some ways," said Michelle, distantly, "that is true."

He thought about trying to say something important about the past, and the future; but decided against it. "Tell me about Alexandra," he said instead. When she had explained about Alexandra Michelle began to cry, and he comforted her, and murmured to her everything encouraging he'd ever heard about people who got cancer, which wasn't much.

"Barbara's looking after the shop," said Michelle. "I told her I didn't know how long I'd be gone. Maybe I can persuade Allie to come home, if things look bad. But if I can't . . . then I'm going to have to stay with her."

"Of course," he said. "Of course." He said it firmly, and filled his voice with love before he spoke, but there was an ache in him much bigger than anything his cracked ribs could produce.

Soon he decided that he'd better go home.

"If I hadn't come over here," he said, "would you have called me? Or would you have just left for New York without a word?" He was getting dressed but had had to stop and rest for a minute. He looked pale, and haggard with pain.

"I don't know," said Michelle. "I hope I would have called you. But I don't know." She got out of bed, naked, and helped him into his shirt. He put his hands around her waist and pulled her close and began kissing her stomach, working his way down. But she stopped him, stepped back, and put on her robe. "No more," she said firmly. "You've got to drive home, and you've overdone it already." She reached out to trace with a finger the deep lines across his forehead. "You have to get home, take a pill, go to sleep."

She helped him down the stairs to the front hall. George ran down ahead of them.

"I know it's not going to be easy," said Casey, at the door. "I know we have to talk about it. We're both going to be—it's going to be hard."

Michelle didn't say anything. George, hoping to go for a walk, was sitting next to her, quivering with anticipation.

"But I think we should do it. Go for it."

Michelle looked at the floor.

"Even if it hurts for a while."

She couldn't think properly. When he'd left her house maybe all the pain and all the anger would come back, and maybe she'd regret having weakened at the sight of him; confided in him, made love to him. Maybe she'd regret that.

"How's your mother?" said Casey.

"Fine. Good," said Michelle, scratching George behind the ears.

"Good," said Casey, nodding. "That's good."

"She's thought it over, and she's going to marry him after all," said Michelle. "But quietly. No guests, no reception. Then they'll go away for a while."

"My father's here," said Casey, and Michelle looked up in surprise. "I'd like you to meet him."

"Well," said Michelle. "I leave on Saturday, you know."

"Maybe we could get together tomorrow."

"I don't know," said Michelle uneasily.

He stepped close to her and put his hands on either side of her face. "Don't chicken out on me," he said, and kissed her, gently but for a long time. "Please don't."

"Oh, Casey. I don't know if I'm brave enough for this."

He held her close to him. "We can do it, you know. If we love each other enough."

"But do we?" said Michelle, crying into the crook of his neck. "Maybe we don't."

"Maybe. But don't you want to find out?"

He hugged her, gasped, and let her go.

"Are you all right?" She wiped her cheeks with her hands.

"Yeah, sure. By the time you get back I'll be as good as new."

"You look awful. Your nose is so swollen and sore looking."

"I'm not surprised that it looks sore. It's damned sore. Can I see you tomorrow?"

"I've got so much to do," she stammered.

Casey sighed, and opened the door. "Okay. Call me when you get to New York, though, will you? Just to let me know you got there safely?"

"Sure. Okay," said Michelle.

He went out onto the porch and down the stairs, very slowly and cautiously. When he got to his car, George suddenly ran out of the house to join him. Casey stooped down, wincing, and stroked her.

Michelle called George, who ignored her, so she had to come down the steps and grab the dog's collar.

"Listen, I've just had a brilliant idea," said Casey. "I'm going to look after George for you."

"Don't be silly. It's all arranged. She's staying in a kennel."

Casey looked at her in disgust. "You can't do that to her. What are you, crazy? This dog would—she'd pine away in a kennel." He reached down, carefully, to rub George's neck. "Jesus, I don't know how you could even consider it. This dog—well, she's just not a kennel-type dog. God knows what would happen to her in a kennel. She wouldn't eat, that's for sure. You'd come back, go out to pick her up, probably find a corpse."

"It's an extremely good kennel," said Michelle indignantly.

Casey slowly straightened. "I'm going to look after her."

"Casey, you can't do that. I'm serious."

He stood with a possessive hand on George's head. "Not half as serious as I am, lady. This dog will be my hostage." Michelle couldn't tell whether he was smiling or not. "When you come back from New York, you don't get George back unless you're willing to take Corky and me as well."

"And Donald?" said Michelle dryly. "Do I have to take him, too?"

He shuffled uncomfortably from one foot to the other.

"Oh, my God," said Michelle.

"Probably not," said Casey quickly. "I'm pretty sure he'll want to go home, after a while."

"Oh, my God," said Michelle.

"He's very nice," said Casey sincerely. "You'll like him."

He hesitated, then stepped close and put his arms around her. "I'll pick George up tomorrow," he said.

She made sure she didn't hug him tightly. She held him carefully, like a dear but fragile possession. We fit very well together, she thought.

She drew back from him and put her hands lightly on his chest. "Your poor ribs," she said. "Your poor nose. It must be hard to teach anybody to sing when you're all banged up like that."

He thought about telling her that he might not have a job for much longer, anyway. But he decided that she had enough bad news to deal with already.

"I might be gone for a long time," she said. "Weeks."

"That's okay," he said courageously, already missing her. "I'll pick her up in the afternoon, at the store."

She helped him get into his car and stood by the road, holding on to George's collar, waiting to wave when he pulled away.

"Try to be back by November seventh," he called out the window. "If you can."

Michelle nodded. "I know. Your choir."

When his car had disappeared she walked slowly up the steps to her front door, George at her heel.

She thought about all the phone calls she'd refused to accept. She thought about his finally driving all the way over here to see her.

She was suddenly light-headed with relief because she had not slammed the door in his face.

38

He put on the black socks and the white shirt with the pleated front; the black trousers, the suspenders, the cummerbund; the bow tie, the black shoes; finally, the black velvet jacket. He dressed solemnly and with care, as though clothing himself for battle, for worship, or for love.

Shaved, showered, tuxedoed, he then regarded himself absorbedly in the mirror and noticed only that his face was slightly flushed and that he'd forgotten to make time to get a haircut.

Donald, when Casey finally emerged, carrying his score, responded gratifyingly. "I haven't seen you tarted up like that since I can't remember when," he said, standing back to admire his son.

"You ought to come visit me more often," said Casey. "Recitals, the choir—you haven't seen me do a damned thing in seventeen years, you old fart."

Donald nodded. "You're right, Charles. I haven't been particularly paternal in some ways and I regret that, and I fully intend to do something about it, too. But you just got away with calling me an old fart for the one and only time in your life." He looked impatiently at his big round wristwatch. "Isn't it time we got moving? You can't be there too early. Got to soothe the soloists, encourage the chorus, say a few words to the orchestra."

"Pop, kindly mind your own business," said Casey, grabbing his topcoat. "Shit, I'm too warm as it is. Let's go." He hung the coat back in the closet and reached for the door. Corky was sitting in front of it, staring concentratedly at the handle. "Pop," said, Casey. "Did I feed those dogs?"

"There's only one of them, remember?" said Donald. "And I fed her," said Donald. "You go on now, Corky. Hop up on your chair and watch us through the window."

Corky gave him an unpleasant look but did as she was told.

"Wish him luck, Dog," muttered Donald, before he followed Casey out to the car.

Michelle had arrived back in Vancouver two days earlier. She had gone straight to Casey's house, to fetch George. But Casey was out, at a dress rehearsal, and Donald had gone with him. Nobody had remembered to lock the door, though, so Michelle had gone in, retrieved her dog, and left a note.

The next day a ticket was delivered to her at the bookstore. It was accompanied by a feverishly scrawled note: *Glad you're back. Love you. See you after the concert.* He hadn't even signed the damn thing, she thought, looking at it critically. She peered at it closely, unable to remember whether she'd ever seen his handwriting before. It might not even be from him. Yet it looked vaguely familiar, so it probably was.

Besides, who the hell else would be sending her a ticket to the *Magnificat?*

It was a good thing he hadn't been bothering her with phone calls since she got back, she thought. She had been hectically busy—trying to get caught up with what had been going on at the bookstore, becoming reacquainted with George, unpacking, putting her house into some kind of order.

She'd talked twice with Alexandra, who was, it seemed, finally recovering nicely from the infection that had followed her surgery and kept Michelle in New York for more than six weeks. She was due to go back to work on Monday.

"They think they got it all," Alexandra had told her, the words like objects she had to spit delicately from her mouth in precisely the right order or else they wouldn't make any sense. Then she'd raised her eyebrows at Michelle, and wiggled them up and down. " 'Ah, Doc,' I told him. 'I bet you say that to all the girls.' "

"But do you believe him?" Michelle had asked her. "Do you *feel* that everything's okay?"

"I don't know, Michelle. How the hell do you tell a thing like that? I just have to wait and see what happens."

And so Michelle went home, after exacting a promise from Alexandra to keep her fully informed.

On Saturday night she drove out to U.B.C. to hear Casey's choir.

It was a long way from West Vancouver to the campus, so she allowed herself an hour to get there. It was a good thing, too. By the time she'd parked in the visitors' parkade and walked over to the auditorium, people were already starting to fill the rows of seats.

Michelle sat down in the middle of a row about halfway to the stage and looked curiously around her.

It was a proscenium arch theater whose stage had been built out in a semicircle into the house. Musicians dressed in tuxedos who were already tuning their instruments occupied chairs clustered in front and to each side of a podium. Michelle, with a mild shock, realized that the podium was probably for Casey. Huge pots of poinsettias were massed along the curve of the stage, and on stands to the right and left of the risers.

She listened to the instruments and watched the people filling up the seats in the auditorium; then she opened her program. Another shock. The *Magnificat,* which was the second half of the evening's program, was to be conducted by Charles W. Williams. "Charles"? Had he ever told her that his name was really Charles? And what was the W. for?

She remembered that Casey, on the phone while she was still in New York, had told her that his father would still be in town for the performance. She looked around for an elderly man who might be he, but couldn't find anybody who looked appropriate.

Finally the houselights dimmed and there were expectant rustlings among the audience. Then a man Michelle had never seen before walked onto the stage, was greeted with applause, and stepped onto the podium.

Michelle stayed in her seat during the intermission. She watched some young men move risers onto the stage, arranging them in three slightly curving rows.

A few minutes later the musicians reappeared, and one of them placed a score open upon the podium.

After a while the audience returned.

Then the houselights dimmed and the choir filed onto the stage, the men wearing tuxedos, the women in long black skirts and white blouses. As the audience applauded, they took their places on the risers. Then the applause became more enthusiastic, and something surged in her chest as Michelle watched Casey stride onto the stage.

Her heart began to beat faster, and the palms of her hands got sweaty.

He headed straight for the podium, stepped onto it, and picked up the baton which had been lying there. All the musicians had their eyes fixed upon him.

There were hardly any sounds to be heard in the auditorium: a few squeaks, as people shifted position in the wooden seats; a discreet rustle as a program was opened, folded, and laid upon a lap; an almost unheard whisper, quickly silenced.

Casey raised his hands and bowed his head in absolute concentration. For an irrational instant Michelle thought he must be praying. He was completely motionless; the slender white baton lay unmoving upon the air.

Then the baton moved quickly up, and quickly down, and a joyful orchestra exploded into the opening bars of the first movement.

Michelle was pretty sure she'd heard the *Magnificat* before. Maybe on the radio. But she had never been present for a live performance.

She saw only his back, the back of his head, his upraised arms; only the back of him. Yet she could see that the music occupied his body, poured through it; and that it did things to his nerve ends, and his brain cells, and to secret parts of his heart that were inaccessible to everything but this, everything but music.

Michelle thought that his hands were shaping the voices as they emerged from the singers' mouths, the music that issued from trumpet and oboe and strings and the rest.

She wished that she understood exactly what it was that was happening; how Bach, through these live people standing right in front of her at this very moment, was able to create such jubilation that Michelle, only listening, felt it in her blood and in her smile.

She actually saw the music, in Casey's body; sometimes limpid as water, as supple as willow branches; then authoritative, determined; and finally, triumphant. Exultant.

It was joyous music, and for the moments that it filled her life Michelle was joyful, too.

She was startled when it came to an end. It wasn't nearly long enough, she thought.

When the applause began, Casey turned around. He was smiling.

She waited in the lobby when the performance was over, not knowing what else to do, and the audience dispersed, chattering, into the night, and then a big man with white hair and a white moustache approached her.

"You must be Michelle," he said, holding out a large hand. "I'm Donald Williams. Charles's father. He asked me to come and take you backstage."

She tried weakly to argue, feeling uncomfortable at the idea of going back where the performers were, but Donald tucked her hand into the crook of his elbow and hurried her back through the auditorium, up onto the stage, through the wings and down a hallway to a large room full of musicians and their admirers.

Michelle pulled back firmly. "I'll wait here in the hall," she said.

Donald gestured vigorously and called, "Charles!"

He was talking to several members of the choir.

He looked up, saw Donald, saw Michelle, and waded through the crush of people toward her.

"Well?" he said worriedly. "What did you think?" His hair was mussed and his tie was askew.

She put her arms around him, under the jacket of his tuxedo. His back was very warm, and damp. She looked closely at his face and saw that it was damp, too, and flushed. "It was wonderful," she said.

"You really liked it? Good!" He hugged her tightly. "Isn't it a glorious piece of music?"

"Oh, dear," said Michelle. "Oh, Casey. The things I don't know about you."

He held her at arm's length. "Yeah. There's a whole lot I don't know about you, too." He wrapped his arms around her again. "It's going to be fun, isn't it."

"He's a pretty good conductor, all right." said Donald, who was leaning against the wall, his arms folded. "He sings pretty good, too. You ever heard him sing?"

"Not really," said Michelle. "Not yet."

"I'll sing to you tonight," said Casey, close to her ear.

"Is there a party or something?" said Donald, beaming. "Just to round out the evening?"